Phineas Garrett

Popular Dialogues

Comprising a great variety of original material expressly prepared by a corps of

experienced writers

Phineas Garrett

Popular Dialogues
Comprising a great variety of original material expressly prepared by a corps of experienced writers

ISBN/EAN: 9783337386214

Printed in Europe, USA, Canada, Australia, Japan

Cover: Foto ©Andreas Hilbeck / pixelio.de

More available books at **www.hansebooks.com**

Popular Dialogues

COMPRISING

A great variety of original material expressly
prepared by a corps of experienced
writers

———

Arranged by

PHINEAS GARRETT

Editor of the "100 Choice Selections" Series

———

Philadelphia
The Penn Publishing Company
1898

CONTENTS

POPULAR DIALOGUES

WAITING FOR THE STAGE.

CHARACTERS.

SIMPLE SIMON, JR., a victimized Western youtn.
BROADBRIM BRAITHWAITE, a Friend.
SILAS PARTRIDGE, commercial traveller.
MR. STUNNER, a Southerner.
JAMES PLUSH, a nice young man.
FRANZ MAHLER, artist.
AMELIA, sister of Franz, just from Germany.
MRS. FLYNN, Irish grocery-woman.
DANIEL AND ELLEN, her children.
MRS. BUNCH, elderly lady.
LUCELIA FLUTTERBY, } fashionable misses.
FLORA FENTON,

*Office of Puckertown Stage—Dingy little room—Hard-looking
settees—Floor untidy with dirt, tobacco spittle, cigar-stumps,
and litter—Walls covered with stage and railway handbills, notices, &c.*

STUNNER [*addressing Broadbrim, the only passenger yet
in waiting*].—So we've got to wait an hour and better
before the stage starts ?
BROADBRIM.—Thee'll not see the stage before three
o'clock, friend.
STUNNER.—It's mighty tedious, this yer waitin'! It's
right smart to three yet, I reckon. [*Taking out watch.*]
Humph! She's stopped!
BROADBRIM.—Thee has friends in Puckertown ?
STUNNER.—My nephew lives out several miles on the
road. It's some years now since I've travelled that way.
Yesterday was a juicy day—I didn't think I'd get to go
to-day. However, it has turned out pretty enough.
BROADBRIM.—Fine day for harvesting.
STUNNER.—Yes—since the blackberry rain the crops

5

have had a smart chance to ripen. How do things look about you?

BROADBRIM.—Very well—very well indeed. [*Pause.*]

[*Simple Simon enters and looks around inquiringly—finally, having perused the bills on the walls, seats himself.*]

I don't know when grain has looked finer. I think not for years.

SIMON.—I say, strănger [*to Broadbrim*], do you know whether anybody round these diggins wants help? I thought as you spoke of harvestin' it mought be you'd know where a chap like me could get a job.

[*Stunner devotes himself to the handbills.*]

BROADBRIM.—Thee wasn't raised in these parts, I observe.

SIMON.—No—most likely I wasn't. 'Pears like as if I was pretty much run agin a stump in 'em, anyhow! [*Attempting to laugh.*]

BROADBRIM.—Does thee speak of some misfortune? Perhaps thee has not fared well, or has lost something?

SIMON.—Not exactly lost any thing.

BROADBRIM.—I trust thee's not fallen into bad company. Thee certainly looks as if thee was not accustomed to such.

SIMON —You're right, strănger; I begin to think I was a fool for leaving the shebang. I could whip my weight in wildcats, if I was only once on the perary agin.

PARTRIDGE [*entering—catching the last part of remark—halts*].—You never heerd tell of 'Bije Skinner round Chicager or Iówer, did you, boy? [*To Simon.*]

SIMON.—Nary Skinner. But how'd yer know I come from Chicager?

PARTRIDGE.—I guessed as much from your yaller skin and your trick of the tongue. Don't hev no fever'n ager out that way, do you? They hev it *jest beyond*, don't they?

SIMON.—Whatever you may signify by that, you won't find such rantankerous scoundrels—not by a long shot—as walk the streets to the east'ard.

PARTRIDGE.—I didn't mean to rile your feelings—couldn't take offence at what I said. I'll leave it to the gentleman [*turning to Broadbrim*].

BROADBRIM.—Indeed, I think not. The young man seems a little uneasy about something that has occurred outside. I was just thinking where he might find busi-ness this way.

PARTRIDGE [*to Simon*].—O—h! Lost your chist?

SIMON.—Bein' as you act like you were inclined to hear, I'll give you jest a mite of my history. [*Plush enters and becomes a listener.*] You see as how I was raised out toward the frontier whar people make each other mighty welcome and jine aginst the Ingins. I've had some experience in that line myself, though I've only jist turned of age. I've lived through dumb-ager and the like, but the gold fever got me bad a few weeks ago, and the folks tried to help me off. We scraped together, among us all, money enough to pay my shot to Australy; but them as has knocked around this way before told me over and over agin not to let them New Yorkers cheat me—and the fact is, strănger, I've ben and gone and done it, without the least notion of hevin' it done.

PARTRIDGE.—You don't say! Du tell!

SIMON.—Yes, but I do, though—and sorry enough I am to do it, too. Why [*leaning forward with his elbows on his knees and emphasizing with his hands*], I'd got clear down to the Australy steamer, lookin' for a ticket-office, when a good-lookin' feller with his biled shirt and store-clothes on come along, and I asked for a little in-formation. "Oh, goin' to Australy!" said he, "I've ben there—I'll show you where to git your ticket; or just hand me your money, and I'll git it for you!" And so I did, like a catawampous fool—but he was gone, like shot off a shovel, and the perlice couldn't help me. It's meaner'n any skullduggery we have out in our ked'ntry. The sneakin' painter! He jest pulled the wool right over my eyes, and I came mighty near hevin' nary red left to my name. I promised to send 'em some word hum, but I'll be lynched if I ain't ashamed to let 'em know how owdaciously I've ben gulled. It puts me back a heap, I tell *you*. Never expected I should come so near goin' up in all my life.

PARTRIDGE.—That's the game of these confidence men. "Misery likes company," they say; and I might tell how I went through 'bout the same kind of dicker. The feller pretended to know all my first wife's relations—and hang me if I stopped to think, all the time he was jabberin', that I never was married! Fact, I declare! Now talk about your fools—will yer? 'Twill do you good! Did me—nothin' like gettin' your eye-teeth cut early! Ye'll look out sharper next time. What are ye goin' to du?

SIMON.—Work my passage out or back agin.

BROADBRIM.—Thee seems honest, friend.

SIMON.—Middlin', I reckon. I say, strânger, have you turned it over yit whether thar's work anywhar about you?

BROADBRIM.—Thee's welcome to my entertainment till thee has judged whether thee can be suited.

SIMON.—Thank ye, strânger! Glad of so good a port in a storm.

[*Franz Mahler, gentleman with slight foreign air and accent, has meanwhile entered with Amelia, neatly dressed but somewhat noticeable from the foreign look of her attire —points her to a seat—she sits with a curious satchel in hand, looking about—he takes out newspaper and reads.*]

PARTRIDGE [*to Broadbrim*].—I think I've seen your face afore, Mister!

BROADBRIM.—Thee has the advantage of me, then, friend!

PARTRIDGE [*to Stunner*].—That young man [*pointing to Plush who has taken a seat by Stunner*] ain't your son —is he?

STUNNER.—Not that I ever heard mentioned. 'Pears like a sort of somebody, though—if he didn't make me think of a lieutenant that took off some of my horses during the war.

PLUSH.—I'm not the sort they make those characters out of, sir! [*somewhat resenting the insinuation.*]

STUNNER.—I should think not. Them chaps did a heap of stealin' over and above what they had any authority for. I owed the whole set a grudge afore they stole half my property. I never bought or sold a man in my life but that emancipation swindle took off fifty blacks born and raised on the place I inherited from my father.

PLUSH.—It did! What a loss! And you git nothin' from Gover'ment for all that?

STUNNER.—All my horses stolen and threats that I'd

have to vamose the ranch myself if I didn't look out ! I laughed in my sleeve some when they thought to take me for givin' aid to the South; and thinks I to myself, "Young man, there's a case against you for takin' the horse that carried the man that carried the money to my son in the Confederate army, down in Georgy !"

PLUSH.—Well !—I declare !

STUNNER.—Now, here's a thing I've thought of [*rolling a quid in mouth*], and I've asked a good many and never got any answer—[*taking out greenback*]—how, when you give your note to a man, it isn't worth any thing—is it— if your name is printed on it ? You must sign it—mustn't you ?

PLUSH.—Of course you must.

STUNNER.—Well, then [*Broadbrim draws near*], here are these notes all over the country, promisin' millions — not one of 'em signed. Who's responsible ? Did you ever think of that ?

PLUSH.—Well—I declare—that's a puzzler to me !

STUNNER.—It may be one of my old-farmer notions, but I'd like to see any lawyer prove the constitutionality of that ! What is perishable is not legal tender—only gold and silver are legal tender. I wouldn't give a picayune for all the government bonds in existence.

BROADBRIM.—Friend, thee'd better stick to thy calling. Politics is less honorable and profitable than farming.

STUNNER.—A man can speak his mind, I reckon, in some parts of this country, yet, sir.

[*Misses Lucelia and Flora, dressed in the extreme of fashion, rush in—look around and talk loudly, with an affected drawl.*]

LUCELIA.—Why, Flor, there isn't no ticket office ! [*whirling around to look for her companion.*]

FLORA.—Of course not—only a box to wait in.

LUCELIA.—Well, I'm not going to wait here—that's fixed ! [*standing with nose elevated and chewing tip of parasol.*] Come, Flor.

[*Their attention arrested by the appearance of Amelia ; they stand staring, till Amelia, overcome by modest sensi- tiveness, blushes—her eyes drop, and tears fall—they smile contemptuously and pass away.*]

LUCELIA [*as she retires*].—Did you ever, Flor ? I thought it would kill me dead !

PARTRIDGE.—Carried consid'ble sail—them are ! [*spitting*].

FRANZ [*looking up from paper and surprised to see sister weeping*].—Was ist mit dir, Amelia ? Du weinst !

AMELIA.—Ich weiss nicht. Ich habe nichts gethan !

PARTRIDGE.—Them little chits needn't have been quite so sassy as to stare and laugh a body so out of countenance 'cause that body didn't cut just so outlandish a figger as they did ! Do 'em good to be taken down a notch or two !

FRANZ [*rising and walking about*].—'Tis but a sample of American politeness ! [*warmly.*] Everywhere in dis country one is struck by de vulgarity of its men and women. Gentlemen and ladies, dey do call themselves; but who, except demselves, can recognize dem by dat title? I speak of dem as a class. Dey are so seldom wurdy dat distinction. Dey are destitute of de first element dat goes to make such characters. One dat travels can most easily notice de difference. A woman can claim so much in dis country and presume upon her prerogatives ! 'Tis too much, unless she have sense enough to know her place. Pardon me, gentlemen, I did not intend to say so much ; but wid de repeated instances I have witnessed, I am doroughly disgusted. When a woman does unsex herself and drow away her dignity, I have just as much right to slap her face as I have to slap a man's—and I would do it, too ! Dese American snobs ! Pf-st ! Dey do excite one now and den almost beyond his reason ! [*vehemently.*]

PARTRIDGE [*to Plush*].—Putty plucky little furrinér, anyhow !

FRANZ.—I am republican—I don't say Black Republican to narrow the word—but I speak broadly. I have been an exile dese seventeen years for dat cause—for de boyish dreams. I secure de privilege of visiting my faderland by much trouble. I do despise dese people who make money deir standard—whose only title to nobility is noding but money—who have no past, no brains, no anyding but vulgar airs ! I have seen too much equality, even in despotic countries—where all races, ranks, and colors meet togeder, receiving respect for deir humanity —not to be ashamed of de type of republicanism one sees in cars and omnibuses and on the streets! [*Pauses.*]

PARTRIDGE.—My! ain't his dander riz!

FRANZ [*boot unluckily hit by an ejected quid*].—Ladies! Gentlemen! *Pfui!* Bipeds, that shpit and shpit and shpit demselves all to shpit! Shpit here—[*pointing*]— shpit dere — shpit everywhere! [*Gesticulating.*] In Germany gentlemen shpit nowhere. [*Turns to Amelia, who, not understanding him, looks somewhat frightened and wondering:* Ist nichts, Amelia! Ist nichts! *Resumes seat and reads. Door opens—Mrs. Bunch, with a bundle, smiling and trotting along, looks for a seat. Franz jumps up and offers his, into which she sinks, smiling still more.*]

MRS. B.—We're a heap of trouble! Ha — ha — ha! [*Plush whistles* "Wait for the Wagon!"]

FRANZ.—Not at all, madam!

MRS. FLYNN [*rushing in, loaded with budgets and bundles, followed by her children*].—Find a sate thare! Find a sate, chilther! Misther, jest give the chilther the tip end of nothing—will yees? [*To Broadbrim, who, near the end of the settee, manages to give a little more room.*] Have you the umberil, Ellie?

ELLEN.—Yas, mither!

BROADBRIM [*interested in boy's appearance*].—What is thy name, my little man?

DANIEL [*bashfully*].—Dân-yel.

BROADBRIM.—Daniel! Thee must prove a good man to merit thy name.

MRS. F. [*looking over budgets, thinks she has lost something.*]—Holy mither! Ellie, where iver did the man put the shoes?

ELLIE.—In the baskit, mither—at the bottom.

MRS. F.—Let me look and be shure—or I lose me day's work! [*After rummaging, finds them and composes herself*]

BROADBRIM [*offering seat*]. — Thee will find it more comfortable to sit than to stand.

MRS. F. [*accepting.*]—Thank ye, sir! Much obleeged to yees, sir! Thank ye, sir—savin' yer prisince, ye's a most lady-like gintleman! Here, darlints! [*Handing each child a ginger-cake.*]   Ate, and make yersilves as asy as ye can !

PARTRIDGE [*to Franz, putting away paper*]. — What's the news, mister ?   How's gold ?

FRANZ. — 140, I believe.

PARTRIDGE. — Goin' up — ain't it ?   What's the reason, now, I wonder ?

FRANZ. — France anticipates war, I believe.

PARTRIDGE. — You don't come from France, I calkerlate ?

FRANZ. — No — I am from Hanover.

PARTRIDGE. — Now, where's that ?   Much of a place ? When I've managed to pile away a few rocks I mean to spend a day or two lookin' round over there.   Never ben to Nyagery — have ye ?   You oughter go there.   You look like one of them as makes picters — ain't ye ? [*Awaiting a reply.*]

FRANZ. — I am an artist, sir — and have seen Niagara.

PARTRIDGE. — I thought's much.   Wall, as I was goin' to say, when I was there once an old chap was along who didn't seem to know what to say about it.   " That's majestic !" says I.   " Thank you !" said he, " I was at a loss for a word !"   " It's the most beautifullest, majesticest thing I ever seen," says I.   I expect he hain't got away yit, the old feller.   That's your sister — ain't it ?

FRANZ. — Excuse me, sir — I cannot tolerate your impertinence longer !   [*Walking away.*]

PARTRIDGE. — 'Pears a leetle huffy !   [*Drawing towards Mrs Bunch.*]   Trav'lin' alone ?

MRS. B. — Yes — nigh on to thirty yeer since he went. He was a nice good man — he was !   He was a peacemaker — Mr. Bunch was !   And I trust he went straight to Beelzebub's bosom — I do !

PARTRIDGE. — You don't say !   Was he rich ?   Any children ?

MRS. B. — I didn't quite understand you, sir !   Yes — out to my son-in-law's — owns a pretty large farm — seven children — three boys and four girls — all down with the small-pox or suthin' a bit ago — Doctor called it measles gone astray.   I don't know what it was.

STUNNER [*to Broadbrim*]. — Three and better — isn't it ? I'll lay we've waited here more'n two hours.

BROADBRIM [*looking at watch*].—Thee's wrong, friend, It lacks seven minutes of three.

PARTRIDGE [*to Mrs. Flynn*].—Better git your traps together, marm—hadn't ye ? Stage'll be along d'rectly !

MRS. F.—Who are ye, sir ? I've been over this road many a day, an' niver a bit without payin' me fare, sir ! But I niver saw the likes of ye here before !

LUCELIA [*rushing in with Flora*].—Oh dear ! I'm just dead ! I thought we should miss it, after all !

FLORA.—Aren't we lucky ? Just in time !

[*Plush rises and offers seat. Flora seats herself. Lucelia looks as if Mr. Stunner should relinquish his, remarking :* " No gentleman ! Not to give a seat to a lady !" *Horn is heard.*]

PARTRIDGE.—Hooray ! The hominy-pot's arriv ! [*rushing out to secure a seat.*]

[*Stunner seizes portmanteau and frantically endeavors to get out.*]

PLUSH [*to Lucelia and Flora*].—Shall I secure the back seat for you, ladies ?

BOTH.—Please, sir !

[*Plush leaves, folloved by them*]

BROADBRIM [*to Simon awaking from a nap*].—Friend, thee accompanies me, I believe ?

SIMON.—As you say, stranger !

[*Mrs. Bunch hobbles out after Mrs. Flynn, children and bundles. Franz follows with Amelia.*]

FRANZ [*to Broadbrim*].—Deliver us from bundles, 'baccy and boxes — the universal accompaniment of American travelling !

[*Curtain falls.*]

THE TROUBLESOME INVESTMENT.

DRAMATIZED FROM

J. T. TROWBRIDGE'S "COUPON BONDS."

DRAMATIS PERSONÆ.

Mr. Ducklow, a miserly old farmer.
Mrs. Ducklow, his wife.
Thaddeus, adopted son of Mr. Ducklow.
Miss Beswick, a tall, gaunt spinster, dressing old style.
Reuben, a returned soldier, also adopted son of Mr. Ducklow.
Sophronia, his wife.
Ruby, their little son.
Ferring, ⎱ neighbors of Reuben.
Jepworth, ⎰
Josiah, son-in-law of Mr. Ducklow.
Laura, his wife.
Dick Atkins, friend of Thaddeus.
Farmer Atkins, and others.

Scene I.—*A kitchen—Mrs. Ducklow sitting knitting by the light of a kerosene lamp—A table set with a single plate, knife and fork, etc., etc.*

Taddy [*behind the stair door, reluctantly kicking off a pair of trousers*].—Say, ma, need I go to bed now [*starting to pull on trousers*]? He'll want me to hold the lantern for him to take care of the hoss.

Mrs. Ducklow.—No, no, Taddy. You'll only be in the way, if you set up. Besides, I want to mend your pants.

Tad.—You're always wantin' to mend my pants [*whining*]. I wish there wasn't such a thing as pants in the world.

Mrs. D.—Don't talk that way, after all the trouble and expense we've been to clothe you! Where would you be now, if it wern't for me and your Pa Ducklow!

TAD. [*muttering.*]—I shouldn't be goin' to bed when I don't want to!

MRS. D.—You ungrateful child! Wouldn't be goin' to bed when you don't want to! You wouldn't be going to bed when you *want* to, more likely; for ten to one you wouldn't have a bed to go to. Think of the sitewation you was in when we adopted ye, and then talk that way!

TAD. [*thrusting his hand into his pants and tearing the hole larger, talking to himself.*]—If she likes to patch so well, let her.

MRS. D.—Taddy, you are tearing them pants.

TAD.—I was pullin' 'em off. I never see such mean cloth. Can't tech it but it has to tear. Say, ma, do you think he'll bring me home a drum?

MRS. D.—You'll know in the morning.

TAD.—I want to know to *night*. He said maybe he would. Say, can't I set up?

MRS. D.—I'll let ye know whether ye can set up after you're been told so many times [*lays down her knitting and seizes a rattan, and Taddy elopes*].

TAD. [*up-stairs.*]—I'm a-bed! Say, ma, I'm a-bed; I'm 'most asleep a'ready!

MRS. D.—It's a good thing for you, you be [*gathering up the pants Taddy dropped.*]—Why, Taddy, how ye did tear them! I've a good notion to give you a trouncing now. [*Taddy snores, Mrs. D takes up the pants and examines them.*] It is mean cloth, as he says. For my part, I consider it a great misfortune that shoddy was ever invented. Ye can't buy any sort of a ready-made garment for•boys now-a-days, but it comes to pieces, on the least wear or strain, like so much brown paper [*sits down and shapes the patch—sounds of wheels without—looks out into the darkness*]. That you?

MR. D.—Yes.

MRS. D.—Ye want the lantern?

MR. D.—No, jest set the lamp in the winder, and I guess I can get along. Whoa!

MRS. D. [*in low voice.*]—Had good luck?

MR. D.—I'll tell ye when I come in.

TAD. [*shouting from the bedroom.*]—Has he brought me a drum?

Mrs. D.—Do ye want me to come up there and tend to ye?

Tad.—No, I don't.

Mrs D.—You be still and go to sleep, then, or *you'll* get *drummed!*

[*Mrs. D. busy setting up the meal.   Enter Mr. D., with packages of sugar, tea, box of matches, etc., etc.*]

Mrs. D [*relieving him of his bundles.*]—Did you buy—

Mrs. D.—[*points inquiringly at the stair door.*]

Mrs. D.—Taddy?   Oh, he's abed! though I never in my life had such a time to git him off out of the way; for he'd somehow got possessed of the idee that you was to buy something, and he wanted to set up and see what it was.

Mr. D.—Strange how children will ketch things sometimes, best ye can do to prevent !

Mrs. D.—But did ye buy ?

Mr. D.—Ye'd better jest take them matches and put 'em out of the way, fust thing, afore ye forgit it ; matches are dangerous to have layin' round, and I never feel safe till *they're* safe [*Mr D. hangs up his hat, takes his overcoat off and lays it across a chair very cautiously*].

Mrs. D.—Come, what is the use of keeping me in suspense : did ye buy?

Mr. D. [*taking down the bootjack.*]—Where did ye put 'em ?

Mrs. D.—In the little tin pail, where we always keep 'em, of course.   Where should I put 'em ?

Mr. D. —You needn't be cross!   I asked, because I didn't see you put the kiver on.   I don't believe ye did put the kiver on, either ; and I shan't be easy till ye do.

[*Mrs. D. goes to the pantry, in anger, and puts on the lid. Mr. D. leans over the chair, and hears it.*]

Mr D. [*pressing the heel of his right boot in the jack, and steadying the toe under the round of a chair.*]—Anybody been here to-day ?

Mrs. D. [*crossly.*]—No !

Mr. D.—Ye been anywhere?

Mrs. D.—Yes !

Mr. D [*mildly*]—Where?

Mrs. D. [*angrily.*]—No matter.

13

MR. D [*sighing deeply.*]—Wal, you be about the most uncomfortable woman ever I see.

MRS. D.—If you can't answer my question, I don't see why I need take the trouble to answer yours. [*Turns with compressed lips to her sewing.*] Yer supper's ready; ye can eat it when ye please.

MR. D. [*in a very mild tone.*]—I was answering your question as fast as I could.

MRS. D [*sewing away.*]—I haven't seen any signs of yer answering it.

MR. D.—Wal, wal! Ye don't see every thing. [*Drawing gently his second boot, a paper falls out, which he picks up and hands triumphantly to Mrs. Ducklow.*]

MRS. D. [*taking it.*]—Oh, indeed! is this the —— [*Examines with satisfaction.*] But what made ye carry 'em in yer boot so?

MR. D. [*in a suppressed voice.*]—To tell the truth, I was afraid o' being robbed. I never was so afraid of being robbed in my life; so jest as I got clear of the town I tucked it down my boot-leg. Then all the way home I was skeer'd when I was riding alone, and still more skeer'd when I heard anybody coming after me. You see it's jest like so much money. [*Closes the window curtain, explains.*] This is the bond, ye see, and all these little things that fill out the sheet are the coupons. You have only to cut off one of these, take it to the bank when it is due, and draw the interest on it in gold.

MRS. D.—But suppose you lose the bonds?

MR. D.—That's what I've been thinking of; that's what made me so narvous. I supposed 'twould be like so much railroad stock, good for nothing to nobody but the owner, and somethin' that could be replaced if I lost it. But the man to the bank said no, 'twas like so much currency, and I must look out for it. That's what filled all the bushes with robbers as I came along the road. And I tell ye 'twas a relief to feel I'd got safe home at last, though I don't see now how we're to keep the plaguy things so we sha'n't feel oneasy about 'em.

MRS. D. [*turning pale.*]—Nor I neither! Suppose the house should take fire or burglars break in? I don't wonder you was so particular about the matches. Dear me, I shall be frightened to death. I'd no idee 'twas to be such dangerous property! I shall be thinking of fires and burglars. [*Taddy at the stair door.*] O—h—h—h! [*Taddy falls headlong towards the papers. General confusion.*]

Mrs. D.—Thaddeus! How came you here? Git up! Give an account of yourself! What ye want? What ye here for? [*Snatching him up by one arm and shaking him.*]

Taddy [*rubbing his eyes drowsily.*]—Don't know. Fell.

Mr. D. [*savagely.*]—Fell! How did you come to fall? What are you out of bed for?

Tad. [*snivelling and rubbing his eyes.*]—Don't know; didn't know I was.

Mrs. D.—Got up without knowing it! That's a likely story! How could that happen you, sir?

Tad.—Don't know, 'thout it was, I got up in my sleep.

Mr. D.—In your sleep?

Tad.—I guess so. I was dreamin' you brought me home a new drum—tucked down yer boot-leg.

Mr. D. [*glancing at his wife.*]—Strange! But how could I bring a drum in my boot-leg?

Tad.—Don't know, 'thout it's a new kind, one that'll shet up. [*Looking eagerly around. Mrs. D. tucks the bonds into the envelope.*] Say, did ye, pa?

Mr. D.—Did I? Of course I didn't. What nonsense! But how came ye down here? Speak the truth.

Tad.—I dreampt you was blowin' it up, and I sprung to ketch it, when fust I know'd I was on the floor like a thousand o' brick. [*Rubbing his knees.*] Mos' broke my knee-pans. [*Whimpering.*] Say, didn't ye bring me home nothing? What's them things?

Mr. D.—Nothing little boys know any thing about. Now run back to bed agin. I forgot to buy you a drum to-day, but I'll get you somethin' next time I go to town, if I think on't.

Tad.—So you always say, but you never think on't.

[*A knock at the door.*]

Mrs. D.—There! There! Somebody's comin'! What a looking object you are to be seen by visitors. Run.

[*Exit Taddy.*]

[*Mr. D. turns anxiously to his wife, who is hiding the bonds in her palpitating bosom.*]

Mr. D.—Who can it be this time o' night?

Mrs. D.—Sakes alive! I wish, whoever it is, they'd keep away. [*Resuming her seat and patching.*] Go to the door, why don't you?

Mr. D. [*opening the door and looking out.*]—Ah! Miss Beswick, walk in!

[*Enter Miss Beswick, with shawl over her head for a bonnet.*]

Mrs. D. [*in surprise.*]—What? that you? Where on airth did ye come from? Get her a chair, why don't ye, father?

[*Mr. D., slipping his feet into a pair of old slippers, hastens to comply.*]

Mr. D. [*apologetically.*]—I've only jest got home. Jest had time to kick my boots off, ye see. Take a seat.

Miss B.—Thank ye. I 'spose ye'll think I'm wild— making calls at this hour. [*Sits down and drops her shawl.*]

Mrs. D.—Why, no, I don't. Ye'r just in time to set up and take a cup of tea with my husband. Ye better, Miss Beswick, if only to keep him company. Take off yer things, won't ye?

Miss B.—No, I don't go a visitin' to take off my things and drink tea this time of night. I've just run over to tell you the news.

Mrs. D. [*laying her hand on her bosom.*]—Nothin' bad, I hope? No robbers in the town? For massy sake——

Miss B.—No; good news—good for Sophrony, at any rate.

Mrs. D.—Ah! she has heard from Reuben.

Miss B.—No! no!

Mrs. D.—What then?

Miss B.—Reuben has come home.

Mr. and Mrs. B.—Come home? home?

Miss B.—Yes!

Mrs. D.—My! how you talk! I never dreamed of such a——when did he come?

Miss B.—About an hour'n a half ago. I happened to be in Sophrony's. I had jest gone over to set a little while and keep her company—as I've often done. She seemed so lonely livin' there with her two children, alone in the house, with her husband away. Her friends hain't been none too attentive to her in his absence; so she thinks, and so I think.

Mrs. D.—I hope you don't mean that as a hint to us, Miss Beswick.

Miss B.—You can take it as such, or not, jest as you please. I leave it to your own consciences. You know best, whether you have done your duty to Sophrony and her family, whilst her husband has been off to the war, and I shan't set myself up for a judge. You never had any boys of your own, and so you adopted Reuben, just as you have lately adopted Thaddeus, and I suppose you think you've done well by him, just as you think you will do by Thaddeus, if he's a good boy and stays with you till he's twenty-one.

Mr. D.—I hope no one thinks or says to the contrary, Miss Beswick.

Miss B. [*with slight toss of head.*]—There may be two opinions on that subject. Reuben came to you when he was just old enough to be of use to you about the house and on the farm, and if I recollect right, you didn't encourage idleness in him long. You didn't give his hands much chance to do "some mischief still." No, indeed! Nobody can accuse you of that weakness. [*Her features tighten with a terrible grin.*]

Mrs. D. [*excitedly.*]—Nobody can say we ever overworked the boy or ill-used him in any way.

Miss B.—No, *I* don't say it. But this I'll say, for I've had it on my mind ever since Sophrony was left alone—I couldn't help seein' and feelin', and now you've set me a talkin', I may as well speak out. Reuben was always a good boy, and a willin' boy, as you yourself, Mr. Ducklow, must allow, and he paid his way from the first.

Mr. D. [*taking up his knife and fork and dropping them in agitation.*]—I don't know about that. He was a good and willin' boy, as you say, but the expense of clothin' him and keeping him to school——

Miss B. [*slowly.*] *He paid his way from the first.* You kept him to school winters, when he did more work 'fore and after school than any other boy in town. He worked all the time summers, and soon he was as good as a hired man to you. He never went to school a day after he was fifteen, and from that time he was better than any hired man, for he was faithful, and took an interest, and looked after, and took care of things as no hired man ever would or could do, as I've heard you yourself say, Mr. Ducklow.

MR. D.—Reuben was a good, faithful boy. I never denied that! I never denied that!

MISS B.—Well, he stayed with you till he was twenty-one—did ye a man's service for the last five or six years ; then you give him what you called a settin'-out—a new suit of clothes, a yoke of oxen, some farmin' tools, and a *hundred* dollars in money. You with your *thousands,* Mr. Ducklow, give him *a hundred dollars in money.*

MR. D.—That was *only a beginnin',* only a beginnin', I have always said.

MISS B.—I know it; and I s'pose you'll continue to say so till the day of yer death. Then, maybe, you'll remember Reuben in yer will. That's the way! Keep puttin' him off, as long as you can possibly hold on to your property yourself, then when ye see you've got to go and leave it, you give him what you ought to have given him years afore. There ain't no merit in that kind of justice, did ye know it, Mr. Ducklow. I tell you what belongs to Reuben, belongs to him *now*—not ten or twenty years hence, when you've done with it, and he most likely won't need it. A few hundred dollars now'll be more useful to him, than all your thousands will be by-and-by.

After he left you, he took the Mosely farm ; everybody trusted him, everybody respected him, he was doin' well everybody said. Then he married Sophrony, and a good and faithful wife she's been to him ; and finally he concluded to buy the farm, which you yourself said was a good idee, and encouraged him in it.

MR. D.—So it was. Reuben used judgment in that, and he'd a got along well enough if it hadn't been for the war——

MISS B.—Jest so ! if it hadn't been for the war. He had made his first payments, and would have met the rest, as they came due, no doubt of it. But the war broke out and he left all to sarve his country. Says he, "I'm an able-bodied man, and I ought to go," says he. His

business was as important, and his wife and children
were as dear to him as anybody's, but he felt it his duty
to go, and he went. They didn't give no such big boun-
ties to volunteers then, as they do now, and it was a sacrifice to him every way, when he enlisted. But says he,
" I'll jist do my duty," says he, "and trust to Providence
for the rest." You didn't discourage his goin', and you
didn't encourage him neither, the way you'd ought to.

MR. D. [*pouring his tea into his plate, and buttering
his bread with a teaspoon.*]—My! what on airth, Miss
Beswick! Seems to me you've taken it upon yourself to
say things that are uncalled for, to say the least. I can't
understand what should have sent you here to tell me
what's my business and what ain't in this fashion, as if I
didn't know my own duty and intentions.

MRS. D. [*sewing nervously.*]—I s'pose she's been talking with Sophrony, and she has sent her here to interfere.

MISS B. [*with a withering look of scorn*]—Mrs. Ducklow, you don't s'pose no such thing. You know Sophrony
wouldn't send anybody on such an arrant, and you know
I ain't a person to do such arrants, or be made a cat's-
paw of by anybody. I ain't hansum, not partic'larly,
and I ain't worth my *thousands*, like some folks I know,
and I never got married for the best reason in the world
—them that offered themselves I wouldn't have, and them
I would've had didn't offer themselves—and I ain't so
good a Christian as I might be I'm aware. I know my
lacks, as well as anybody, but bein' a spy and a cat's-
paw ain't one of them. I don't do things sly or under-
hand. If I've any thing to say to anybody, I go right
to 'em, and say it to their faces, sometimes perty blunt,
I allow; but I don't wait to be sent by other folks. I've
a mind of my own, and my own way of doin' things,
that you know as well as anybody. So when you say
you s'pose Sophrony, or anybody else, sent me here to
interfere, I say you s'pose what ain't true, and what you
know ain't true, Mrs. Ducklow. As for you, Mr. Ducklow,
I haven't said you don't know your own duties and intentions. I have no doubt you think you do at any
rate.

MR. D. Very well, then. why can't you leave me to do

what I think's my duty—everybody ought to have that privilege.

MISS B.—You think so?

MR. D.—Sartain! Miss Beswick, don't you?

MISS B.—Why, then, I ought to have the same.

MR. D.—Of course nobody in this house 'll prevent you from doin' what you're satisfied is your duty.

MISS B.— Thank ye, much obleeged! That's all I ask. Now I'm satisfied it's my duty to tell ye what I've been tellin' ye, and what I'm goin' to tell ye. That's my duty, and then it'll be your duty to do what you think's right. That's plain, ain't it?

MR. D.—Wal! wal! I can't hender yer talkin', I s'pose, though it seems, a man ought to have a right to peace and quiet in his own house.

MISS B.—Yes! and in his own conscience, too! And if you'll hearken me now, I'll promise you'll have peace and quiet in your conscience, and in your house too, sich as you never had yit. I s'pose you know your great fault, don't ye? *Graspin'*—that's yer fault—that's yer besettin' sin, Mr. Ducklow. You used to give it as an excuse for not helpin' Reuben more, that you had your daughter to provide for. Well—your daughter has got married; she married a rich man—you looked out for that—and she's provided for, fur as property can provide for any one. Now, without a child in the world to feel anxious about, you keep layin' up, and layin' up, and 'll continue to lay up, I s'pose, till ye die, and leave a great fortin' to your daughter, that already has enough, and just a pittance to Reuben and Thaddeus.

MR. D. [*excitedly.*]—No, no! Miss Beswick! You're wrong, Miss Beswick! I mean to do the handsum thing by both on 'em!

MISS B. [*smiting her lap with her hands.*]—*Mean to!* *Ye mean to!* That's the way ye flatter yer conscience and cheat yer own soul. Why don't you do what you mean to at once, and make sure on 't? That's the way to git the good of your property! I tell ye the time's comin', when the recollection of havin' done a good action will be a greater comfort to ye than all the property in the world! Then you'll look back and say: " Why didn't I do this, and do that, with my money, when 'twas in my

power, 'stead of hoardin' up, and hoardin' up, for others to
spend after me?" Now, as I was goin' to say, you
didn't discourage Reuben's enlistin', and ye didn't in-
courage him the way ye might. You ought to have said
to him : " Go, Reuben, if ye see it to be yer duty, and, as
far as money goes, ye sha'n't suffer for it ; I've got enough
for all on us, and I'll pay your debts if need be, and see
't yer fam'ly's kep comf'table while yer away." But that's
jest what ye didn't say, and that's jest what ye didn't do.
All the time Reuben's been saving his country, he's had
his debts and family expenses to worry him ; and you
know it's been all Sophrony could do, by puttin' forth
all her energies and strainin' every narve, to keep herself
and children from going hungry and ragged. You've
helped 'em a little, now and then, in driblets, it's true ;
but—dear me !

[*Mrs. D., biting her lips with anger, sews the pants to
her apron. Silence broken by Mr. D. picking up his knife
and fork and letting them drop again.*]

Mr. D.—Wal ! wal ! you've read us a perty smart lec-
tur', Miss Beswick, I must say. I can't consaive what
should make ye take such an interest in our affairs ; but
it's *very kind, very kind* in ye, to be sure !

Miss B.—Take an interest ! Haven't I seen Sophrony's
struggles with them children ! and haven't I seen Reuben
come home, this very night, a sick man, with a broken
constitution, and no prospect before him but to give up
his farm, lose all he has paid, and be thrown upon the cold
charities of the world with his wife and children ? And
if the charities of his friends are so cold, what can he
expect of the charities of the world ? Take an interest !
I wish you took half as much ! Here I've sot half an
hour, and you haven't thought to ask how Reuben looked,
or any thing about him !

Mr. D.—Maybe there's a good reason for that, Miss
Beswick. 'Twas on my lips to ask a half-a-dozen times ;
but you talked so fast, ye wouldn't give me a chance to
git a word in edgeways.

Miss B.—Well, I'm glad you've got some excuse, though
a very poor one.

Mrs. D. [*meekly.*]—How is Reuben ?

Miss B.—All broken to pieces—a mere shadow of what

he was. He's had his old wound troublin' him agin.
Then he's had the fever; that came within one of taking
him out of the world. He was in the hospital, ye know,
for two months or more; but finally the doctors seed his
only chance was to be sent home, weak as he was. Oh,
if you could have seen him and Sophrony meetin' as I
did, then you wouldn't sneer at my takin' an interest
[*puts her handkerchief to her eyes*]. I didn't stop—only
to put him to bed, and to fix things a little; then I left 'em
alone, and ran over to tell ye. It's a pity you didn't
know he was in town when you was there to-day, so as
to bring him home with ye; but I s'pose ye had yer in-
vestments to look after. Come, Mr. Ducklow—how many
thousand dollars have you invested since Reuben's been
off to the war, and his folks have been sufferin' to home?
You may have been layin' up hundreds, or even thousands
that way this very day, for aught I know; but let me tell
ye, ye won't git no good of sich property. It 'll only be
a cuss to ye, till ye do the right thing by Reuben—mark
my word! [*Long silence—Miss B. rises to go.*]

MRS. D.—Ye ain't goin', be ye, Miss Beswick? What's
yer hurry?

MISS D. [*pulling her shawl over her head.*]—No hurry
at all; but I've done my arrant and said my say, and
may as well be goin'. Good-night. Good-night, Mr.
Ducklow.

[*Exit Miss Beswick.*]

MRS. D.—Did you ever?

MR. D.—She's got a tongue.

MRS. D.—Strange she should speak of your investin'
money to-day. D'ye 'spose she knows?

MR. D. [*rising from the table and pacing the floor in
trouble.*]—I don't see how she can know. I've been
careful not to give a hint on't to anybody; for I knew
jest what folks would say:. "If Ducklow's got so much
money to dispose of, he'd better give Reuben a little."
I know how folks talk.

MRS. D. [*indignantly.*]—Coming here to browbeat us!
I wonder ye didn't be a little more plain with her, father.
I wouldn't have sot and been dictated to as tamely as
you did.

MR. D.—You wouldn't? Then why *did* ye? She

dictated to you as much as she did to me; and you scarce opened yer mouth. Yer didn't dare to say yer soul was yer own.

Mrs. D.—Yes, I did! I——

Mr. D.—You ventured to speak once, and she shet you up quicker'n light'nin'. Now tell about yer wouldn't have sot and been dictated to like a tame noodle, as I did!

Mrs. D.—I didn't say a tame noodle.

Mr. D.—Yes, ye did! I might have answered back sharp enough, but I was expectin' you to speak. Men don't like to dispute with women.

Mrs. D. [vexed.]—That's your git off. You was jest as much afraid of her as I was. I never seed ye so cowed in all my life.

Mr. D. [scowling, and taking his boots from the corner.] —Cowed! I wasn't cowed, neither. How onreasonable now for ye to cast all the blame onto me——

Mrs. D.—Ye han't got to go out, have ye? I shouldn't think ye'd put on yer boots just to step to the barn, and see to the hoss.

Mr. D.—I'm going over to Reuben's.

Mrs. D.—To Reuben's! Not to-night, father.

Mr. D.—Yes, I think I'd better. He and Sophrony'll know that we heard of his gettin' home, and they're enough inclined already to feel we neglect 'em. Haven't ye got somethin' ye can send 'em?

Mrs. D. [curtly.]—I don't know. I've scarce ever been over to Sophrony's but I've carried her a pie, or cake, or somethin', and mighty little thanks I've got fur it, as it turns out.

Mr. D.—Why didn't ye say that to Miss Beswick when she was runnin' us so hard about our never doin' any thing for 'em?

Mrs. D. —It wouldn't have done no good. I knew jest what she'd say. "What's a pie or a cake now and then?" That's jest the reply she'd have made. [Rises and finds the garment fast to her apron.] Dear me! what have I been doin'? So much for Miss Beswick. [Unties her apron and throws the united garments on the floor.] I do wish such folks would mind their own business and stay to home.

Mr. D. [*putting on his coat.*]—You've got the bonds safe?

Mrs. D.—Yes; but I won't engage to keep 'em safe. They make me as narvous as can be. I'm afeard to be left alone in the house with 'em. Here, you take 'em.

Mr. D.—Don't be foolish! What harm can happen to them or you while I'm away? You don't s'pose I want to lug 'em around with me wherever I go, do you?

Mrs. D.—I'm sure it's no great *lug*. I s'pose you're afear'd to go across the fields with 'em in your pocket. What in the world we're goin' to do with them I don't see. If we go out we can't take 'em with us for fear of losin' 'em or bein' robbed, and we sha'n't dare to leave 'em to home for fear the house 'll burn up or git broke into.

Mr. D.—We can hide 'em where no burglars can find 'em.

Mrs. D.—Yes, and where nobody else can find 'em neither, provided the house burns down, and neighbors come in to save things. I don't know but it 'll be about as Miss Beswick said: we sha'n't take no comfort in property we ought to make over to Reuben.

Mr. D.—Do you think it ought to be made over to Reuben? If ye do it's new to me.

Mrs. D.—No, I don't. I guess we'd better put 'em in the clock-case for to-night, hadn't we?

Mr. D.—Jest where they'd be discovered if the house was robbed. No, I've an idee. Slip 'em under the sittin'-room carpet. Let me take 'em. [*Puts the bonds under the carpet, and sets a chair over them.*]

[*Thaddeus at the door.*]

Mrs. D.—What noise is that?

Mr. D. [*springing to the door.*]—Thaddeus, is that you? What do you want now?

Tad.—I want you to scratch my back.

Mrs. D. [*seizes her rattan and strikes him on the back.*] —I'll scratch yer back for yer. There, sir; that's a scratchin' that 'll last ye for one while. [*Exit Ducklow.*] Away to bed, and don't show yer mug agin to night!

[*Taddy obeys, crying, and sobs himself to sleep.*]

Mrs. D. [*going to the door.*]—Father! you know what time it is? It's nine o'clock. I wouldn't think of going

over there to-night.   They'll be all locked up, and a-bed
and like enough, asleep.

Mr. D. [*entering.*]—Wal, I suppose I must do as ye say.

Mrs. D. [*lighting a candle and preparing for bed.*] —
Father, hadn't ye better put a few tacks in the carpet
where ye put the bonds?   If robbers should break in,
they'd be sure to knock over the chair and turn up the
carpet.

Mr. D.—Don't see much use, but I can do it.   [*Gets
hammer and tacks.*]   Keep the light away ; a spark might
do the mischief.

Mrs. D. [*retires with the candle.*]—Father, don't ye
smell somethin' burnin' ?

Mr. D.—No ; I can't say I do.   Do you?

Mrs. D.—Jest as plain as ever I smelt any thing in my
life.   [*Snuff, snuff.*]

Mr. D. [*snuffing.*]—Seems to me I do smell something.
It can't be them matches, can it ?

Mrs. D.—I thought of the matches, but I certainly
covered 'em up tight.

[*Mr. and Mrs. D. snuff, first one and then the other.*]

Mr. D.—Oh, it was nothing but your imagination.
Let me see if I can get this tacked.   Good gracious !

Mrs. D.—What now?   They're not gone, are they ?
You don't say they're gone ?

Mr. D.—Sure as the world—No, here they be—I didn't
feel in the right place.

Mrs. D.—How you did frighten me !   My heart almost
hopped into my mouth.   Come now, let's get to bed
some time.   Done ?

Mr. D.—Yes.

[*Exit scene.*]

Scene II.—*Ducklow's house in the morning—Mr. and
Mrs. Ducklow just rising from their frugal breakfast—
Taddy sitting on the floor, putting on his shoes.*

Mr. D.—Now, mother, I'll run over and see Reuben.

Mrs. D.—Why not harness up and let me ride over
with ye?

Mr. D.—Very well; maybe that'll be the best way.

Come, Taddy [*looking round*], get those shoes on—fly round—you'll have lots o' chores to do this morning.

TADDY [*provoked*]. — What's the matter with my breeches? Some plaguy thing's stuck to them. [*Runs round and round.*]

MR. D. [*laughing heartily.*]—Wal, wal, mother! you've done it. You're dressed for meetin' now, Taddy.

MRS. D.—I do declare, I can't for the life of me see what there is so funny about it. [*Takes the scissors and cuts the apron loose. Mr. and Mrs. D. prepare to go.*]

MRS. D.—Taddy, Taddy, now mind, don't you leave the house, and don't you touch the matches, nor the fire, nor don't go ransacking the rooms, neither; ye won't, will ye?

TADDY.—No, ma'am.

[*Exit Ducklows.*]

TADDY [*watches till they are gone, slily gets the hammer, pulls out the tacks, turns up the carpet, and takes out the bonds. He examines them with curiosity. Soliloquizes.*] —Whew! won't they make me a nice kite? They're nothing but paper anyhow. [*Folds up a newspaper and puts it in the envelope under the carpet.*]

[*Exit scene.*]

SCENE III.—*At Reuben's house—Reuben lying on a couch, propped up with pillows—Sophrony sitting by him, with little Ruby on her knee—Miss Beswick moving about the room—Neighbors Jepworth and Ferring talking to Reuben —Enter Mr. and Mrs. Ducklow.*

MR. D.—Wal, Reuben, glad to see ye ! This is a joyful day I scarce ever expected to see. Why, you don't look so sick as I thought you would—does he, mother?

MRS. D.—Dear me! I'd no idea he could be so very, so very pale and thin—had you, Sophrony?

SOPHRONY.—I don't know what I thought. I only know I have him now. He has come home. He shall never leave me again—never!

MRS. D. [*in a whisper.*]—Wasn't it terrible to see him brought home so?

Sophro.—Yes, it was; but, oh, I was so thankful, I felt the worst was over, and I had him again. I can nurse him now. He is no longer hundreds of miles away, among strangers, where I cannot go to him, though I should have gone long ago, as you know, if I could have raised the means, and if it hadn't been for the children.

Mrs. D.—I—I—Mr. Ducklow would have tried to help you to the means, and I would have taken the children, if we had thought it best for you to go. But ye see it wasn't best, don't ye?

Sophro.—Whether it was or not, I don't complain. I am too happy to-day to complain of any thing, to see him home again; but I have dreamt so often that he came home, and woke up to find that it was only a dream, I am half afraid now to be as happy as I might be.

Reuben [*in a weak voice*].—Be as happy as you please, Sophrony; I'm just where I want to be, of all places in this world or the next world either, I may say, for I can't conceive of any greater heaven than I'm in now. I'm going to get well too, spite of the doctors. Coming home is the best medicine for a fellow in my condition. Not bad to take either. Stand here, Ruby, my boy, and let your daddy look at you again! To think that's my Ruby, Pa Ducklow. Why he was a mere baby when I went away.

Sophro. [*leaning over Reuben.*]—Reuben! Reuben! you're talking too much! You promised me you wouldn't, you know.

Reuben.—Well, well, I won't. But when a fellow's heart is chock full it's hard to shut down on it sometimes. Don't look so, friends, as if you pitied me: I ain't to be pitied. I'll bet there isn't one of ye half as happy as I am at this minute.

Sophro. [*Miss Beswick approaching.*]—Here's Miss Beswick, Mother Ducklow: haven't you noticed her?

Mrs. D. [*surprised.*]—How do you do, Miss Beswick?

Miss B.—Tryin' to keep out of the way and make myself useful. [*Exit Miss Beswick.*]

Sophro.—I don't know what I should do without her. She took right hold and helped me last night. Then she came in, the first thing this morning. "Go to your

husband," says she to me; "don't leave him a minute; I
know he don't want ye out of his sight, and you don't
want to be out of his sight either. So you tend right to
him, and I'll do the work. There'll be enough folks
comin' in to hender, but I've come in to help," says she.
And here she's been ever since, hard at work, for when
Miss Beswick says a thing there's no use opposing her,
that you know, Mother Ducklow.

MRS. D. [*with a peculiar pucker.*]—Yes, she likes to
have her own way.

SOPHRO.—It seems she called at the door last night, to
tell you Reuben had come.

MRS. D.—Called at the door! Didn't she tell you she
came in and made us a visit?

SOPHRO.—No, indeed! Did she?

MRS. D.—Oh, yes; a visit for her. She ain't no hand
to make long stops, you know.

SOPHRO.—Only when she's needed; then she never
thinks of going, as long as she sees any thing to do.
[*Turning towards Reuben, who is conversing with Jepworth.*] Reuben, you mustn't talk, Reuben.

JEPWORTH.—I was saying it will be too bad now, if you
have to give up this place, but he ——

SOPHRO. [*interrupting.*]—We are not going to worry
about that after we have been favored by Providence so
far, and in such extraordinary ways. We think we can
afford to trust still further. We have all we can think of
and attend to to-day, and the future will take care of
itself.

MR. D.—That's right, that's the way to talk. Providence will take care of ye, ye may be sure.

FERRING.—I should think you might git Ditson to renew
the mortgage. He can't be hard on you under such circumstances, and he can't be so foolish as to want the
money. There's no security like real estate. If I had
money to invest I wouldn't put it into any thing else.

MR. D.—Nor I. Nothing like real estate.

JEP.—What do you think of gov'ment bonds?

MR. D.—I don't know. I haven't given much attention to the subject. It may be a patriotic duty to lend
to gov'ment if one has the funds to spare

JEP.—When we consider that every dollar we lend to

gov'ment, goes to carry on the war and put down this cursed rebellion.

MR. D.—I believe if I had any funds to spare I shouldn't hesitate a minute, but go right off and invest in gov'ment bonds.

FERRING.—That might be well enough, if ye did it from a sense of duty, but as an investment 'twould be the wust ye could make.

MR. D. [*quickly.*]—Ye think so?

FERRING.—Certainly, gov'ment will repudiate. It'll have to. This enormous debt never can be paid. Your interest in gold is a temptation just now, but that won't be paid much longer, and then your bonds won't be worth any more than so much brown paper.

MR. D. [*alarmed.*]—I—I don't think so. I don't b'lieve I should be frightened, even if I had gov'ment securities in my hands. I wish I had. I really wish I had a good lot of them bonds. Don't you, Jepworth?

JEP.—They're mighty resky things to have in the house. That's one objection to 'em.

FERRING.—That's so! I read in the papers almost every day 'bout somebody having his *coupon* bonds stole.

JEP.—I should be more afraid of fires.

REUBEN.—But there's this to be considered in case of fires. If the bonds burn up, they won't have to be paid, so what's your loss is the country's gain.

MR. D.—But isn't there any remedy?

REUBEN.—There's no risk at all, if a man subscribes for registered bonds. They're like railroad stock. But if you have the coupons you must look out for them.

MR. D. [*rises hurriedly.*]—Wal, Reuben, I must be drivin' home I s'pose. Left every thing at loose ends. I was in such a hurry to see ye, and find out if there's any thing I can do for you.

REUBEN.—As for that I've got a trunk over in town which couldn't be brought last night. If you will have that sent for, I'll be obliged to you.

MR. D.—Sartin, sartin.

[*Exit Mr. D.*]

FERRING.—One would think that Ducklow had some of them bonds on his hands, and got scared—he took such a sudden start. He has, hasn't he, Mrs. Ducklow?

14

Mrs. D. [*engrossed with her knitting.*]—Has what?
Ferring.—Some of them coupon bonds. I rather think he's got some.

Mrs. D.—You mean government bonds? Ducklow got some! 'Taint at all likely he'd spec'late in 'em without saying something to me about it. No! he couldn't have any without my knowing it, I'm sure.
[*Exit Scene.*]

Scene IV.—*Taddy in sitting-room playing marbles. Mr. Ducklow on the road—Alarm of fire without.*

Mr. D. [*heard shouting*].—Git up! git up! fire! fire! O them bonds! them bonds! Why didn't I give the money to Reuben! Fire! fire! fire! Why don't ye go long! [*Slap, slap. His hat falls off.*] Whoa! whoa! whoa——
[*Fire! fire! fire! by many voices in the distance. A false alarm! a false alarm!*]
[*One fellow says, "* Seems to me ye ought to have found that out 'fore you raised all creation with yer yells."]
[*Another hallooing, "* Ye look like the flying Dutchman. This your hat? I thought it was a dead cat in the road."]
Atkins —No fire! no fire! only one of Ducklow's jokes.
[*Boys still shout "* Fire!*" Thaddeus puts on his hat to go out, but meets his Pa Ducklow.*]
Mr. D.—Thaddeus! Thaddeus! Where are you going, Thaddeus?
Tad.—Goin' to the fire!
Mr. D.—There isn't any fire, boy!
Tad.—Yes, there is! Didn't ye hear 'em? They've been yelling like fury!
Mr. D.—It's nothing but Atkins' brush.
Tad.—That's all! I thought there was goin' to be some fun! I wonder who was such a fool as to yell fire jest for a darned old brush-heap.
Mr. D.—I've got to drive over to town and get Reuben's trunk. You stand by the mare while I step in and brush my hat. [*Hastens to look after bonds.*] Heavens and airth!
[*Ducklow gropes under the carpet and finds his package, discovers Taddy looking in at the door.*]
Mr. D.—Didn't I tell you to stand by the old mare?

TAD. [*shrinking back.*]—She won't stir!

MR. D.—Come here! [*Grasps him by the collar.*] What have you been doing? Look at that!

TAD. [*whimpering and putting his fists in his eyes.*]— 'Twarn't me!

MR. D. [*shaking him.*]—Don't tell me " 'twarn't you "! What was you pullin' up the carpet for?

TAD. [*snivelling.*]—Lost a marble.

MR. D.—Lost a marble! Ye didn't lose it under the carpet, did ye? Look at all that straw pulled out! [*Shakes him again.*]

TAD.—Didn't know but what it might a got under the carpet—marbles roll so!

MR. D.—Wal, sir! [*Boxes him on the ears.*] Don't you do such a thing again if you lose a million marbles.

TAD.—Hain't got a million! [*Weeping.*] Hain't got but four! Won't you buy me some to-day?

MR. D.—Go to that mare and don't leave her again till I come, or I'll marble ye in a way ye won't like. [*In deep trouble, pacing the floor.*] Why ain't she to home! These women are forever a-gaddin'. I wish Reuben's trunk was in—Jericho. Where shall I put 'em! A—h! now I know; I'll slip 'em down in that trunk of worthless old rubbish where no one would ever think of lookin' for 'em, and resk 'em.

[*Exit Scene.*

SCENE V.—*Ducklow's sitting-room. Taddy sitting on the floor, making his kite.*

[*Enter Mr. Ducklow.*]

MR. D.—Did that pedler stop here?

TAD.—I hain't seen no pedler.

MR. D.—And hain't yer Ma Ducklow been home neither?

TAD. [*hiding the kite frames.*]—No!

MR. D.—Wal, come here and mind the mare! [*Taddy obeys. Mr. D. soliloquizes.*]—I don't see no way but for me to take the bonds with me. [*Takes the bonds out of the old trunk and fastens them in his breast-pocket with six large pins.*] There, now, they're safe!

[*Going out, Taddy appears.*]

TAD.—There's suthin' losin' out o' yer pocket! [*Mr. D. puts his hand, quick as lightning, to his breast, and stumbles.*] Yer side pocket! It's one of yer mittens.

MR. D.—You rascal! how you skeer'd me! [*Skins his shin and pulls up his pant-leg.*]

TAD.—Got any thing in yer boot-leg, to-day, Pa Ducklow?

MR. D.—Yes, a barked shin, and all on yer account too. Go and put that straw back and fix the carpet, and don't let me hear ye speak of my boot-leg again, or I'll boot-leg ye.

[*Exit Mr. Ducklow.*]

[*Taddy gets his kite and goes out. Enter Mrs. Ducklow out of breath.*]

MRS. D.—Thaddeus! Thaddeus! The house deserted! Carpet torn up! Straw pulled out, and bonds gone. Mr. Ducklow never could have done it getting the bonds! Somebody must have taken them! [*She rushes frantically from the house calling "Taddy! Taddy! Taddy!" and, after a few minutes, enters, breathless, pulling Taddy.*] Look here, boy! how came the carpet up? O——

TAD.—I pulled it up hunting for a marble.

MRS. D.—And the—-the—the thing tied up in a brown wrapper——

TAD.—Pa Ducklow took it.

MRS. D.—Ye sure?

TAD.—Yes, I seen him!

[*Exit Taddy.*]

MRS D.—Oh, dear! I never was so beat! Oh, dear! I'm half dead! Oh, dear! Oh, dear!

[*Enter Mr. Ducklow.*]

MRS. D.—-Did ye take the bonds?

MR. D.—Of course I did. Ye don't suppose I'd go away and leave them in the house, not knowin' when you'd be comin' home!

MRS. D.—Wal, I didn't know—I didn't know whether to believe Taddy or not. Oh, I've had sich a fright! Oh, dear!

MR. D.—What frightened ye?

MRS. D.—Wal, I came home and found the carpet all torn up, and bonds gone. Just as I came in I see'd an old chaise goin' up the road, and as Taddy was not about

I very naterally thought the house had been robbed, and
bonds and Taddy both taken. So I run fast as I could
through the mud, hollering loud as I could, " Stop thief!"
" Stop thief!" but he paid no attention. After a while I
got round the hoss and cried, " Stop, sir, you've robbed
my house!" I didn't look at all, till I said it, and who
should it be but Mr. Grantley, the minister! Oh, dear!
Oh, dear!

Mr. D. — Massy on us! How could you make such a
fool of yourself! It'll git all over town, and I shall
be mortified to death. Jest like a woman, to git frightened.

Mrs. D. — If you hadn't got frightened at Atkins' brush-
heap, and made a fool of yourself yelling fire, 'twouldn't
have happened.

Mr. D. — Wal! Wal! Say no more about it. The
bonds is safe!

Mrs. D. — Where?

Mr. D. — I went to the bank, and asked 'em if they'd
lock 'em up in their safe, and they said they would, but
wouldn't give no receipt for 'em, or hold 'emselves responsible for 'em. I didn't know what else to do, so I
handed 'em the bonds to keep.

Mrs. D. — I want to know if you did now?

Mr. D. [unfolding his weekly paper.] — Why not?
What else could I do? I can't lug 'em about with me,
and as for keepin' 'em in the house we've tried that.
[He reads.]

Mrs. D. — I wouldn't have left the bonds in the bank!
My judgment would have been better than that. If they
are lost I shan't be to blame. [Mr. Ducklow starts with
surprise.] Why, what have ye found?

Mr. D. [turning pale.] — Bank robbery!

Mrs. D. — Not yer bank? Not the bank where yer
bonds are?

Mr. D. — Of course not! but in the very next town.
The safe blown open with gunpowder. Five thousand
gov'ment bonds stole.

Mrs. D. — How strange! Now what did I tell ye?

Mr. D. — I believe ye'r right. They'll be safer in my
own house, or even in my own pocket.

Mrs. D.—If you was going to put 'em in any safe, why not put 'em in Josiah's? He's got a safe, ye know.

Mr. D.—So he has! We might drive over there and make a visit Monday, and ask him to lock 'em up Yes, we might tell him and Laury all about it, and leave 'em in their charge.

Mrs. D.—So we might!

Mr. D. [*pacing the floor.*]—Let me see! To-morrow's Sunday. If we leave the bonds in the bank over night they must stay there till Monday.

Mrs. D.—And Sunday is jest the day for burglars.

Mr. D.—I've a good notion—let me see—[*looking at the clock*]—twenty minutes after twelve—bank closes at two—an hour and a-half—I believe I could make it—I'll go immediately.

[*Exit Scene.*]

Scene VI.—*Josiah's house. Josiah, Laura, Mr. and Mrs. Ducklow present.*

Mr. D. [*turning to Laura.*]—Josiah's got a nice place here. That's about as slick a little barn as ever I see'd Always does me good to come over here and see you gettin' along so nicely, Laury. •

Laura.—I wish you'd come oftener, then.

Mr. D.—Wal, it's hard leavin' home, ye know. Have to git one of Atkins' boys to come and sleep with Taddy the night we're away.

Mrs. D.—We shouldn't have come to day, if it hadn't been for me. Says I to your father, says I, "I feel as if I wanted to go over and see Laury; it seems an age since I've seen her," says I. "Wal," says he, "s'pos'n we go," says he. That was only last Saturday, and this morning we started.

Mr. D.—And it's no fool of a job to make the journey with the old mare.

Laura.—Why don't you drive a better horse?

Mr. D.—Oh, she answers my purpose. Hoss-flesh is high, Laury. Have to economize these times.

Laura.—I'm sure there's no need of your economizing. Why don't you use your money and have the good of it.

Mrs. D.—So *I* tell him.

Mr. D. [*accidentally.*]—What do you think of gov'-ment bonds, Josiah?

Josiah.—First-rate.

Mr. D. [*encouraged.*]—About as safe as any thing, ain't they?

Josiah.—Safe! Just look at the resources of this country. Nobody has begun yet to appreciate the power and undeveloped wealth of these United States. It's a big rebellion I know, but we're going to put it down. It'll leave us a big debt, very sure; but we'll handle it easily. It makes us stagger a little, not because we are not strong enough for it, but because we don't understand our own strength, or how to use it. It makes me laugh to hear folks talk about repudiation and bankruptcy.

Mr. D.—But s'pos'n we do put down the rebellion, and the States come back, then what's to hender the South and secesh sympathizers in the North, from jinin' together and voting that the debt sha'n't be paid?

Josiah.—Don't you worry about that. Do you suppose we're going to be such fools as to give the rebels, after we've whipped 'em, the same political privileges they had before the war? Not by a long chalk! Sooner than that we'll put the ballot into the hands of the freedmen. They're our friends. They've fought on the right side. I tell ye, in spite of all the prejudice there is against black skins, we a'n't such a nation of ninnies as to give up all we're fighting for and leave our best friends and allies, not to speak of our own interests, in the hands of our enemies.

Mr. D. [*growing radiant.*]—You consider gov'ments a good investment then, do ye?

Josiah.—I do, decidedly,—the very best. Besides you help the government, and that's no small consideration.

Mr. D.—So I thought. But how is it about the *cowpon* bonds? A'n't they rather ticklish property to have in the house?

Josiah.—Well, I don't know. Think how many years you'll keep old bills and documents and never dream of such a thing as losing them! There's not a bit more danger with the bonds. I shouldn't want to carry them around with me to any great amount, though I did once carry three thousand dollar bonds in my pocket for a week. I didn't mind it.

MR. D.—Curious! I've got three thousand dollar bonds in my pocket this minute.

JOSIAH.—Well, it's so much good property.

MR. D.—Seems to me, though, if I had a safe as you have, I'd lock 'em up in it.

JOSIAH.—I was travelling that week. I did lock them up pretty soon after I got home.

MR. D. [*as if the thought had just struck him.*]—Suppose you put my bonds into your safe, I shall feel easier.

JOSIAH.—Of course! I'll keep them for you, if you like.

MR. D —It will be an accommodation. They'll be safe, will they?

JOSIAH.—Safe as mine are. Safe as anybody's. I'll insure them for twenty-five cents.

[*Ducklow is very happy. Mrs. D. goes to her husband, and with a pair of scissors cuts the stitching, they having been previously stitched in for safety.*]

JOSIAH.—Have you torn off the May coupons?

MR. D.—No.

JOSIAH.—Well, you'd better. They'll be payable now soon, and if you take them you won't have to touch the bonds again till the interest on the November coupons is due.

MR. D.—A good idee! [*Takes the envelope, unties the tape, and removes the contents. The glow of comfort on his face changes to consternation. There are no bonds, but three Sunday-school Visitors instead.*]

JOSIAH.—Hallo! What ye got there?

MRS. D.—Why, father! Massy sakes!

LAURA.—What does it mean, father?

[*Mr. Ducklow cannot speak. He opens the envelope again, turns it inside out, and shakes it with a trembling hand. They are gone. Looks for his hat.*]

MR. D.—Wal! Wal! Mother, hadn't we better go right home? Those rascals must have stolen them at the bank.

JOSIAH.—There'll be not the least use in going to-night. If they were stolen at the bank, you can't do any thing about it till to-morrow; and even if they were taken from your own house, I don't see what's to be gained now by hurrying back. It isn't probable you'll ever see them again; and you may just as well take it easy, go to bed and sleep on it, and take a fresh start in the morning. The best way will be to advertise.

[*Laura passes out.*]

JOSIAH [*taking his hat*].—Excuse me; I'll be back in a few minutes.

[*Exit Josiah.*]

MR. D.—If we had only given the three thousan' dollars to Reuben ! 'Twould have jest set him up, and been some compensation for his sufferin's and losses goin' to the war.

MRS. D.—Wal, I had no objections. I always thought he ought to have the money eventooally; and as Miss Beswick said, no doubt it would a' been ten times the comfort to him now it would be a number of years from now. But you didn't seem willin'.

MR. D.—I don't know ! 'Twas you that wasn't willin'. But it's no use talkin' [*holding the envelope in his hand, and giving it an occasional shake*]. I've not the least idee we shall ever see the color of them bonds again. If they was stole at the bank, I can't prove any thing.

MRS. D.—It does seem strange to me that you should have had no more gumption than to trust the bonds with strangers, when they told you, in so many words, they wouldn't be responsible.

MR. D.—If you have flung that in my teeth once, you have done it fifty times !

MRS. D.—Wal, I don't see how we're going to work to find 'em, now they're lost, without making inquiries; and we can't make inquiries, without letting it be known that we have bought.

MR. D.—I been thinking about that. Oh, dear ! [*with a groan*] I wish the pesky coupon bonds had never been invented ! Very like, somebody got into the house that morning, when the little scamp run out, before you got to home from Reuben's; and then I don't see any way left but to advertise, as Josiah said. [*Sighing.*]

MRS. D.—And that 'll bring it all out ! Oh, dear ! if you only hadn't been so imprudent !

MR. D.—Wal ! wal !   [*Exit scene.*]

K

Scene VII.— *Reuben's house — Reuben, Sophronia, and Ruby, present — Reuben watching Sophronia. Enter Mr. and Mrs. Ducklow looking as mournful as the grave.*

Mrs. D. [*solemnly.*]—Good-morning.

Mr. D. [*soberly.*]—How are you gettin' along, Reuben?

Reuben.—I am doing well enough. Don't be at all concerned about me. It ain't pleasant to lie here, and feel it may be months—months—before I'm able to be about my business ! but I wouldn't mind it—I could stand it first-rate—I could stand any thing—any thing, but to see her working her life out for me and the children ! To no purpose, either ! That's the worst of it ! We shall have to lose this place, spite of fate !

Sophro. [*hastening to him and laying her hand upon his forehead.*]—Oh, Reuben ! why won't you stop thinking about that ? Do try to have more faith ! We shall be taken care of, I'm sure !

Reuben.—If I had three thousand dollars—yes, or even two—then I'd have faith ! Miss Beswick has proposed to send a subscription-paper around town for us ; but I'd rather die than have it done ! Besides, nothing near that amount could be raised, I'm confident. [*Mr. D. utters a groan.*] You need't groan so, Pa Ducklow ; for I ain't hinting at you. I don't expect you to help me out of my trouble. If you had felt called upon to do it, you'd have done it before now ; and I don't ask—1 don't beg—of any man ! [*proudly.*]

Mr. D.—That's right ! I like yer spirit ! But I was sighin' to think of something—something you haven't known any thing about, Reuben.

Mrs. D.—Yes, Reuben, we should have helped you, and did take steps towards it——

Mr. D.—In fact, you've met with a great misfortin, Reuben, unbeknown to yourself. You've met with a great misfortin ! Yer Ma Ducklow knows.

Mrs. D.—Yes, Reuben, the very day you came home your Pa Ducklow made an investment for yer benefit. We didn't mention it, you know—1 wouldn't own up to it, though I didn't exactly say the contrary, the morning we was over here.

Mr. D.—Because we wanted to surprise you ! We was

keepin' it a secret till the right time; then we was goin' to make it a pleasant surprise to ye.

REUBEN [*in bewilderment, looking from one to the other*].—What, in the name of common-sense, are you talking about?

MR. D. [*groaning.*]—Cowpon bonds! Three thousan' dollar cowpon bonds! [*another groan.*] The money had been lent, but I wanted to make a good investment for you, and I thought there was nothing so good as gov'-ments.

REUBEN.—That's all right! Only, if you had money to invest for my benefit, I should have preferred to pay off the mortgage the first thing.

MR. D.—Sartin! sartin! and you could have turned the bonds right in if you had so chosen, like so much cash, or you could have drawed yer interest on the bonds in gold, and paid the interest on your mortgage in currency, and made so much; as I rather thought you would.

REUBEN [*eagerly raising on his elbow.*] — But the bonds?

[*Enter Miss B., with shawl over her head.*]

MRS. D. [*with anxiety.*]—We was just telling about our loss—*Reuben's loss!*

MISS BESWICK [*slipping the shawl from her head and sitting down*].—Very well, don't let me interrupt you. [*Listens, in a prim, sarcastic manner.*]

REUBEN.—I see—I see. You had kinder intentions towards me than I gave you credit for. Forgive me if I wronged you.

MR. D.—Wal, wal, if we only had them. They were all invested for your benefit.

REUBEN.—But don't feel so bad about it. You did what you thought best. I can only say the fates are against me.

MISS B. [*stretching up her neck and clearing her throat.*] —Hem! hem! So them bonds you had bought for Reuben was in the house the very night I called.

MRS. D.—Yes, Miss Beswick; and that's what made it so uncomfortable to us, to have you talk the way you did.

MISS B. [*stretching her neck still further and clearing her throat.*]—Hem! 'Twas too bad. Ye ought to have told me. You'd actually bought the bonds—bought 'em for Reuben, had ye?

MR. D.—Sartin! sartin!

MRS. D.—To be sure; we designed 'em for his benefit —a surprise, when the right time come.

MISS B.—Hem! well! When the right time come? Yes. That *right time* wasn't somethin' indefinite, in the fur futur, of course? Yer losin' the bonds didn't hurry up yer benevolence the least grain, I s'pose? Hem! Let in them boys, Sophrony.

[*Sophronia opens the door. Enter Dick Atkins, followed reluctantly by Taddy, who begins to whimper.*]

MR. AND MRS. D.—Thaddeus! what are you here for?

MISS B. [*arbitrarily.*]—Because I said so! Step along, boys! step along! Hold up yer head, Taddy, for ye ain't goin' to be hurt while I'm 'round. Take yer fists out of yer eyes, and stop blubberin'. Mr. Ducklow, that boy knows somethin' about *Reuben's coupon bonds!*

MR. AND MRS. D. [*angrily.*]—Thaddeus! did you tech them bonds?

TADDY [*whimpering*].—Didn't know what they was.

MRS. D. [*grasps Taddy by the shoulder.*]—Did you take them?

MISS B. [*sternly.*]—Hands off, if you please! I told him if he'd be a good boy, and come along with Richard, and tell the truth, he shouldn't be hurt [*raising her hand with a majestic nod*]. If you please! [*Mrs. D. takes her hand off of Taddy.*]

MR. D.—Where are they now? Where are they?

TADDY —Don't know.

MR. D.—Don't know? You villian! [*approaches Taddy angrily.*]

MISS B. [*raising her hand.*]—If you please! [*Mr. D. sinks back.*]

MRS. D.—What did ye do with 'em? What did you want of 'em?

TADDY.—To cover my kite.

MR. D.—*Cover your kite? your kite?* Didn't you know no better?

TADDY.—Didn't think you'd care. I had some newspapers Dick gave me to cover it, but I thought them things would be puttier, so I took 'em, and put the news-papers in the wrapper.

Mr. D.—Did ye cover yer kite?

Taddy.—No. When I found out you cared so much about 'em, I darsent. I was afeard you'd see 'em.

Mrs. D.—Then what did you do with 'em?

Taddy.—When you was away, Dick came over to sleep with me, and I—I—sold 'em to him.

Mr. D.—*Sold 'em* to Dick!

Dick [*stoutly*].—Yes; for six marbles, and one was a bull's eye, and one an agate, and two alleys. Then when you come home, and made such a fuss, he wanted 'em agin, but he wouldn't give me back but four, and I wa'rn't goin' to agree to no sich nonsense as that.

Taddy.—I'd lost the bull's eye and one common.

Mr. D.—But the bonds—did you destroy 'em?

Dick.—Likely I'd destroy 'em after I'd paid six marbles for 'em. I wanted 'em to cover my kite with.

Mr. D.—Cover your—Oh! Then you've made a kite of 'em?

Dick.—Well, I was goin' to, when Aunt Beswick ketched me at it. She made me tell where I got 'em and took me over to your house jest now, and Taddy said you was over here, and so she put a-head and made us follow her.

Mr. D. [*impatiently.*]—But where are the bonds?

Dick.—If Taddy 'll give me back the marbles——

Miss B.—That 'll do! Reuben will give you twenty marbles, for I believe you said they was Reuben's bonds, Mr. Ducklow.

Mr. D.—Yes; that is——

Mrs. D.—Event-oo-ally.

Miss B.—Now look here! what am I to understand—be they Reuben's bonds, or be they not? "That's the question."

Mr. D. [*slowly.*]—Of course they're Reuben's.

Mrs. D.—We intended all the while——

Mr. D.—To do jest what he pleases with 'em.

Miss B.—Well, now, it's understood. Here, Reuben, are your coupon bonds. [*Draws them from her bosom and lays them in Reuben's hands.*]

Reuben [*opening them*].—Glory! Sophrony! Ruby—

you've got a home! Miss Beswick, you angel from the
skies, go order a bushel and a half of marbles for Dick,
and have the bill sent to me. Oh, Pa Ducklow, you never
did a nobler, or more generous thing in your life. These
will lift the mortgage and leave me a nest-egg besides.
Then, when I get my back pay and my pension, and my
health again, we shall be independent.

[*Exit scene.*]

THE PURITAN'S DILEMMA.

CHARACTERS.

CAPT. MILES STANDISH.   JOHN ALDEN.   PRISCILLA.

SCENE I. *By the sea-side.*

MILES STANDISH [*walking, soliloquizes*].
Aye! Plymouth is fair—no goodlier spot
Could gladden the heart out of England,
Standing so like the Angel of Vision—
Her one foot on sea, the other on land,
While the hem of her garment touches low
On the beach and the woodland.
Dear, dear to the pilgrim is rest—the hope
That his labors in measure are ended.
How snug seem those huts our own hands have builded,
Gleaming like palaces in October's sun;
And, to eke out the fancy, yon tower,
Our fort, lifting up its rude cannon, seems
Fearful enough in the glorious autumn
To frighten a host of dusky invaders.
Ah! what would betide to the colony
Should the fury of winter set early in?
I fear that nought would be left—none to tell
Of the fate of companions, should this year,
Like the last, shroud our hopes in despair.
God forbid that our foes and the weather—

The wild blasts and the savages wilder—
Should count on our weakness to conquer—should hope
To bury beyond resurrection this seed
His right hand has sifted.   Bible and home!
These unmolested we longed for.   We find
Them in prospect for children, perhaps, while
Our hearts must be rent through manifold woes,
—Oh, Rose of my heart! Your grave on the hill,
Now bristling with corn-blades and displaying full ears,
Seems a Providence speaking directly to me!
  ALDEN [*approaching*].
Captain Standish!   [*Capt. does not hear.*]
    Standish, Captain of Plymouth!
  STANDISH [*recognizing*].
Ah, Alden, my friend!   From the Governor now ?
  ALDEN.
Yes, with message for you.—Your pardon, I trust,
For breaking the thought that held you intent;
But 'tis danger foreboding that brings me in haste.
The Indians, they say, are prowling in sight.
Your good word as ever, your right arm as well
We count on for safety.
  STANDISH.
     I'll with you at once.
  ALDEN.
Go to the Governor—other mission is mine.
When behests are all given and action complete
We'll meet and converse according to wont—
Discuss doctrines, books, and talk of the village.
  STANDISH.
As you say, my young friend.   I always find strength
In counsels with you.   Good-bye, then.   [*Exit.*]
  ALDEN.
    Farewell!   [*Exit.*]

  SCENE II.—*Room in a house.*

  STANDISH [*striding impatiently*].
This parleying with savages never has done—
Never will do!   So I've settled the matter—
Accepted their challenge—stand ready for fight.
Snake-skin and arrows after treaties of peace!

Powder and shot pressed down in good measure—
They'll understand that, I warrant—yes, feel
Its significance early to-morrow.

ALDEN.

We discuss retribution then, I surmise.

STANDISH.

We'll not stop to discuss it, but deal it—
Deal to the death—to the cowardly tribes
That sneak on our borders to ravage and kill;
That promise good faith, but only to lull
Our wary suspicion, more surely to kill.
Depravity total what man can doubt
Who has treated with red men—a doctrine
We hold by strongly as saints' perseverance !
—Hear me, John Alden ! Faith in humanity
Doesn't mean faith in Indians, I verily think !

ALDEN.

So the army of Plymouth goes out with the dawn !

STANDISH.

Yes—few, tried men, and staunch—their lives in their
        hands
And death for those treacherous redskins ! Oh, man,
A saint might swear at their villanous tricks !

ALDEN.

But, Captain, my friend, may we not here perceive
How God, in his mercy, bears long with us all ?
Should his wrath be extended and justice done——

STANDISH [interrupting].

True, true, John—we soldiers forget. You scholars
And peace men have time to reflect, to order
Your lives right seemly indeed. We war men, howbeit,
Grow rough—I fear wicked—and oftentimes need
Your kind admonitions and breathings of heaven.
—Oh, how a man pines for the blessing of home !
The light of mine quenched, I oft seem to myself
Adrift without compass ; and e'en the Good Book
Seems less full of comfort than when Rose and I
Together betimes sought its teaching with prayer.
You remember her well, and the heavenly grace
That shone on her brow from her nearness to God—
You know how her spirit passed hence when he called.
—But, friend, who can know of the void in my heart ?

ALDEN.

As the Psalmist hath said—" We go unto them,
" But they cannot come back unto us"—" Truly
" A gift from the Lord is a wife good and true."

STANDISH.

When I tarry in camp or in combat strive,
" What boots ᐧ me my life," I frequently ask,
" Since no hearthstone is mine to which to return—
" No tie here on earth but my duty to do ?"

ALDEN.

Yet that is well done; and a father to all
You prove by your valor, since you are our hope
In such times of distress.

STANDISH.

        That all may be true;
Yet that is such light   as the traveller sees
In the cot from afar, when out on the moor.
It warms not, scarce cheers with its bright slanting ray—
Only gives him a hope such bliss to attain.

ALDEN.

Is friendship no boon ?

STANDISH.

        Aye, certainly, Alden—
Such as ours well may call for gratitude deep;
But nought passing love of a woman I've found.
Since talk has turned thus, I will venture to tax
Your friendship for once with a thought that has lain
Smouldering for weeks till this call gives it vent,
When it bursts into flames, and will not be quenched,
But free air it craves.   You know fair Priscilla:
Think you she would share a roof with a warrior—
Give her heart unto me—her hand into mine ?

ALDEN.

None fairer, none worthier, than she could one name
To stand where Rose stood, as first in your heart!
But ask her, my friend, and put to the proof
Your skill in heart-weapons—your valor in love.

STANDISH.

Just there, my friend, I falter. I long, but can't speak ;
And would beg for your service. Ere I go,
I ask you to tell her how lone is my plight—
I love her, albeit my manner is rude.

I trust to your words and your most courtly ways
To win her approval and her heart for me.
ALDEN.
A strange errand this for a young man like me,
Who ne'er yet addressed a woman himself;
While you, urged by memory, might enter a claim
No womanly heart could withstand, and secure
A prize for yourself worth the winning. Indeed,
If time fails ere you must buckle on steel,
Write out your petition—its bearer I'll be.
STANDISH.
No, John, I've no words, though a full heart is mine.
Break it, I pray, in most elegant phrases,
In which you're reputed by all to excel.
You're a friend in my need ; and when I return,
Let me hear from your lips your success, which is mine.
Yes, early to-morrow I marshal my band—
God guide us and you, John! Your hand—and good-bye!
[*Exit.*]
ALDEN.
He would not take nay.—My friend and companion,
How, telling your wishes, you pictured my own!
I could not say nay, he so leaned on my friendship—
Nor could I reveal my depths of emotion. No—
The elder, needier by reason of loss—
My hope must give way, "preferring another,"
As well saith the Scriptures, "unto myself!"
Why have I been tardy? How could I suspect
Another would covet the jewel I saw?
Why not? Fair as the sun she shines unto all!
Why falter? A friend I can prove, though to love
Be denied me. By waiting, I'm tempted
To be false to my friend and myself—my suit
To prefer—his to—I'll straight to Priscilla!
[*Exit.*]

SCENE III.—*Room in house— Priscilla at work.*

PRISCILLA [*to Alden entering*].
Good-morrow, John Alden—good-morrow!

ALDEN.

The same

I bid you.

PRISCILLA.

Good wishes are well when the place
Is well nigh deserted—a guard but for women
And children remains. Indeed, 'tis very gloomy
The prospect—with war and with winter at hand!
You saw, then, our army depart?

ALDEN.

Yes, saw them,
And bade them God-speed!—an army terrible too,
With banners and weapons and courage to strike
The foe dumb.

PRISCILLA.

The flower of our Plymouth has gone—
The pride of the Mayflower. Oh, pity if they
Should fail!

ALDEN.

Doubtless we die, if they do. Surely
You give not up to misgivings like these! Why
The Lord's on our side, and Miles Standish—Standish,
Who knows not defeat in matters of warfare—Standish,
Whose fame every household in England
Was proud to repeat! Quicker work he will make
With these tribes than with phalanx on phalanx
Of men for years trained in battles in Europe.

PRISCILLA.

Yes, Standish is notable and one to trust
In emergency. But vain is the help of man
If God be not on our side.

ALDEN.

Now we're speaking
Of Standish, I'll state my purpose in main
In calling this morning so early. A charge
He has given me as his friend, and as friend
I will faithfully try to discharge it. Deep,
Deep are the wounds that love makes—deeper, I trow,
Than sabre-cuts that bring high renown. Standish
Boasting honorable scars yet confesses
A vulnerable spot in his heart. The smart
That was left when Rose died still unabated,

He deems but one remedy sure—thinks that you
Perhaps——
PRISCILLA [*in astonishment*].
     I marry Miles Standish, the Captain!
ALDEN.
If you knew that he loves and desires it—might——
PRISCILLA.
Pray, what knows the Captain of love—a fighter?
Of tender regard for a woman?
ALDEN.
       ——forget
His calling and possible roughness of manner,
And share home with him who fireside has none——
PRISCILLA.
Forget all a woman feels and discovers
By her God-given instincts alone? Well, a love
One can't show, nor yet speak, must, I ween, a queer
Sort of malady prove! Did Standish suppose
That such wounds could be healed by proxy alone,
Or through negotiations? [*Laughing derisively.*]
ALDEN.
     He, doubtless, himself
Had pleaded his cause, had not duty called hence.
PRISCILLA.
What duty can call one away to prevent
His settling himself his affairs with his God?
Or, if need is so great, with the woman he thinks
A helpmeet to journey with him to that God?
ALDEN.
His friend, he desired me to open the case,
Which most likely he intends when returned
Himself to prosecute.
PRISCILLA.
     What friend, pray, is that
Whom any man needs to interpret himself
To his wife? What marriage were that where a man
Might be at such loss every day, I suspect,
Translating himself?
ALDEN.
    But what saith the Lord, pray,
Of living alone? Saith he not, " 'Tis not good?"
And a man like Miles Standish has surely most need

Of companion, of comfort, caresses—all,
In short, to preserve a fair balance in life.
What were the lone dove without mate ?   All nature
Shows types blessing union of heart and of life—
And, indeed —
     PRISCILLA.
                    With such views you have never— ?
John Alden, why do you not speak for yourself?
               [*Curtain falls.*]

A SCENE IN COURT.

CHARACTERS.

JUDGE SOBER, presiding
COUNSELLOR SHARP, prosecuting attorney.
BLUSTER SNAP, counsel for prisoner. ⁻
PHELIM O'SHAUGHNESSY, prisoner.
HANS PUMPERNICKEL, ⎫
FRAU PUMPERNICKEL, ⎬ witnesses for prosecution.
CONSTABLE FERRET, ⎭
TERRENCE BRADY, ⎫
BRIDGET SPALPEEN, ⎬ witnesses for prisoner.
MRS. McJERK, ⎭
CLERK, JURORS, CRIER and BAILIFFS.
SPECTATORS, *ad lib.*

―――

Court-room with usual accompaniments. Loud conversation suspended on the entrance of Judge, who takes his seat.

JUDGE.—Mr. Crier, you may open the Court.

CRIER.—O yes! O yes! O yes! All persons having any business before this Honorable Court, which stood adjourned to this time and place, draw near and give their attendance, and they shall be heard!

JUDGE.—Any thing ready this morning, Mr. Sharp?

SHARP.—Yes, your Honor! State against O'Shaughnessy, for larceny, was assigned, and the witnesses for the prosecution are all here, I believe.

JUDGE.—Call the prisoner, Mr. Clerk.

CLERK.—Phelim O'Shaughnessy!

PHELIM [*sitting near his counsel*].—Here, your worship! [*rising and pulling his forelock.*]

JUDGE.—Let him be arraigned.

BLUSTER.—I appear, if your Honor pleases, for Mr. O'Shaughnessy. We waive the arraignment and plead "Not Guilty." [*Phelim sits.*]

JUDGE —Has the jury been sworn?

CLERK.—Yes, your Honor.

JUDGE.—Proceed, Mr. Sharp.

BLUSTER.—Before going any further, if your Honor pleases, I have here a motion [*holding paper in hand*] to quash the indictment. The prisoner is indicted for the larceny of one *hog*, the property of Hans Pumpernickel. My point is, that the description of the animal alleged to have been stolen is too vague and indefinite— and that the indictment, therefore, is fatally defective in not stating whether the animal laid is a hog, or a sow, or a boar, or a barrow, or a shoat, or a pig. Such an indictment, your Honor, can never be sustained for a fraction of a moment in a court of law. I would refer your Honor—if indeed your Honor has any doubt upon so clear a point—to the case of Regina *v.* Tims, Vol. 989, English Common Law Reports, page 3001. I have the case here, your Honor [*producing book*], and will read it to you. This was a case——

JUDGE [*interrupting*].—Have you any thing to say, Mr. Sharp?

SHARP [*smiling*].—Nothing, your Honor.

JUDGE.—The Court will not trouble you, Mr. Snap. I overrule the motion to quash.

BLUSTER.—Your Honor will note an exception, then [*seating himself*].

JUDGE.—Certainly [*making memorandum*]. Proceed, Mr. Sharp.

SHARP.—Gentlemen of the jury, this is an indictment against Phelim O'Shaughnessy, the prisoner at the bar, for the larceny, on the twenty-fourth of last December, of one hog, the property of Hans Pumpernickel. The facts in the case you will learn from the witnesses who will be produced before you. Call Hans Pumpernickel.

CRIER.—What name?

CLERK.—Hans Pumpernickel.

CRIER [*calling*].—Hans Pumpernickel!

HANS [*coming forward*].—Yah—yah—he ish here.

SHARP.—Take the stand, Hans. [*Clerk swears witness.*] Now, Hans, tell these gentlemen here [*pointing to jury*] and the judge all you know about losing your hog last winter.

BLUSTER.—If your Honor please, in a case of so much importance to my client I must ask that all the witnesses in the case except the one testifying shall be excluded.

JUDGE.—Certainly, if you wish. Mr. Clerk, call the names of the witnesses. [*Clerk calls names of witnesses, Bluster having handed him a list of prisoner's.*] All the witnesses whose names have been called, except the one now on the stand, will leave the court-room and remain outside till they are called.

[*Witnesses withdraw, the opposing witnesses scowling defiance at each other.*]

SHARP.—Now, Hans, speak up loud, so that all these gentlemen can hear you.

HANS.—Yah—yah. Don't nobody bodders me, and I dells you der troot and nodin' but zhoost der troot. You sees I says to mine frow, says I, " Katareen "——

BLUSTER [*loudly*] —You needn't tell what you said. to your wife, sir.

SHARP.—Never mind that, Hans.

HANS.—Den Katareen, she says, " Vat you vants, Hans?" Den——

BLUSTER.—Don't tell us what your wife said, sir.

SHARP.—No, Hans. Go on and tell us about your losing your hog.

HANS.—Yah—yah. Dat ish zhoost vat I vas dryin' to dell you. Zhoost all lets me be and I dells you all about mine hog and dat Irishman's shtealing him.

BLUSTER.—This, certainly, is not evidence, your Honor.

SHARP.—Hans, hark to me now, and answer the questions which I ask you.

HANS.—Yah—yah.

SHARP.—Did you lose a hog last winter, Hans?

HANS.—Yah—I loses one goot hog—so goot as never vas mit me before.

SHARP.—What time in the winter was it ?

HANS.—Grismas vas der neksht day.

SHARP.—The day before Christmas—the twenty-fourth of December then. What kind of a hog was it?

HANS.—I dells you he vas one goot hog. Oh, *so goot!* So pig—so——

BLUSTER [*interrupting*].—A pig? I thought you just now swore it was a hog. [*Looking meaningly at jury.*]

SHARP.—So he did, Mr. Bluster. He was going to say how big it was.

HANS —Yah—yah—dat ish so. He vas so pig as das. [*Touching fingers of both hands and describing a circle with his arms.*] Me and mine frow, we never takes round him eder of us. And so fett! [*Smacking lips.*] So fett as butter never vas !

BLUSTER.—So what ?

SHARP.—*Fat*, he means.

HANS.—Yah—yah. Das ish so. Oh, *so* fett!

SHARP.—You lost him, you say, on the 24th of December last ?

HANS.—Grismas was der neksht day

SHARP.—When did you see him again after you lost him ?

HANS.—Ven I sees him more? Oh, dree, four week. Den der gonstable he brings mine hog pack.

SHARP.—That's all, Mr. Snap. He is your witness.

BLUSTER [*squaring himself off for cross-examination*]. What is your name, sir ?

HANS.—Hans Pumpernickel.

BLUSTER.—How long have you lived in this country, sir ?

HANS.—How long in dis guntree? Sieben year.

BLUSTER.—What do you say ?

SHARP.—Seven years.

BLUSTER [*turning to Sharp*].—I'll attend to the witness in my own way, if you please, sir. [*To Hans.*] Now, sir, upon your oath, how long have you been in this country ?

HANS.—I zhoost dells you—*sieben year.*

BLUSTER.—That doesn't answer my question, sir.

JUDGE.—Really, Mr. Snap, the witness has answered the question twice already; and, moreover, it is an entirely irrelevant question. The time of the Court cannot be frittered away in such trifling. If you are unable to understand the witness, and will not avail yourself of Mr. Sharp's suggestions, the interpreter of the Court must be called.

BLUSTER [*somewhat subdued*].—Yes, your Honor. [*To Hans.*] Seven years, you say ? What kind of a hog did you lose ? Had he any marks about him ?

HANS.—I dells you he be a goot fett hog—goot pig large hog. Nobody could not mark him—the fett runs out of him if dey do.

BLUSTER.—Then he had no marks on him? How did you know him, then, sir?

HANS.—How I knows him? I did know him when he vas a little so pig hog [*making a small circle with his thumbs and forefingers*], ven he vas nodin but one baby hog—yah. Den I cuts one ear and der oder ear—once twice—den I knows he vill all der dime be mine own hog.

BLUSTER.—Oh! Then you did mark him after all? [*looking to jury.*]

HANS.—I dells you I cuts his both ear.

BLUSTER.—What time in the day did you miss him on the 24th of December?

HANS.—I mish him not, I loses him ven der Irishman he steals him.

BLUSTER [*loudly*].—Take care what you say, sir, about stealing. Answer my question: when did you lose him that day?

HANS.—I eats mine dinner—I goes to mine hog's pen —and he vas dare no more ash ever vas.

BLUSTER.—You missed him directly after dinner? You said the constable brought him back to you—what constable?

HANS.—Der gonstable ash ish here zhoost now—Misder Ferret.

BLUSTER,—And you swear it was your hog that the constable brought you? Upon your oath—your solemn oath—remember?

HANS.—I dells you, and I dells you now, I shwears it.

BLUSTER.—That's all, sir.

SHARP.—That's all, Hans. You may sit down. [*To bailiff.*] Call Frau Pumpernickel. [*Bailiff returns with Frau, who is sworn.*] Frau, did Hans lose a hog last winter? If so, when?

FRAU.—Der day before Grismas vas me and Hans loses our fett hog.

SHARP.—When did you see him again?

FRAU.—He ish gone bigger dan tree week ven der gonstable he dells me and Hans dat der Irishman——

BLUSTER.—Never mind that, ma'am.

SHARP.—What constable are you speaking of?

FRAU.—Misder Ferrett, he brings me and Hans' hog pack wid him.

SHARP.—You are sure that the hog the constable brought was your hog?

FRAU [*raising both hands and looking around the room*]. —I knows dat hog—dat hog Peter—so vell I knows mine own child.

SHARP.—Cross-examine, Mr. Snap.

BLUSTER.—How did you know the hog was yours? You say the hog belonged to you and Hans? Are you his wife?

FRAU.—Yah, I be his frow.

BLUSTER.—How did you know the hog?

FRAU.—How I knows der hog? How I knows mine child? I knows him so well I knows him.

BLUSTER.—What marks had he on him?

FRAU.—Marks! [*holding up hands.*] Himmel! You dinks me and Hans marks dat hog? Nein, nein! [*emphatically.*] Dere vas no marks on him He vas so fett no marks could stay dere. I sees Hans shlit his ears mineself.

BLUSTER.—Both ears?

FRAU.—Now one, and den der oder—so—[*making motion as if drawing a knife across her hand.*]

BLUSTER.— You swear positively that the hog which Constable Ferret brought back was yours, do you?

FRAU [*looking at him with the utmost contempt*].—I dells you nodin' more; you be too doom for me.

BLUSTER.—That's all, then.

FRAU —So I dinks [*leaving the stand in disgust, before Sharp has given her permission, which is done as she leaves*].

[*Sharp directs Ferret to be called and sworn.*]

SHARP —Mr. Ferret, state to the Court and jury what you know relative to a hog lost by Hans Pumpernickel last winter.

FERRET.—I learned from Hans on Christmas last, that his hog had been missing since the day before. I knew the hog well, and some time afterwards—on the 11th of last January—I saw the animal in O'Shaughnessy's pen. I told a woman there, who I understood to be the prisonér's wife, that that hog had been stolen from Hans, and she flew at me with curses and an iron spoon which she had in her hand, when the prisoner came in, and wanted to know what it was all about. I told him who the hog belonged to, and he abused me with every thing he could lay his tongue to. He said, "No Dutchman ever owned a pig like that." I said he did—and so on. At last he got summat peacified, when I told him that I should restore the hog to his rightful owner. Then he fell to again—and I don't know what more wouldn't have happened, if some of his friends hadn't over-persuaded him, and I drove the hog home to Hans.

SHARP.—Your witness, Mr. Snap.

BLUSTER.—You knew the hog to be what's-his-name's, did you?

FERRET.—I knew he was Hans Pumpernickel's hog.

BLUSTER.—How did you know it, sir?

FERRET.—I live near Hans and had seen it almost every day, off and on, since it was a little pig.

BLUSTER.—Oh, you lived near the hog, did you? [*No answer—witness looks contemptuously at B.*] Any marks about the animal by which you could recognize him?

FERRET.—One slit in his right ear and two in his left.

BLUSTER.—Sure of that, sir?

FERRET —Yes, sir.

BLUSTER —'Twasn't one in his left ear and two in his right, was it? Be cautious, now; you are on your oath, remember, Mr. Constable.

FERRET—I have told you already—one slit in his right ear and two in his left.

BLUSTER.—You removed that hog from Mr. O'Shaughnessy's pen without any warrant—didn't you, sir?

FERRET.—I knew it was Hans' hog, and I took him home.

BLUSTER.—You may stand down, sir. [*As Ferret steps away Bluster remarks in an audible tone*, "You'll hear from me shortly, sir!" *Ferret replies*, "Thank you, sir, happy to hear from you at any time!"]

SHARP [*to Court*].—The case for the prosecution is closed.

JUDGE.—Any witnesses for the defence, Mr. Snap?

BLUSTER.—Yes, your honor. But before I call any, I

ask your Honor's decision upon a point of law. To my mind, there is an essential variance between the indictment and the proof—essential and fatal. This hog is laid in the indictment as the property of one Hans Pumpernickel; the proof is that he belonged jointly to Hans and his wife.

JUDGE.—There is nothing in that point, sir. Mrs. Pumpernickel, I presume, like some others of her sex, proceeds upon the theory that what is her own is her own, and what is her husband's is her own also. [*Smiles in court at this judicial witticism.*] Proceed with your defence, Mr. Snap.

BLUSTER.—Yes, your Honor—an exception will be noted? [*Judge nods affirmatively.*] Gentlemen of the jury, our defence is that this hog was our hog—and I shall prove it. [*Takes his seat with a pompous flourish.*] Call Terrence Brady! [*to bailiff, who returns with the witness, and the latter is sworn.*] Mr. Brady, are you acquainted with Mr. O'Shaughnessy?

BRADY.—Is it that ye say? Do I know Phalim? Faix, and do I know mysilf thin, if I haven't known Phalim O'Shaughnessy since he was ivir that high, your worship! [*Lowering his hand to the level of his knee, to indicate the height.*]

BLUSTER.—You live near him—don't you?

BRADY.—Right forninst his house.

BLUSTER.—Did Mr. O'Shaughnessy have any hogs last fall?

BRADY.—And didn't he have two of the swatest crathers the blissed saints ivir set eyes on?

BLUSTER.—What became of them, Mr. Brady?

BRADY.—What wint wid them, do ye say? Didn't Phalim and mysilf kill the one of thim in Christmas wake for us and the childer—for didn't mysilf buy the half of him and pay for him like a man, too—didn't I, Phalim? [*To prisoner.*]

PHELIM.—Troth and ye did, my boy!

CRIER.—Silence in court! [*Bailiff approaches Phelim and Bluster is seen enjoining silence upon his client.*]

BLUSTER.—Mr. Brady, you'll talk to the Court and jury.

BRADY.—Yis—and that I will.

BLUSTER.—He killed one in Christmas week, you say. What became of the other?

BRADY.—Of the other is it ye say? Och! and didn't that murtherin' baste of a dirty constable stale him away from Phalim's own pen? And didn't I see him and hear him with my own eyes? And the childer and Biddy cryin' too! The thaving spalpeen that he is! [*Shaking fist at Ferret.*]

CRIER.—Silence in court!

JUDGE.—Witness, you will be committed to jail if you don't conduct yourself as a witness should.

BRADY [*bowing profoundly to Judge*].—Beg your worship's pardon—but ivery hair on my head stiffens into a shillala whin I think of the likes of it.

BLUSTER.—How do you know that that hog which the constable took from Mr. O'Shaughnessy was his own—I mean Mr. O'Shaughnessy's?

BRADY.—Wasn't he the last of a litter of sivin? And wouldn't he have been three years ould if the Blissed Virgin had spared him till the nixt Saint Pathrick's? And didn't this knife of my own [*taking one from his pocket*] slit the ear on the right of him once [*making appropriate motions*], and the ear on the left of him twice the very day he was in his six-wakes' birthday? Know him, is it ye say? Does Terrence Brady know himself? Thin does he know Phalim's swate pig?

BLUSTER.— The witness is yours, Mr. Sharp.

SHARP.—You are positive that that hog was Phelim's?

BRADY.—As certain as that I'm here before yer Honor. Can a man say more? And that man an Irishman?

SHARP [*smiling*].—I should think not. You may take your seat. [*Brady steps off the stand.*]

BLUSTER.—One question I forgot to ask you, Mr. Brady.

BRADY [*resuming stand*].—Any question ye likes, and Terrence Brady's yer boy, if he was there.

BLUSTER.—Was anybody present when you slit the hog's ears?

SHARP.—It is not strictly legal—but, to save time, go on.

BRADY.—Was anybody prisint? Wasn't Biddy Spalpeen and Misthress McJerk? And didn't Biddy say,

" Now, Terrence, bc as aisy as iver ye can and don't hurt the swate crathur?"

BLUSTER.—That's all, Mr. Brady. You may stand down. [*Brady leaves ; and bailiff, at Bluster's direction, calls Bridget Spalpeen, who is sworn.*] Miss Spalpeen, do you remember any thing about Mr. Brady's marking a pig at any time for Mr. O'Shaughnessy?

BRIDGET.—It's Terrence and Phalim and the six-wakes' pig ye mane. Terrence's knife wasn't what it should have bin for the likes of that—and didn't I plade with him not to hurt the poor dumb baste?

BLUSTER.—How old was the pig?

BRIDGET.—Just six wakes to a day.

BLUSTER.—When did you see that pig last?

BRIDGET.— When he stole him away from Phalim's pin. [*Pointing to Ferret.*] Bad 'cess to him! [*shaking head.*]

BLUSTER.—You are sure it was the same animal?

BRIDGET.—Shure—is it? If it were the last breath that iver I breathed, I would kiss the book a thousand times to the truth of it! [*earnestly.*]

BLUSTER [*to Sharp*].— Any questions? [*Sharp shakes head in negative.*] You may be seated. [*To bailiff.*] Call Mrs. McJerk.

SHARP.—I suppose she is to corroborate the slitting?

BLUSTER.—Yes—and to identify the hog. [*Bailiff enters with Mrs. McJerk.*]

SHARP.—I'll admit that she'll testify to the same as the last witness.

BLUSTER.—Never mind, Mrs. McJerk. You may bo seated. I shall not want you.

MRS. McJ.—And don't I know it all—bad luck to yees? [*tossing her head towards Hans and company.*]

CRIER.—Silence in court!

JUDGE.—Well, gentlemen, is this to be argued?

SHARP.—I have no desire to take up more time, your Honor.

BLUSTER.—My duty to my client, your Honor, renders it obligatory upon mc to say a few words.

JUDGE.—Proceed, sir.

BLUSTER [*During his speech witnesses for prisoner exchange nods and glances of approval and scowl defiantly at witnesses for prosecution*].—May it please the

11

Court and you, gentlemen of the jury! Precious as your time is, gentlemen, and valuable as my own time is, gentlemen, I should not address you at the present time, gentlemen, did I not feel it incumbent upon me, as one in whose hands my client has placed what is dearer to him than life itself—his reputation—to call your attention to some points which it is quite possible, considering the hurry of this trial, may have escaped your attention.

My client, it is true, is but a common laboring man—having, however, the proud distinction of belonging to a race which, however some may affect to sneer at, contains —I say unhesitatingly—some of the most pre-eminent names upon the roll of fame, in this or any other land. And I declare to you, gentlemen of the jury, that, whatever others may say, the wheels of time will yet—and at no distant point of time—roll round the day when for a man to be able to say "I am an Irishman" will place him in a more enviable position than that once occupied by him who could say "I am a Roman citizen!"

My client, gentlemen of the jury, is charged with stealing a hog Let not what may, perchance, be your estimate of an animal of that species—as of but comparative slight money value—shut from your minds the fact, that to my client as a laboring Irishman such an animal is, next to the wife of his bosom, the most valuable possession which a benignant Providence can bestow upon him. I forget not his children. Far be it from me to overlook those sweet solacers of the day's toils, those refreshing companions of the night. No, gentlemen of the jury, I do not forget the children ; but I except them not. Without the pig the children could not live—and what boon were they then ?

The evidence, gentlemen of the jury, upon which the State seeks to convict my client, an Irishman, of having stolen a pig, an Irishman's second great earthly blessing, is before you.

The law in the case his Honor [turning to Judge and bowing profoundly] will give you. The facts, you, gentlemen, are to deal with in the light of the law.

With these remarks, gentlemen—without which I could not have laid my head upon my pillow this night, feeling that I had discharged my duty to my client—I leave the case with you, confident that you will never in your deliberations upon it forget that great maxim, without which the life of each were a weary burden to be borne as best we might through this Sahara of a world—that transcendent maxim, "*Fiat justitia, ruat cœlum!*" Gentlemen, I have done!

JUDGE.—Gentlemen of the jury: This is a case of conflicting testimony. You have the evidence upon both sides, and its decision I leave with you.

[*Bailiff is sworn by clerk to take charge of jury, when the foreman announces that they have agreed upon a verdict—the jury have consulted together in their seats during the swearing of the bailiff.*]

JUDGE.—Take the verdict. [*To Clerk.*]

CLERK.—How say you, Mr. Foreman, is Phelim O'Shaughnessy, the prisoner at the bar, guilty or not guilty?

FOREMAN.—Not guilty.

CLERK.—Hearken to your verdict as the Court shall record. You say that Phelim O'Shaughnessy, the prisoner at the bar, is not guilty. So say you, Mr. Foreman —so say you all. [*Each juror nods affirmatively.*]

[*Amid expressions of intense satisfaction on the part of Phelim and friends and corresponding indignation and surprise on the part of Hans and friends, the curtain falls.*]

THE MUTUAL DEVELOPMENT SOCIETY;

Or, CAPITAL vs. LABOR.

DRAMATIS PERSONÆ.

HON. EZEKIEL TYRANNUS.
MRS. EZEKIEL TYRANNUS.
HON. OBEDIAH CRINGEY, a lawyer.
MRS. FAIRPLAY,
MISS MANSFIELD,
MISS OLIVE BRANCH,
MISS GRACE ROBINSON, } factory women.
MISS LOU ATHERTON,
MISS ELLA EDGAR,
BILLY, an errand boy.

In one Act, three scenes.

SCENE I.—*Parlor in the house of Tyrannus—Mr. and Mrs. T. seen sitting—she sewing—he reading the paper.*

MR. TYRANNUS [*throwing down the paper, jumps to his feet, and paces up and down the room*].—Just as I expected, Mrs. T! I told you that it would be so! I knew it would—and now, for the fortieth time, have my predictions again been verified——

MRS. T. [*interrupting.*]—What in the world has come over you again, Mr. T.?

MR. T.—Come over *me?* Nothing, madam, nothing! [*excitedly*] do you understand me? absolutely nothing! But did I not emphatically declare that if 'Squire Jones allowed those factory girls to hold their [*sneeringly*] Mutual Development Society meetings in his hall, that they would run mad, and we should all be compelled to stop our factories until sane persons could be procured.

MRS T.—Is that all, Mr. T.? Then why get into such a terrible rage about it? your girls have not left you, nor have those from any other mill that I have heard of. I don't see that the least harm in the world can come out of such a society among those working girls; but it

seems to *me*, Mr. T., as if the universal failing of your
sex is to deny women the privilege of exercising the
powers which God has given them, and any act or effort
on their part which would tend to elevate them in the
scale of humanity, *you*, and such like you, immediately
set about to cry them down, and would, no doubt, lose
no chance to make their lives more miserable than even
now [*rising*]. Mr. Tyrannus, I am ashamed of you!
[*leaves the room.*]

MR. T. [*looking towards the door.*]—There's a model of
love, honor, and obey, for you, Ezekiel! [*folding his arms,
looks to the floor.*] Well, I guess women have some rights
[*shakes his head*]; but it would never do to give them a
chance—they're too tyrannical—man could not endure it!
Now, if I don't knock that Mutual Development Society
so far into the middle of next week that it will never again
be heard from, then my name is not Ezekiel Tyrannus,
the honorable ex-member of the New Jersey Legislature!
I'll go and see Deacon Smythe [*starting to the door, meets
Cringey*]. Good-morning, Mr. Cringey [*shake hands*].

MR. C. [*shakes Tyrannus' hand violently.*]—Good-morning, my dear Tyrant—Tyrannus—excuse me—I am de-
lighted to see you looking so well this morning! May I
venture to ask how is Mrs. T. this morning?

MR. T.—In an ill-humor, Cringey—in an ill-humor! Do
you know that ever since those factory women took it
into their heads—the nonsensical idea!—that there was a
higher and nobler station for every one of them than at
their places doing their work, the very deuce has been to
pay! My wife indorses every word and act of the [*contemptuously*] "Mutual Development Society"—and there
is war brewing [*handing Cringey a chair*]. Take a seat
[*both sit down*].

MR. C.—What society did you say?

MR. T.—Mutual Development Society.

MR. C.—Oh, I understand—a James' nasium!

MR. T.—No, no! nor a *Jim*-nasium; but a society where
they meet together to debate, read, sing, and undoubtedly
lay plans whereby they may render man their slaves and
very humble servants.

MR. C.—But, my dear boy—excuse the familiarity!—

but—it is the custom of all lawyers—you're married, are you not?

Mr. T. [*interrupting.*]—Of course I am!

Mr. C.—Then you have nothing to fear! Look at me —an old bachelor—I'm one of those who should tremble and fear such a formidable combination as you complain of; but I tell you, Tyrannus, I am glad to see those hardworked women initiate these steps to raise themselves out of the serfdom which capital has imposed upon their labor.

Mr. T.—But, Mr. Cringey, did you never reflect, and compare the superiority of the minds of men over that of women? Have you forgotten that man was created *first*, and woman *gave* to him, *afterwards*, as a helpmeet? Had it not been the wisdom of the Great Creator to bestow upon man the honor of being his first great work, he would have created——

Mr. C. [*interrupting.*]—Well, I admit that man was created first.

Mr. T. [*interrupting.*]—That's what I said!

Mr. C.—I mean *before* woman!

Mr. T.—That's what I mean!

Mr. C.—The beast was created before man, was it not?

Mr. T.—Certainly.

Mr. C.—Then, since the lowest order of animal nature was created *first*, then man, then woman, it stands to reason that woman must be superior to man, if man is to the brute, on the simple idea of progression—the glorious theme you used to harp upon so much. How now?

Mr. T.—I don't see it in that light, Cringey.

Mr. C.—No—but in a far less just one! Now, let me turn prophet for once, Tyrannus, and prophesy that the day will come when you capitalists will be brought up the round turn, and that, too, by the brains of women [*rising*].

Mr. T.—Nonsense! I don't believe there are as much brains in the whole thirteen hundred of my factory girls as in the head of your cane!

Mr. C.—We'll see. Good-morning.
[*Exit Cringey.*]

Mr T.—Old Cringey has labored hard to move me in my ideas. I'll not give in, though all the world shall decide against me! I know I'm right; but why others cannot see the evil of these combinations of women, as

tending to demoralize the community, as I do, is a mystery [*puts on his hat and leaves the room*]
[*Curtain drops.*]

SCENE II.—*Society-room. Rows of girls dressed in factory
suits on either side of room. Mrs. Fairplay, chairwoman,
in the centre. Miss Mansfield, secretary, at her right.*

MRS. FAIRPLAY. — Does any member of our little
Spartan band know of any person who is in sorrow or
distress?

MISS OLIVE BRANCH [*rising*]. — There is one in my
district—the girl who lost her hand in the machinery
one week since—her mother is also very ill, and want is
evident from their surroundings. I called upon Mr.
Tyrannus, of the mill where she worked, but he refused
to aid them. His excuse was that her injury had spoiled
over ten dollars' worth of muslins for him and she de-
served the punishment for her carelessness. I gave her
one-half of my week's wages—only one dollar and a-half
it is true—and they were very thankful and blessed our
Society. [*Sits down.*]

MRS. F.—Noble girl! While it is not in our power to
reimburse you now, you may rest assured that you shall
never want while there is a member of this organization
to assist you. Sisters [*to all*], here is a worthy example
set us—let it prompt us to follow it, and go about doing
good. Has any member aught to say in behalf of our
Society?

MISS ROBINSON [*rising*].—As chairwoman of the committee appointed at our last meeting to prepare an
address to our much oppressed sisters in the factories of
this country, I have the pleasure to offer the following
for the consideration of the Society. [*Reads from a
paper.*] "To the oppressed and down-trodden women
of the whole world: We, your sisters and co-workers,
employed by capitalists in the —— of —— (*using the
name of any place desired*), in order to more effectually
promote our social, moral and intellectual worth to such
a degree as our individual talents may admit, to promote
the well-being of our co-laborers, relieve their necessities

in sickness and distress, do most sincerely and earnestly
offer for your consideration the subject-matter of this
circular.

"We believe that the creation of man by the All-Wise
Intelligence was for protection and not oppression. We
do most emphatically believe that in women may be
found all the accomplishments—moral and intellectual—
that were ever attributed to man as an individual.

"We do, in the grossness of our scourging by the capitalists, offer up our prayers for the speedy deliverance
from the imposed servitude of our oppressed sisters in
factories and shops throughout the entire world; con-
demning, as inhuman, the unlicensed course pursued in
taking us while helpless children from the care and protection of our parents, and placing us in the workshops
of capitalists to weary fully three-fourths of the hours
twenty-four over our labors, thus preventing us from
realizing an education, alike beneficial to posterity as
ourselves.

"We cry aloud against all nations who thus permit
their moneyed men to pervert the creatures of circumstances to their pecuniary aggrandizement, to the detri-
ment of hundreds of lives annually, and a peopling of
the community with thousands of semi-illiterate women.

"We appeal, therefore, to you to lend us your aid in
our high and laudable efforts to suppress this growing
and unholy evil. Organize bodies for reading and mutual
culture; take under your charge the friendless orphans,
teach them, watch over them, and to your best means
relieve their wants in sickness and distress, and from the
indication of our own young band we predict that the
future will give to the world many bright minds, from
out even the dusky factory We are for raising the
standard of individual worth up! up!! promising to you,
as we mutually do to each other, to 'weary not in well-
doing.'

"Even now the importance and influence of our little
Spartan band is being felt by those who, at the expense
of life and limb, have become millionaires.

"In closing this appeal, we disclaim any intentions or
aspirations to assume a station with man politically.

We have aimed higher, and in so doing we ask your hearty co-operation."

Signed by the Committee.

[*Sits down.*]

MRS. F.—What will you do with your Committee's report?

MISS ATHERSON [*rising*].—For one, I heartily indorse it, and move that the report be received and adopted. [*Sits down.*]

MRS. F.—In the absence of objection, it is so ordered. [*Pausing.*] So ordered, Miss Mansfield.

MISS MANSFIELD [*rising*].—I have a communication addressed to our Society.

MRS. F.—Let it be read.

MISS M. [*reads.*]—" To whom it may concern :—This is to give notice that any and all employees of my factory belonging to, or sympathizing with, the so-called ' Mutual Development Society' are hereby discharged, and will call upon the Cashier for settlement. Signed Ezekiel Tyrannus" [*sits down*].

MRS. F.—Place it in the waste-paper basket [*pausing*]. No—I have a better plan—we will all stop work! You all know what a flurry he has been in for the last ten days ? He is compelled to fill his government contract by day after to-morrow. We'll stop, girls, and he will be forced to accede to our terms. Shall that be our mutual plan ?

ALL.—Yes.

MRS. F.—In the absence of further business, we will now adjourn—Miss Edgar first singing one of her songs.

[*Miss E. sings, the whole company joining in a chorus.*]

[*Curtain drops.*]

SCENE III.—*Curtain rises—Mr. Tyrannus seated at a table reading letters—Dress, morning-wrapper.*

MR. T.—Well, that's a respectable order ! [*reads from letter :*] "If you will furnish us seventy thousand yards of sheeting, in six weeks from the first proximo, we will pay two cents a yard extra for the accommodation" [*counting his fingers*]—Why, I'll make twelve thousand dollars out of that. [*Opens another letter — reads:*] " Sir :—We shall hold you to your agreement - the Government officers hold us to ours. The balance of those goods *must*" [*looking up*]—M-U-S-T, in great capitals— [*reads*] "*must* be delivered this week, or you forfeit forty thousand dollars" [*rising*]. Pshaw! they need not be afraid—they'll be done! [*Enter small boy.*] Well, Billy, what's wanting?

BILLY.—Please, sir, the Cashier says that all the girls have quit, and they want their money, because——

MR. T. [*interrupting.*]—Quit? What for? They sha'n't do any thing of the kind! I won't let them! I'll show them that they can't trifle with me! Go! send the fore-woman to me! [*exit Billy.*] Quit! I can buy every one of them, body and soul! I'll show them that they can't balk Ezekiel Tyrannus before they are twenty-four hours older! I'll starve every one of them! [*Enter Billy.*] Where's Miss Edgar?

BILLY.—There she comes.

[*Enter Miss Edgar.*

MR. T. [*to Miss Edgar.*]—What's all this hubbub about? Are all the girls mad, or are they going to throw them-selves away on some worthless young men, and get mar-ried?

MISS E.—No, sir! They have thrown the best part of their lives away already, and you, sir, have gathered to-gether their sorrow and turned it into riches [*producing a letter*]. Did you write that letter? [*hands it to him.*]

MR. T. [*looking at the letter.*]—Yes, I did. What right have you to question it? [*hands it back.*]

MISS E.—The right, as one of the members of that Society.

MR. T.—Do all the girls belong to it? I thought it was made up of a few crack-brained old maids.

MISS E.—Every factory girl in the county is a member of the Mutual Development Society—thousands through-out the land are joining in the movement—and let me respectfully inform you, Mr. Tyrannus, *our* time has come! We have been like the bundle of fagots—sepa-rated, you crush us singly! joined together in unity, fra-ternity, and equality, as we are to-day, there is no power, save high Heaven, which can break our bonds of united strength! Now, sir, what will you?

MR. T. [*holding the two letters, one in each hand, aside.*]

—Forty thousand dollars forfeit, twelve thousand four hundred dollars profit—[*to Miss E.*] Tell the girls to go to work. I will make it all right.

MISS E.—You have been paying from one dollar and fifty cents to four dollars per week.

MR. T.—Well, that's enough; it is as much as any one else pays.

MISS E.—Enough for you to give, but not enough for us to receive. We ask that the one dollar and fifty cents be made four dollars and fifty cents, the four dollars be made twelve.

MR. T. [*in a rage.*]—Won't stand such extortion! [*Looks at his letters again.*] I'll give it this week.

MISS E.—We want it for one year, sir.

MR. T. [*aside.*]—I'll promise, but I'll never pay them at all! not a cent! I'll learn them a lesson. [*To Miss E.*] Very well, go to work; I'll engage you all for a year at those rates.

MISS E. [*producing a paper.*]—Then sign this agreement which the girls have drawn up.

MR. T [*smilingly.*]—Certainly. [*Aside.*] It will not do to back out now, and knowing, as I do, that there is not one girl in my factory who has had one-quarter's schooling, they haven't got brains enough to bind me very close. I'll sign it without reading it, this will make them think I am overly sincere, but my retribution will come. I'll make them sue for bread on their bended knees yet. [*To Miss E.*] Give me the paper.

MISS E.—Shall I read it to you? It is written quite poorly, but I done the best I knew how.

MR. T. [*takes the paper.*]—No! don't you think that I have confidence enough in you girls to sign your paper without reading it? You all thought that I was a hard-hearted employer, but you find that I am not, am I? [*Aside.*] A little soft soder will make them feel good, but revenge is mine. [*Goes to the table, sits down and writes his name, while Mrs. T., Cringey, Billy, and all the factory girls enter unobserved by him.*] You will want this witnessed, forewoman. [*Hands it back of him.*] You should have brought a witness with you.

MRS. C. [*takes the paper.*]—I'll witness your signature [*aside*] to the death-warrant of capital monopoly.

MR. T. [*rising, turns round, surprised.*]—What, you here, Lawyer Cringey? and these girls, too! [*Cringey sits down and writes his name.*] What does all this mean?

MR. C.—L-e-t m-e s-e-e [*putting on his spectacles reads, slowly*]. "Articles of agreement made and entered into this — day of — 18—, by and between the Honorable Ezekiel Tyrannus of the one part, and Miss Ella Edgar, forewoman, of the other part, both of the town of —, in the county of —, and State of—, Witnesseth:

" The said party of the first part hereby agrees to retain his entire force of factory operatives for the term of fifty-two weeks from this date, and agrees to pay the said party of the second part four dollars and fifty cents per week for each operative who has heretofore received one dollar and fifty cents, and twelve dollars per week for all those who have heretofore received but four dollars weekly, and for the faithful performance of this agreement he, the said Ezekiel Tyrannus, pledges all his property, both personal and real estate. Witness my hand and seal the day and date first above written. Signed, Ezekiel Tyrannus. Witness, Obadiah Cringey." This wants an internal revenue stamp to make it complete.

ALL [*closing around Cringey, offering a stamp*].—Here's one.

MR. C. [*takes one from Billy, reads.*]—Internal revenue proprietary, Brandreth's pills [*handing it back*], that won't do, Billy, it wouldn't do to increase the dose just now; your boss has got a very bitter pill on hand already. [*Billy retires—Cringey takes one from his pocket and puts it on.*] Signed, stamped [*handing it to Miss Edgar*], and delivered.

MR. T.—What does this mean, I say?

MR. C.—Why, simply that there is more legal ability in your factory than justice in your heart. They have got you handsomely—the law will now protect and defend them in their rights [*turning to the audience*], and I dare say that there is not a man, woman or child who learns of this fact but will rejoice, and give three rousing cheers for this, the first triumph of labor over the tyrant, Capital Monopoly.

[*Curtain falls.*]

PATENT MEDICINE.

CHARACTERS.

NATHAN WORRY, a dyspeptic farmer.
DR. OLDSCHOOL, physician.
MRS. WORRY, wife of Nathan.

SCENE I.—*Room in private house.*

MR. WORRY [*seated in easy chair, looking generally miserable*].—If I've got to call this misery life [*groaning*] the sooner I am out of it the better! Not a single hour of comfort have I had for more'n a year now. I've tried ev'ry thin', and ev'ry thin' fails. Somehow or 'nother nothin' 'pears to agree with me—ev'ry thin' goes agin the grain!

MRS. W. [*converses in a dismal, cheerless tone.*]—You don't feel a bit better to-day—do you, Nathan? [*Sitting.*] You're lookin' mis'rable—mis'rabler than I've see'd you yit, I reely b'lieve! Stick out your tongue! [*He complies—she leaves chair to inspect.*] I declare to you it's furred thicker'n pie-crust! [*Resuming seat.*] It's my actil 'pinion, Nathan, that none of them doctors knows any thin' what's the matter with you.

MR. W. [*groaning.*]—No more do I. I grow worser and worser ev'ry day I live. I'm goin' fast—and, the way I feel 'most all the time, now-a-days, I'm 'bout glad on't!

MRS. W.—Nathan, you've no business as a professin' man to talk in that way. You know you're sinnin' when you do it. What if you are goin' fast—and it's putty plain to me you are—you've no call to be glad on't, you know well's as I do! You must git resigned, Nathan—that's what you want and oughter have!

MR. W.—I am resigned. I feel as if I could put up with any thin' after what I've gone through.

MRS. W.—'Taint the right kind, and you know it. Your head don't feel any comfortabler, I s'pose?

MR. W.—Not a mite—feels jest as if I had forty camp-meetin's in it in full blast.

MRS. W.—And your food don't set well on your stom-ick any more—does it?

MR. W —No—I don't relish any thin', and if I did, 'twould nearly kill me to eat any thin'.

MRS. W. [*looking wise.*]—I'm jest as certain it's your liver, Nathan, as I'm certain that I'm a livin' woman. You know I've stuck to it from the very fust that it's your liver and nothin' else. I stick to it yit, and I shall till you're dead and gone. I do wish you'd a-heered to me a long while ago and did as I wanted to have you. You might have ben a great 'eal better this very minit. Who knows?

MR. W.—Didn't I go to see that doctor you told me of? What's his name?

MRS. W.—Doctor Lobely?

MR. W.—Didn't I go to see him—and didn't I take more'n fifty bottles of his blood-root bitters? And they didn't do me a bit of good! I only wish I'd kep' on with Dr. Oldschool!

MRS. W —Well you didn't, I can tell you, Nathan! You'd a-ben carrid out feet foremost long afore this if I hadn't a-got you out o' the notion o' list'nin' to him! I hope I may be forgiven for't, but I actilly think he'd be properer named if he's called old fool! Didn't he say he wouldn't give you a hooter of med'sin?

MR. W.—More'n he didn't—I b'lieve now I was on the mend fast.

MRS. W.—On the mend, Nathan! Lawful sakes! You're goin' out o' your head, Nathan! Didn't 'Zuby Pepper say over and over agin—day in and day out—and you know she seed you's often 's three or four times a day—that you were failin', failin', all the time? Now, didn't she?

MR. W.—So you said, I b'lieve. But it 'pears to me like I oughter know as much 'bout myself as 'Zuby Pepper or anybody else.

MRS. W —But you can't, Nathan! Sickness 's mighty deceivin'. You think you're goin' to git up and about right away, and the fust thing you know you're stone-dead—go off jest like that [*snapping finger*]. I reely

don't think—you know I never didn't—that you treated
Doctor Lobely fair. I don't think—as a Christian woman I don't think—you gin his med'cin a fair try.

Mr. W. [*getting somewhat animated.*]—What would
you have a man do, woman alive? Isn't more'n fifty
bottle enough, I'd like to know? You wouldn't drown a
man clean out—would you?

Mrs. W.—Now don't take on so, Nathan! Jest keep
yourself's easy 's you can! You're bad enough off,
goodness knows—and you 'll only git worse if you git
so excited. As I was sayin', I don't actilly think you
took bitters enough. No more does 'Zuby Pepper—that
I know—for I heerd her say jest them very words with
my own ears, Nathan. And if anybody knows any thin'
'bout any kind o' sickness in these parts I should think
'Zuby oughter! She's laid out more'n twenty folks, old
and young—some on 'em sick one way and some 'nother
—and she's been 'round the country nussing upwards of
a dozen year! Plaguey few doctors she can't teach a
few things to, I tell you! Didn't 'Zekiel Harlow have
the matter with his liver—and didn't Dr. Lobely 'tend
him—and didn't 'Zuby nuss him, night an' day, all the
living time he 's sick?

Mr. W.—He died, didn't he?

Mrs. W.—What do you ask sech a question as that for,
Nathan? You know he did. Didn't we go to hear his
fun'ral preached—and don't you mind my sayin' to you
as we was a-comin' home, what an improvin' 'casion we'd
hed? 'Zekil Harlow's dead and buried, certain—and it's
a mighty mean stone his widder's gin him. I'll do
better for you'n that, Nathan, if you're called fust—
you may depend on't. Wal—'Zuby studied into 'Zekil's
liver, and studied, and studied till she got to know all
about it—all about it—'cept them doctor names, which
don't amount to shucks, anyhow; and says she to me the
very day I told her how that you had gin over takin' any
more of Doctor Lobely's med'cin—and I didn't tell her
right off quick's you stopped, 'cause I wasn't willin' to
let on what you'd ben and done—howsomever, says 'Zuby,
says she, soon's I'd told her, says she, "Axy, Nathan hasn't
took enough of that med'cin by a great sight," says she.
"Zekil Harlow," says she, "took a hundred and forty-

two on 'em to my certin knowledge," says she. "Arter
the d'scase's sot and took root," says she, "in the systim,
it takes a power of bitters to clean it out." That's what
she said to me—did 'Zuby Pepper that very day. And
then she went on and explained all about this liver sickness jest for all the world as if she was a born doctor.
I seed right through it all in a minnit. You see, Nathan,
the liver's—I'll show you so you'll know all 'bout it
plain as preachin'. [*Going towards Nathan.*]

MR. W.—Now, Axy, don't worry me! I feel mis'r'ble
enough now.

MRS. W.—I won't hurt you, Nathan—it's all for your
own good. [*Drawing chair by his side, and seating.*] I
was goin' to tell you jest 'zactly as 'Zuby explained it all
to me. You see the liver's here. [*Touching his left side
on the chest.*]

MR. W. [*wincing.*]—Oh, don't, Axy, I say!

MRS. W.—Didn't I say 'twas your liver that ailed you?
And that jest proves it. The liver's right down under
the borax—jest touches it like—ain't fastened fast to
it, but moves back'ards and forreds kinder towards it.
Wal, all the blood's in the liver, you see—and when you
take a long breath—so—[*expanding her chest and inhal-
ing*] it brings the liver up agin the borax—and when
you let your breath out agin—so—[*illustrating*] the
liver goes back agin where 'twas afore—kinder slump!—
jest as if you'd throwed some cold mush agin the wall.
Now, you see, [*growing oracular and bringing forefinger
of her right hand forcibly down into the palm of her left
as she makes a point,*] if you breathe quick much—jest as
you allers do when you're a-movin' or a-workin' hard—
the liver keeps a-goin' forred and back —thumpity-thump
—thumpity-thump agin the borax—and if it's kep' at it
long, the outside of the liver—the bag-like, you know—
gits worn through with, and the good blood that's in the
liver—comes in, you see, from your vittles that you eat—
runs out o' the holes, and the bad blood—that's stickin'
to the inside of the borax all round the liver—jest as the
water does to the puddin'-bag when I put it in to bile—
the bad blood gits in—keeps a-gittin' in 'till the liver
matterates, and matterates, and keeps on matteratin' 'till
the matter gits to the heart—and then this matter-stuff

clogs and chokes up the heart and it can't beat any more
—and then we're dead !

MR. W.—That's what's the matter—is it?

MRS. W.—Nathan, you oughter be ashamed of yourself! Jokin' 'bout sech scr'ous subjicks.! You understand—don't you—what I jest explained?

MR. W.—I guess I do—I was 'most asleep, some of
the time—'bout the borax and liver—wa'n't it? [*Yawning.*]

MRS. W.—Now, Nathan, that ain't a-treatin' on me
right. Sick a man as you are—and I a-takin' pains to
explain to you somethin' for your good—and you a-tryin'
to go to sleep! What good is it to do me, I'd like to
know? And I think it very ungrateful in you—mebbe
a dyin' man soon—not to hear me out.

MR W. [*yawning again.*]—I am so sleepy, Axy. Go
on, if you want to; I'll do my best to keep awake.

MRS. W.—Where was I? Le'me see. Oh, 'bout them
bloodroot bitters of Doctor Lobely's. 'Zuby didn't explain this out to me, but the Doctor he did. This blood-
root, you see, 's most all the same kind of stuff as the
good blood—that is, the juice on't, and that's steeped
out so it comes e'enamost reel pure blood—what's put in
along it's only somethin' to keep it from spilin'—some
essence of some 'arb or t'other——

MR. W.—Guess it's liquor, ain't it?

MRS. W.—You know better, Nathan Worry; you
know better'n that. Ain't Doctor Lobely the president
of the teetotle? What do you mean?

MR. W.—Nothin'; go on, if you want to; only I
b'lieve it's liquor.

MRS. W. [*earnestly.*]—'Taint, and you know 'taint.
Don't take on so, Nathan. You must save yourself long
as you can. This bitters, you see, goes into the liver—
and bein' as it's thicker'n the blood, it crowds into the
holes that are worn out, as I jest explained to you, and
fills 'em up by'n by—up chuck—and there can't no more
blood git out, and you git well, you see. But you have
to keep a-takin' and keep a-takin' on't till all the holes is
stopped up—sometimes sooner and sometimes later.
Nathan Worry, you're asleep, as I'm livin'! Nathan!
[*loudly.*]

Mr. W. [*waking and rubbing eyes.*]—Go on, if you want to.

Mrs W.—You've ben and gone asleep jest at the important pint.

Mr. W.—I heerd you, Axy, about the bitters filling up chuck.

Mrs. W.—Wal, do for massy's sake, keep awake now! When you've took bloodroot bitters enough to stop all the holes up, then arter that you only jest want to take some catnip tea to keep the pores open so's to let the air into the liver to venterlate the blood—and you'll never die unless you die of some other disease. Now do you understand?

Mr. W.—I understand. How happened 'Zekil Harlow to die, then?

Mrs. W.—Jest his own tomfoolery Might a-ben alive and hearty now, fur 's aught I know, if he'd a-done's the Doctor told him. But no! he wouldn't do it—he allers was one of your so smart men that knows a precious deal more'n anybody else—he wouldn't tend to takin' the catnip—and so he died—died along o' want o' venterlation of the borax—so Doctor Lobely told me himself—and not o' liver. I reely b'lieve this bloodroot's a nateral medicine—provided for us by God himself! Many and many's the time I've seen the dumb critters— the hens and the lambs and the pigs—a-nippin' and a-nippin' at it 'round in the paster—and that's what's keepin' them so healthy, I reely b'lieve! You never knowed any of sech to die of the liver—now did you?

Mr. W.—Never examined, and can't tell. Let's talk 'bout somethin' else. I b'lieve it makes me sicker to hear you talk about that stuff than I'd be if you'd only let me alone.

Mrs. W.—How can you expect ever to be any better, Nathan, if you don't do somethin' for yourself? You know you've got the liver bad— you couldn't help a-hollerin' when I jest kinder touched you softly-like——

Mr. W.—I called it a putty good punch, Axy.

Mrs. W.—You know better, Nathan! You've got it on you, I say; and you're a-lettin' it run on and run on —a-doin nothin' for it in the way of docterin'.

Mr. W.—And I don't want to, unless I can git hold of some sound doctrine.

Mrs. W.—Don't bother me with your nonsense, when I'm advisin' with you—poorly off as you be, too—and a-jokin' like as if you'd a right to. You're a-lettin' it run on till it'll run away with you pûtty quick, if you don't look out sharp. You haint took no med'cin no kind for more'n three days now—have yer?

Mr. W.—No; and what's more, ain't goin' to neither, unless Dr. Oldschool tells me to. I'm a-goin' to have him come and see me this very day.

Mrs. W.—You act like as if you were persessed, Nathan. Didn't you say you wouldn't never hev him set foot inside your door again?

Mr. W.—You said that, Axy; I didn't.

Mrs. W.—Did you say a lisp agin it?

Mr. W.—No—and more fool I. Fact is, Axy, I've ben thinkin' a little 'bout some things some days now, as I've ben sittin' and mopin' round here, and I've come to the conclusion that it's 'bout time for me to strike out for myself now. You've had your say, Axy, a good bit now—and you see what's come of it. I'm goin' to have my say for's long, and if I don't git any better, I'm tol'bly certain nobody's say won't mar or make me.

Mrs. W.—Nathan, do you reely mean that you're a-goin' to call in Dr. Oldschool?

Mr. W.—I shall do it, Axy—shall send for him to come around this afternoon.

Mrs. W.—Your blood will be upon your own head, then, Nathan Worry! [raising her hands.] I won't have nothin' to do with it! You've got to run your own resk.

Mr. W.—So I've ben thinkin'! Set down, Axy, and hear me out. I listened to you, a bit ago, you know.

Mrs. W. [seating herself resolutely.]—I won't git asleep, Nathan. But you can't talk me 'round, and you needn't waste your breath a-tryin'.

Mr. W.—I shouldn't try any thin' like that, Axy, you know. [Faint attempt at a smile.] 'Cute as you are, you forgit some things well's other folks; and I want to tell you a little, which, like's not, you disremember.

17

When I fust begun to ail you know I wanted to do as Dr. Oldschool said. You said "No," and I let you have your way. You was so scary about my takin' great lumps of pisin stuff that you got me to try Dr. Pellet. He gin me 'bout's much sugar as'd stay on the pint of a needle in a damp day, and made me hold my breath if any of the smell from the lalocks was 'round.

Mrs. W. — Dear knows his med'cin couldn't hurt you, if it didn't do you any good ! And that's more'n you can say of some others !

Mr. W.—I knew he wasn't doin' me any good, and arter a while you find it out and pester me to try Dr. Baden.

Mrs. W.—Pester you ! How can you say that, Nathan ? Wasn't I a-workin' and a-conjurin' all for your good ?

Mr. W.—In your way, Axy. Dr. Baden he puts me to soak in the mornin' — takes me out at noon — sets me under the dam through the afternoon—and makes a water-tank out of me durin' the night. You found I was gittin' to hate water so that you was afraid I'd break the pledge, and you wanted I should try Dr. Ninny.

Mrs. W.—Cold water never did hurt anybody yit in this born world.

Mr. W.—They say drownin's the easiest death—them who've tried it. Dr. Ninny he kep' me hold of them nibs with the wires hitched to 'em while he turned the crank of the machine till I cut such a figure a-jumpin', a-hoppin', and a-dancin'—feelin' all the time jest as a feller might who'd eaten hearty of herrin'-bones—that you was glad enough to call him off and git me home agin.

Mrs. W.—You know's well as I do, Nathan, that 'lectricity's good for folks !

Mr. W.—A feller gets too much on't sometimes, Achsah — 'specially in thunder-gusts. Then you got me to see Dr. Fumbler, who rubbed me, and pulled me, and stretched me, and twisted me, and jerked me about so that you were mortal 'feard you'd have to take me home in pieces—and as you wasn't certain you could put me together agin right, you made him let me alone.

Mrs. W.—Now, Nathan, what is there that's better in this cold, onfeelin' world than symperthy ? And you

know that was the symperthetic treatment. If you hadn't
a-ben so onresliss-like I expect 'twould a-taken all the
kinks out of you.

MR. W.—That's what I was thinkin' at the time—and
laid me out straight enough. Then comes Dr. Hum—
the feller that teched you where your dinner hurts you
and rolled up his eyes and jabbered somethin', and said
you were healed of every disease.

MRS. W.—So you would a-ben, if you'd only had faith
and b'lieved him.

MR. W.—I had faith enough to b'lieve him a thorough-
bred, full-blooded humbug—but it didn't cure me for all
that. Then that female doctor—but I won't say any
thin' 'bout that, 'cause you got riled when she was goin'
to have you killed off fust and begun to talk about my
secon' wife.

MRS. W.—I allers b'lieved she was nothin' but a man
dressed up in woman's clothes.

MR. W.—You giv her an extra dressin' with your
tongue, I remember. Then, when I had a good right to
think I'd a-done my duty by you and might be allowed
to do somethin' like I wanted to, nothin' would do but I
must have Dr. Lobely and his bloodhound biters.

MRS. W.—Blood-root bitters – and the patentest medicine in the whole country—that you may depend upon !

MR. W.—It's patent to me—that's certain ! Howsomever we've talked that stuff enough, and we won't wrangle
any more 'bout it. That's 'bout what I've ben goin'
through with—statin' it fairly and not stretchin' on't a
whit. I've a sorter notion how that I've got to the eend
of that woosted. I'll try Dr. Oldschool, as I told you,
and we'll see what comes of that.

MRS. W.—'Tain't no kind of use tryin' to argufy with
you, Nathan, when you once git your back up, and I
ain't a-goin' to. But - just you mark my words—[*raising
her hand and pointing her forefinger solemnly*]—I never
yit knowed a human bein' speak disrespeckful of them
blood-root bitters who didn't die within a year ! Remember that, Nathan, and don't say I didn't give you
fair warnin'. [*Exit.*]

MR. W.— I guess the time it took him to die'd depend
'bout's much on how long Lobely 'tended him as any thin'

else. Now my mind's made up on that point 'bout which I've had so much fuss with Axy, I declare I begin to feel better'n I have for a long time.

SCENE II.—*Room as before.*

[*Mr. W. in easy chair. Mrs. W.'s voice outside:* "Now, Doctor, don't you dare give Nathan any of your pisen drugs! If you do, I'll throw 'em away, unbeknowings to either of you!"]

DR. OLDSCHOOL [*in the act of opening door*]. — Mrs. Worry, attend to your baking! When I require a consultation, I'll let you know—provided I want you! [*Entering.*] Nathan, good-evening! What are you huddled up in that old woman's chair for? Why aren't you out and stirring 'round?

MR. W.—Fact is, Doctor [*extending hand, which Doctor shakes*], I'm putty nigh used up. Set down—set down. I'm glad to see you and hev ben wantin' a long time to have a chat with you.

DR. [*seating.*]—You must understand, Nathan, that I can have but very little patience with you.

MR. W.—Doctor, if you only knew what I've been through with sence you were here last——

DR.—I know all about it; and that's why I am so out of patience with you. A man of good sense who will suffer himself to be nosed around as you have, don't deserve any sympathy; and precious little he will get from me! Both of us remember what happened when I was last here, and I shan't mince matters at all. Understand, I come to see you—to take charge of you—and no one, in the house or out of it, must interfere. If it is done in a single instance, I am done with you, Nathan.

MR W.—I can't blame you, Doctor. I've been makin' a simpleton of myself.

DR.—"A man's foes shall be they of his own household." We start, then, with a distinct understanding, Nathan?

MR. W.—You may do with me jest what you like. I haven't a word to say agin it.

DR. [*examining chest—feeling pulse—looking at eyes and tongue.*]—Let me see how much they've left of you

Upon my soul, there's more of you than I expected to find. It's well for you that you've such a constitution—or you'd been running on your by-laws by this time.

Mr. W.—Can I ever git well agin, Doctor?

Dr.—Nonsense, man! You might have been in prime order and condition months ago, if you'd followed my directions. You have been tampering with yourself since, and you'll need a longer time to pick up. What do you eat?

Mr. W.—I don't relish nothin'—I hanker arter things which I know I hadn't oughter to have—and what I oughter have don't stay on my stomick.

Dr.—What do you hanker after now, Nathan?

Mr. W.—Seems as if some beefsteak would go good—but I know 'tain't best for me to have it.

Dr.—Oh, you know—do you? Then I don't know what I'm here for. Have you such a thing as a gridiron about the house, Nathan?

Mr. W.—I declare I don't know. [*Calling.*] Axy!

Mrs. W. [*who has been standing at door, pushed ajar, entering, with indications of bread-making about her.*]—Don't ask me to git any thin' for your pisens, Nathan, for I will hev nothin' to do with nothin' of the kind!

Dr.—Mrs. Worry, attend to what I tell you! [*sternly.*] Have you a gridiron in the kitchen?

Mrs. W [*rather cowed.*]—I don't know for certin, Doctor, whether there's any gridiron about. But I'll go look. [*Exit.*]

Dr.—A tender beefsteak—quickly broiled—rare done—will be just the thing for you.

Mr. W.—You know best, in course—but won't it disagree with my liver?

Dr. [*jumping from chair.*]—Liver, Nathan! You haven't any liver! There isn't any sensible man of my acquaintance who has a liver—unless he's sick—and the sickness brings it.

Mrs. W [*entering.*]—I've found one, Doctor—but it's powerful rusty.

Dr.—Have it well cleaned, then; and [*looking at watch*] one hour from this have the table set for Nathan, with a tender beefsteak, broiled quick, rare done—some of your good bread and butter, too!

Mrs. W. [*hesitating.*]—But, Doctor, won't bran bread be better for him?

Dr. [*loudly.*]—Do as you're told [*Mrs. Worry leaving, somewhat startled*]. One moment, Mrs. Worry—add a cup of green and black tea mixed, pretty strong. [*Mrs. Worry exit—her voice heard outside:* "Might as well git his shroud made fast as last!"] Talk about your liver, Nathan! Why, a short time hence, the way you've been going on, you'd either be under the sod or as big a fool as that he-Pepper, 'Zuby—pepper-sass, some call her! Do you want to know what's the matter with you, Nathan? I would have told you a year ago, if I'd been permitted. Now I know that I can say what I please, and that you'll do as I say. You wouldn't have been so ready, then; but you have learned somewhat since. You've called me in at last, because you have become disgusted with your attempts, and you think you can't be any worse off, whatever I may do. I believe, moreover, you have a lingering half-notion that I can do something for you. I can, Nathan—but you must first understand your disease. You are dying, Nathan—dying of *want of a gridiron!*

Mr. W. [*smiling.*]—Never heerd tell of that disease afore, Doctor!

Dr.—I know that—pity you hadn't, though. If you farmers, as a class, don't hear of it soon and apply the proper remedies, there'll be farms enough hereabouts in administrators' hands before long. Nathan, did you ever hear of any animal's being used for food besides the hog?

Mr. W.—'Casionly a beef critter, or so, I b'lieve, Doctor.

Dr.—That's well said—occasionally—and *semi* at that, in this bailiwick. Upon my soul, I believe no greater blessing could be conferred upon our farmers than to have the hog-cholera sweep off all the swine in the country!

Mr. W.—Why, Doctor, bacon allers agreed with me when I was able to work hard.

Dr.—Pish! You aren't able to work hard now, simply because eating so much bacon never did agree with you, I tell you. Pork in its place, Nathan—and that place isn't the human stomach all the time, I assure you. You've gone the whole hog—and now you're paying the penalty. That's why you farmers bristle up so when any-

body talks against your pet notions. You grow a few
bushels of wheat—don't you, Nathan?

Mr. W.—A thousand, last year! [*faintly smiling.*]

Dr.—Don't forget, Nathan, that very excellent bread
can be made of wheat.

Mr. W. [*rising from chair, growing earnest, infected by
the Doctor's manner.*]—A man can work so much better
on good, solid corn-bread, Doctor.

Dr —Pish! You might as well dump the stones from
the pike down into your stomach, and make your stomach
break them! Nathan, remember you're not going to leave
us yet awhile!

Mr. W. [*walking around cheerful.*]—I b'lieve you, Doctor. I feel better than I have for months.

Dr.—You have improved fifty per cent. since I've
been in the room. I've a great mind to charge you for
two visits to-day. You will get well, I say—not because
I shall cure you—but because you'll let your good sense
guide you. Listen! You are troubled with indigestion.
That's what we moderns call it. In old times it was
known as original sin. Here's my prescription: Eat
whatever your stomach craves at regular hours. If
animal food, broiled or boiled or stewed—never fried.
Abjure pork. Enjoy your meals. Eat a light supper.
Tea in preference to coffee. Discard milk for the present.
Feed your corn-meal to your stock. I don't say to your
hogs, for, I take it for granted, you'll kill them and put
their carcasses in the compost heap. Eat cold wheat
bread, never hot. Take active exercise in the open air
in all weathers, with proper precautions against exposure.
This last for a few weeks—after that your farm work will
give you exercise enough. When you go to work again,
don't over-do. Better enjoy a hundred dollars while
you have it, than make a thousand dollars which you can
never enjoy. Two points more: Be sure that, living as I
tell you, nothing will hurt you. That is the first. Be
cheerful. That is the second. And, to secure it [*lowering voice*], don't keep too close at home for some time to
come [*laughing*]. It's a delicate matter, Nathan, but I
must speak out. Have you attended to the prescription?

Mr. W.—Every word on't.

Dr.—And you'll observe it in all respects?

Mr. W.—Faithfully.

Dr.—Then [*slapping him on the shoulder*] I'll warrant you, Nathan,—accidents excepted,—for as long as you'll care about living. You begin to look somewhat like yourself, man—at least around the edges.

Mr. W.—It does me good to see you and hear you talk, Doctor.

Dr.—It ought to. Nathan, do you know my objections to a stone-house?

Mr. W—Because it's so often a jail or a penitentiary?

Dr. [*laughing.*]—No; because it keeps you cold in winter, hot in summer, and damp all the time. I've seen humans very like stone houses, Nathan. Do you know what I would have done if they had made out to kill you off by keeping us apart?

Mr. W.—What, Doctor?

Dr.—Why, Nathan, after they'd put the slab up, I would have stolen in some night—they say we people do that, you know, but it's a vile slander—taken down the lying thing, "Sacred to the memory of," &c.—you know the stereotyped stuff—and put up a neat affair which wouldn't blush to see sunlight, for it would have told the truth—"Died of hog and hominy."

Mr. W.—You think that would have pleased survivors?

Dr.—It would have gladdened every honest man, Nathan. But I must be going.

Mr. W.—Oh, Doctor, don't hurry. You do me more good than medicine.

Dr.—Little I'd do you if I didn't. When you get quite yourself again, Nathan, cheerful and joking as you were before you straddled your hypo, I'll drop in often and see you. By-the-by, I heard the worst conundrum this morning I ever heard in my life.

Mr. W.—That's sayin' a good 'eal, Doctor. What was it?

Dr.—I was at Jim Stokes's—baby sick—and the chimney smoked frightfully. I'd said something or other, trying to be funny—don't remember now what it was —when Jim said to me, "Doctor, why is that chimney like a bird with a crippled wing?" I knew the rascal's tricks, and wasn't going to bother my head with trying to get the resemblance, so I said, of course, that I didn't know. " Because there's a defect in the flue ! (flew,)" said Jim, looking as innocent as if he hadn't done any thing worthy of a beating—which I certainly would have given him if his wife hadn't been there !

MR. W. [*laughing almost heartily.*]—That was bad enough, certin, Doctor.

DR.—You have had time to read the papers. I've been so busy that I haven't. Any thing new ?

MR. W.—You know we've bought Russian Ameriky, don't you ? What do you think about it ?

DR.—Yes, I knew that. I think the best thing that'll come to us from that purchase is the conundrum I concocted about it.

MR. W.—As bad as Jim's ?

DR.—You shall judge. They call the territory Sitka, you know. Hark to the conundrum. What is the most distant portion of the United States ?

MR. W.—I s'pose, in course, yer mean Sitky, but I don't see why.

DR.—You've travelled in the Middle States and in the South, and you'll see the point. Because it is the *fur* corner !

MR. W. [*laughing heartily.*]—I must think on't a bit afore I decide which is the worst—Jim Stokes's or yours !

DR. [*joining laugh.*]—I'll give you till my next call, which will be this time three days hence. Have you any moral reflection, Nathan, suggested by the late Rebellion ? Almost everybody has.

MR. W.—Nothin' partickler. What do you mean ?

DR.—I have. The moral I draw from it is, Never *se*-cede unless you're sure you will *suc*-ceed ! Good-bye, Nathan ! [*going.*]

MR. W. [*accompanying him to door.*]—But you've left me no medicine !

DR.—Yes, I have. *No pork!* That's my PATENT MEDICINE !

         [*Curtain falls.*]

M

THE PREMATURE PROPOSAL.

CHARACTERS.

PETER DOUGHTY.
PATIENCE, his wife, a hypochondriac.
MRS. HASTINGS.
BETSEY ANN HASTINGS, her daughter.

SCENE I.—*A potato-patch—Peter hoeing potatoes.*

PETER [*soliloquizing*].—If our two children had lived perhaps she wouldn't have got so bad. What can ail the woman, I'd be glad to know?
[*Enter Betsey Ann.*]
BETSEY.—Good-morning, Mr. Doughty.
PETER.—Why, Betsey Ann, how d'ye do? How's all at home?
BETSEY.—All's well; and how's Mrs. Doughty? [*with a tinkling laugh.*] We heard she was dying last night, and I thought it no more than neighborly to inquire if you're digging her grave.
PETER [*with an attempt at indignation*].—Betsey Ann! these things ain't to be laughed at, and made light of! I'm getting to be afraid she may actilly die one of these days.
BETSEY [*drawing down her mouth*].—It's barely possible—folks do, now and then. Grandpa says, he never heard of anybody's sticking by the way. And there's one consolation, Mr. Doughty, if she should die you'll certainly be prepared for it. [*Peter smiles.*]
PETER. - Betsey Ann [*confidentially*], I'm dreadful!put to it, to know what ails that woman—the pains shift so, there's no calculating on 'em. I've been reading lately some of these advertisements and things in the papers, and it sounds to me like a snake.
BETSEY.—Like a what?
PETER [*lowering his voice*].—A snake. You know

there is such a thing as drinkin' 'em in water, and they are said to affect the mind very bad.

BETSEY.—Oh, don't think of such dreadful horrors, Mr. Doughty! You really make me shudder. It's the *hypo* that ails your wife, and not a snake. I don't wonder you get fidgety—anybody would, to live such a life as you do, poor man! Good-bye!

[*Exit Betsey Ann.*]

PETER.—I wonder what does make such odds in women folks? Some as chirk as posies, and some as down at the heel as a frizzled-out potato ball.

[*Exit Scene.*]

SCENE II.—*Doughty's kitchen. Patience lying bolstered up on a lounge.*

[*Peter appears at the door.*]

PATIENCE [*gasping*].—Come in here, Peter, for I'm dying—but don't you make tracks on my nice floor. I can't live two minutes, husband! Oh! oh! [*in a louder key.*] Rub your feet on the mat.

PETER.—I'm rubbin' 'em, dear! [*Enters and proceeds without dismay to mix a pitcher of molasses and water, vinegar and ginger—tasting the mixture to get the right proportions—then takes a twisted dough-nut from the cupboard and eats it—takes off his boots and steals like a cat to the couch.*]

PATIENCE [*raising herself on her elbow and looking at him.*] – My dear! [*reproachfully as she sees a crumb on his coat-sleeve*] would *I* help myself to doughnuts if *you* hadn't five minutes to live? [*Peter wipes his mouth on his blue checked handkerchief and looks humble.*] It's reasonable to suppose [*snuffing at the camphor-bottle*] that I can't hold out long. Take a towel, Peter, and tie up my head in a hard knot. [*He obeys.*] Pull tight, for it's going to split. Now take the camphire in one hand and hold it to my right nostril, and the hartshorn in the other hand, and hold it to my left nostril. Oh, dear! Oh, dear! [*Peter obeys, putting the stoppers of the two bottles in his mouth.*] And while you're doing that, if you could only soak my feet it would be a great relief. The fact is, I need somebody to wait upon me, that

knows how better than a man. You do the best you can,
but I need—oh, oh such a spasm. 'Tis worse than death.
Ah, Peter, little you know what it is to have one foot in
the grave. I wish you could know! [*Pause. Peter
sighs.*] I was perfectly speechless before you came in,
and now I'm sure my voice doesn't sound at all natural.
Don't it have a hollow sound, dear, as if it came from a
distance ?

PETER [*unstopping his mouth*].—Yes, I don't know but
what it does. I didn't think of it till you spoke, but now
it strikes me your voice has a kind of a crack in it, like
broken crockery-ware.

PATIENCE.—Did it ever sound so before, Peter? Think
quick !

PETER.—Well, I can't say certain. It was always rather
ha'ash; but now it's so uncommon loud, you know, and
that makes it haa'sher yet.

PATIENCE.—Oh, yes ! oh, yes ! My right lung is 'most
gone, Peter; and that's what I've been afraid of for some
time. I felt a singular numbness in it—no feeling at all
—that was the way I was taken speechless. The left one
adheres to my side—you always knew that; and now the
right one is collapsed, and I might as well bid you good-
bye. Husband, feel in my pocket, and take out my handkerchief. Yes, husband (*with dirge-like voice*], the time
has come, when you will see my face no more ! We've
jogged along together for fifteen years——

PETER.—And a half.

PATIENCE.—And what kind of a wife can you conscien-
tiously say I've been to you, Peter?

PETER.—As good as the common run [*wiping his eyes
where the tears ought to be*].

PATIENCE.—I've worn you about out with my ailings
[*taking a whiff of hartshorn*]—I know I have.

PETER [*kindly*].—No, you haven't—there's a good deal
left of me yet You've died so much nights, that it's made
it rather bad sometimes in harvesting ; but, take it by the
year together, I've generally got my sleep made up.

PATIENCE.—I shouldn't so much mind dying—for this
is a miserable world—if it wasn't for leaving you, Peter.

PETER [*soothingly*].—Oh, don't you worry about that !
I shall get along first-rate.

PATIENCE [*groaning*].—You don't know what you're
talking about, dear—you're so numb, about some things,
so half awake like, Peter. Did ever I see such a man?
[*Peter looks condemned.*] You've always had me to do
for you, and see to you're mending, ungrateful as you are.
A pretty sight you'll be, with your stockings down at the
heel, and holes in your elbows! But 't will be the same
to you—you'll never think of the difference, but the neighbors will. [*Patience groans.*] Besides, you'll make a poor,
drozzling housekeeper, Peter. My best dishes will go to
destruction; and you'll stuff the broken windows with
rags! [*groans again.*] You'll cook horrid messes; for
you've had little experience in cooking, considering the
sickness I've been subject to. And my floors—my nice
floors, that the whole village says are such a beautiful
sight—and my carpets, without speck or grease—where 'll
they be, in a year from this day? Dirt here, dirt there,
and the corners full of it.

PETER [*brightening and speaking in a cheery voice*].—
Oh, well, I'll take the goose-wing, and dig into the cracks—
so don't fret about that! And if you're not going to die
for some hours, I might as well have my dinner going on,
for 'twill soon be noon. I see there's cold potatoes and
fish in the pantry, and I can chop a hash—so you turn
over, dear, and try to go to sleep.

PATIENCE [*screaming with rage*].—To sleep! To sleep!
Just as if I could sleep in such distress as this! Heat a
piece of brown paper wet in vinegar, and clap it to my
forehead! And if I did feel the least disposition to even
wink, do you think, Peter Doughty, I'd let you leave me,
when it would certainly be my last sleep. [*Peter brings
the brown paper, and applies it with awkward fingers.*]
Now I'll finish what I was going to say [*drops of vinegar
course their way down her cheeks*]. You'll certainly have
to marry again, Peter; but I know you'll never think of
it, unless somebody puts the idea into your head.

PETER [*astonished*].—Oh, don't be foolish! You've got
on to a new tack, Patience. I've heard all the rest of your
talk a hundred times over; but you never said any thing
before about another wife.

PATIENCE [*weeping*].—It's because I never got wrought
up to such a pitch before. But I seem to have had a vision

of the state you 'll be in, and the ruinous condition of this
house and furniture; and it's been made clear to my mind
that I ought to see you provided for before I go. It isn't
as if I went without warning, Peter. And now I ask you,
if it would be right for me to die, with my eyes open, as
it were, and not know of somebody that is going to take
my place?

PETER.—It's a curious way you have of joking. Come,
don't take on so! Keep talking—for you cry harder when
you don't talk.

PATIENCE.—Answer me candidly, Peter. When you've
seen me *just alive* so many times, have you ever, even for
a moment, thought of anybody you'd like for a second
wife?

PETER.—No, I never! What an idea!

PATIENCE [*pleased*].—That's just like you, Peter, you
never was any kind of a hand to look out for the future
[*groaning*]; you've the poorest calculation in the world
about preparing for a rainy day.

PETER [*in a deprecatory tone*].—I didn't know it was
customary.

PATIENCE.—Well, it isn't generally, my dear. I'll
admit that it isn't considered just the thing for a married
man to be having his eye out for a second wife. But
circumstances alters cases, Peter; and as I said before,
I'm astonished that you never went so far as to make a
selection in your own mind.

PETER [*twirling his thumbs and looking very foolish*].—
If you'd only given me a hint, you know, but you never
said any thing about it.

PATIENCE [*removing the brown paper from one eye, and
peeping out at Peter*].—I've been more thoughtful for you
than you've been for yourself; I've picked out Phebe
Skillings.

PETER [*alarmed*].—You don't say so! Well, I'll tell
you what it is, Patience Doughty, folks say I'm henpecked, and I suppose I *am* henpecked; but you won't
make me marry that old Phebe Skillings if you stand
over me with a horsewhip!

PATIENCE.—Why, Peter, you needn't look so fierce.
Who ever saw you look so crusty? When I'm only supposing a case! I haven't set my heart on Phebe, not by

any manner of means. Only she does know how to
wash floors like a queen, and makes as good pie-crust
with as little lard as ever I tasted ; I should feel safe to
leave my dishes and furniture in her hands. And she'd
dose you up beautifully, Peter; she understands all
kinds of cough mixtures and plasters.

PETER.—Well, I'll do any thing in reason to please
you, but I don't want to marry Phebe if there's any way
of getting round it.

PATIENCE [*considerately*].—I shan't insist upon it, dear;
hand me the comb and brush, Peter; I suppose I shall
have to see about getting dinner; though I know I'm
too weak to stand, and can't walk a step without fainting
away. But, with regard to your marrying, I only insist
upon one thing, and that is, that you look around and
make your choice of some smart, capable girl; and when
the matter is decided let me know, for I shall die easier
if it's all cut and dried; I've lived through this spasm,
it's true, but it's no sign I shall live through the next
one.   I shan't be with you long, Peter.   [*Exit Scene.*]

SCENE III.—*Peter cutting potatoes alone.*

PETER [*to himself*].—What a curious woman Patience
Smith Doughty is ! But I positively declare there's some
sense in what she says. I should be the poorest hand in
the world to get along alone. 1 shall miss her desper-
ately that's a fact. I haven't known what it was to be in
the house five minutes, without hearing her groan   It
comes about as natural as the ticking of the clock.
Poor Patience ! But she's got to die, I suppose there's
no doubt of that, sooner or later : and as these spasms
keep growing worse and worse, I've no doubt she's
nearer her end than she was a month ago. Says "I shan't
be with you long, Peter." That sounds to me kind of
prophetic. "I only insist upon one thing," says she,
"and that is, that you look around and make your own
choice of a smart, sensible girl," etc., etc. Now what
would you do [*looking at the potato he is cutting*], if you
was in my place? would you look 'round, or wouldn't
you ? I never supposed it was customary; but then, as
Patience says, and Patience is a woman of judgment,

"circumstances does alter cases." One thing is sure now, she's got the notion in her head, and I shan't hear the last of it for some time. Now there's Betsey Ann, but then she's so smart and perty, has been to boarding-school, can play on the piany, and all that sort of thing, I wonder if she would look at a plain fellow like me? I hardly think she would [*sighs*]; but then I might try Yes, I might just speak to her on the subject, so I might. It couldn't do any harm, and as Patience is so anxious about it I'll try.

[*Exit scene.*]

SCENE IV.—*Mrs. Hastings' parlor—Peter, in Sunday best, knocks at the door—Mrs. Hastings goes to the door.*

PETER [*timidly*].—Can I see your daughter Betsey Ann a few minutes, alone?

MRS H.—Certainly, Mr. Doughty. Walk into the back parlor; I'll send her in.

[*Peter passes to opposite side of the stage. Mrs. H. calls " Betsey Ann," who enters.*]

MRS. H.—Betsey, Mr. Doughty wishes to speak with you in private a few minutes.

BETSEY.—With me, mother? That is strange!

MRS. H.—I must confess I have some curiosity to know what the man is after, in his new coat with the brass buttons. He looks so mysterious and so bashful too. His face is as pink as a sweet William.

BETSEY [*gayly shaking her curls*].—Poor soul! most likely he has been reading some more quack advertise-ments, and would like to know my opinion in regard to snakes. Where's my fan? I shall need it to screen my face when I laugh. [*Miss Betsey approaches Peter. Mrs. H. retires.*] Good-evening, Mr. Doughty! How are you this fine evening and how is Mrs. Doughty?

PETER.—Poorly, very poorly! I mean never was better, that is to say I am—Miss Betsey Ann—that is to say, she isn't—in other words, failing fast, worse and worse, and more frequent——

BETSEY [*with a twinkle in her eye*].—I am very sorry, and very glad, that is to say distressed, that is I mean for her, and in other words rejoiced for you.

PETER.—Yes, ma'am. I don't know about that [*blushes*].

BETSEY.—Lovely weather, Mr. Doughty

PETER [*examining the buttons on his coat*].—Yes, ma'am!

BETSEY.—But we need rain !

PETER.—Yes, ma'am, rain.

BETSEY.—The river is very low.

PETER.—The river is. Yes, ma'am.

BETSEY.—Quite dusty!

PETER.—What did you observe, ma'am?

BETSEY.—Dusty, I said, quite dusty, Mr. Doughty!

PETER.—I don't exactly understand you, ma'am, that is, I don't so much as I ought to, perhaps.

BETSEY [*laughing and screening her face with her fan*].—Fine weather, no rain, and too much dust.

PETER [*looks at the ceiling—turns and looks out the window*].—A very pretty evening out doors. [*Balances himself on his heels and turns round with a jerk.*] I thought whether or no, Miss Betsey——

BETSEY.—Well, sir !

PETER.—I thought whether or no, Miss Betsey——

BETSEY.—Very well, Mr. Doughty [*Aside.*] What can he want ! He'll keep me here two hours. I think my mother said you wished to see me, Mr. Doughty.

PETER [*with still redder cheeks, inserting the index finger between necktie and throat*].—Nothing, oh, nothing in particular, Miss Betsey.

BETSEY.—Ah, then it was a mistake of her's—so you'll please excuse me if I leave you now, for I was intending to go out.

PETER.—Stop, Miss Betsey ! won't you please to stop ! Does your father wish to buy a cow ?

BETSEY.—Not that I know of. Shall I call him ?

PETER.—Oh, no, not for the world ! I've got one to sell, one of the best kind, and I've been calculatin' to turn her into another cow, and then beef her. Didn't know but your folks might like to trade. Dreadful rainy weather, Miss Betsey ; never needed dust so much. And is your mother at home ? And how's her health this summer ? Give her my respects ! Is Tommy pretty well, and how is his health ? Is Johnny pretty well, and how is his health ?

M 2   18

BETSEY.—Take a seat, Mr. Doughty, and pray tell me what in the world you have on your mind. I'm ready to befriend you—indeed I am. Why are you so afraid of me? Is there any thing I can do for you, or your wife? You would like me to go and watch with Mrs. Doughty?

PETER.—Oh, no, no, not for the world! She's past hope! You're very kind, Miss Betsey, very kind, that's the general opinion, or I wouldn't have had the heart to come here to-night, for it's something that isn't customary, it certainly isn't, but I'm in hopes you'll understand that circumstances alters cases in all cases, that is, in my case, and won't take offence, Miss Betsey.

BETSEY.—No offence at all, Mr. Doughty. Indeed I can imagine what your errand is before you give it.

PETER.—Can you though, Miss Betsey? Well, that's clever.

BETSEY.—It concerns some of your poor wife's fancies.

PETER.—Well, you are the quickest-witted girl I ever did see, considering I never said a word to a living soul, and you couldn't have guessed it from my actions. I'm very glad you understand my business, for I confess it's very unpleasant to me, and if it wasn't for the peculiar circumstances, I should certainly wait till she was *dead*.

BETSEY.—You take a very circuitous method of expressing yourself, Mr. Doughty, but no doubt you wish to tell me that you have heard something new about snakes.

PETER [*crestfallen*].—I haven't the least idea, Miss Betsey, what snakes you refer to, and that is certainly not my object in coming, though I hope you'll give me time to collect my thoughts, for I am not good at speaking off-hand, Miss Betsey.

BETSEY.—So I perceive, Mr. Doughty.
[*Profound silence.*]

PETER.—Since I've been a-sittin' here I've been a-thinkin'—[*silence again, save the tap of Betsey's foot upon the carpet.*] Since I've been a-sittin' here I've been a-thinkin'. [*Silence.*] Since I've been a-sittin' here, Miss Betsey, I've been a-thinkin'.

BETSEY.—So I should judge.

PETER.—I've been a-thinkin' what I should do for a *second wife.*

BETSEY [*rising and facing him*].—Sir !

PETER [*hurriedly*].—Patience won't be with me long. It's her dyin' wish that I should look 'round and make my ow.. choice of some smart, capable girl, and when the matter is decided let her know, fur she'll die easier when it's all cut and dried.

BETSEY.—Peter—Doughty !

PETER.—She wanted me to look 'round, she didn't hamper me, and I did look 'round, and my choice fell on you. Now I want you to take time to think, for there ain't any hurry—none at all.

BETSEY.—Stop this minute, sir ! I'm going to call my mother.

PETER.—Wait a minute, for pity's sakes, Miss Betsey. I don't mean any harm, I don't expect you to marry me *now*, I'm only looking out for a rainy day. Think, Miss Betsey, there will be only myself and a neat little cotta " · free of all incumberances, for I'm well to do in the wor... if I say it myself.

BETSEY [*laughing and crying hysterically*].—Pete. Doughty, do you know you are an unprincipled, audacious scamp, a wicked Mormon, and an outrageous, unmitigated idiot ! Sir, do you walk out of this house as fast as you can go, and never darken our doors again.

PETER.—But, Miss Betsey ——

BETSEY.—Go this minute, and do you never offer yourself to any other woman till your wife is dead and buried in a Christian manner, which won't be in your day or mine, Peter Doughty.

PETER [*in a faltering voice*].—I guess you don't look at in the right light. I wish I had stayed at home. 'Twill get into the papers—'twill be spread all over town.

BETSEY.—No, sir; do you think Elizabeth Ann Hastings hasn't pride enough to keep such a disgraceful proposal to herself ? Why, you little simpleton, I've too much self-respect to tell it to my own mother !

PETER.—Say that again, Betsey Ann !

BETSEY.—Here's my hand on it, Peter Doughty. And do you hold your feeble, stammering tongue as well. For if you ever tell a living soul what you've said to me to-night I 'll never forgive you as long as I live.

[*Curtain falls.*]

THE MISFORTUNE OF CIVIL WAR.

CHARACTERS.

MR. KAYSER, a blustering old gent.
MRS. KAYSER.
MISS THEODORA KAYSER.
BIDDY, a servant girl.
Soldiers.

SCENE I.—*Family circle—Mr. Kayser reading paper—*
Ladies engaged in sewing.

MR. K.—Indeed, wife, it is a matter of hourly congratu-
lation to me that my inclination did not turn to public
life. The public man is not permitted to make the least
turn, without one of those prickly-pears of society clinging with bombastic vigor to his intentions.

MRS. K.—To whom do you have reference, my love?

MR. K.—To whom could I refer, if not to that abomi-
nable class of persons, the reporters? Your good sense
should have discerned that, without any explanation.
You are aware, my dear, that I am a man possessed of a
remarkably easy disposition; but even my temper could
not withstand [*Theodora smiles*]—What are you laughing
at, girl?

THEO.—Nothing, papa—only my thoughts.

MR. K.—Very well. I say even I could not withstand
the impudence of having my wife, or private property, dis-
cussed in such a style of ownership, as it were. Listen,
wife, to this [*reads*]: "We are happy to announce the
arrival of the able, noble and labor-loving General Slim-
jack, of the Army of the Potomac. Our readers are well
aware how nobly this gentleman has sacrificed health,
home-comforts, and the society of his beautiful and amia-
ble wife, to his country's cause, until his rapidly-failing
strength has made it necessary to leave his laborious position for a time. We hope the tender nursing of his loving
spouse will soon give him back a convalescent. The

General's well-known abilities are such that his presence can illy be dispensed with at the present time. We wish him all the rest and enjoyment this short respite from duty can give—then welcome back to the field of glory!" [*casting the paper aside.*] Such wordy palaver—it disgusts me! I wonder how many baskets of champagne they expect for this! Oh, I thank my good sense that I am not a public man!

Mrs. K.—Such indelicate publicity is not enviable, certainly, however one may enjoy popularity.

Mr. K.—Can a man not be popular without becoming the helpless carcass in the claws of hankering buzzards? Please to answer, madam!

Mrs. K.—If any one aspire to mount the ladder of celebrity, and the public tolerate them, why of course they belong, in a measure at least, to the grounds on which they trespass, and thus must expect to be subjected to the peculiarities of the birds that are at liberty to flap their wings in the field of the aspirer's labors, be it hawk or dove.

Mr. K.—I do not accept the allegory, and still more, I do not choose to give them any such honorable name as *birds.* I will give you a figure that suits them better. The public is a mosquito, and the reporter is the blood-sucker, to be depended on to the same extent. They prepare to excoriate while they serenade you. Then, having gratified their momentary enthusiasm or desire, you may sink into silent oblivion, for all they care. They smell fresher game on the same road. They do not halt to *bury* the fame of the "old love," before they are on to the new; they merely sting you to death, and leave the vultures finish the bad job. Such is public life. Away with the name—I'll none of it!

Theo.—But, papa, think of the glory!

Mr. K.—Glory, indeed! You know nothing about the thing! It is a fraud—a pit for youthful blood! Glory is like sweetmeats. For instance, you over-dose yourself at the table of some good-natured grandmother—the result would be an unpleasant sensation about the region of the stomach—nausea, or something of the kind, would follow.

Theo.—But, papa, I would be discreet, and not be greedy

MR. K.—Glory has no medium state—once get a taste of it and the craving leads you to the other extreme. Now mark the result of the sweetmeats—'tis the same.

THEO.—I think, however, I would risk the nausea rather than go through life a nobody.

MR. K.—Do you mean to tell me I am a *nobody*, Miss?

THEO. [*rising and going to his side, taps him lovingly on the cheek.*]—I mean no such thing, you dear, good, bilious *somebody*. I intended to imply that I should like to become famous by achieving some great feat, con- quer some army, risk life or death in the performance of a duty that required unusual ability or courage—some thing more difficult than devouring sweetmeats!

MR. K.—And then be lauded by the steam of human approbation to the seventh sphere of acknowledged merit, eh?

THEO.—Why, yes; I think I should like to be appre- ciated, else I should have no encouragement for still higher attempts.

MR. K.—Human nature *will* peep out. Well, I sup- pose it *is* natural for us to think more of the noise we make in the world than of the worthiness of the act itself. Praise is very sweet; but, remember, child, honey is ex- cellent—still, it is gathered by the insect that has a vicious sting.

THEO.—Do you think, papa, your simile is exactly ap- plicable? I don't think my greatness ever would bite any one. [*Resumes her seat, laughing.*]

MR. K.—Miss Impudence presumes to question *me!* Really, wife, this is a fearful age, and this detestable war has not bettered matters. I rejoice I have no son, or he would be advising me how to cast my vote, since my daughter would put ideas into her father's head. I thought it was quite enough, when, a few days since, she suggested to you a *superior* mode of making army shirts. Why, when we were children we would have hidden our brazen faces had we so far forgotten ourselves as to address our elders thus.

MRS. K.—I truly hope Theodora intended no disrespect; however, we should remember, we progress with our years, and every year is more progressive than the last, and our children step in where we leave off; therefore we must not expect them to be what we were in our young days. Education is more liberal now than in those days of pay-schools and private tutors. Education is the bed of ideas, and ideas make forward brains.

MR. K.—Upon my soul, madam, has this war affected the women too? Strange development of audacity! Wives would lecture their husbands, and children would play the wise tyrant. [*Rising and pacing the floor indignantly.*] I demand the respect that is my due as the *head* of the house. I do not choose to be reprimanded in the hearing of my child. Really, I do believe the dissenting fever is contagious. [*Sits down, and drums impatiently on the table as Biddy enters.*]

BIDDY.—Plase mum, there's a soger out here as wants to spake wid the misthress.

MRS. K.—Is he begging? Give him something to eat.

BIDDY.—Sure, mum, it's a dainty beggur he is, then. I offered him a bit o' the chicken and a bit o' the purtata, and a bit of all that was left of the dinner, but the crathure is plased to ax for the misthress herself—*the Jarsey cannibal!*

MR. K.—Bring him in here. I will see the man.

BIDDY.—It's afeared he is o' the masther. He tould me to see the misthress; her good heart would do better nor him. [*Aside.*] An' that's a fact, troth!

MR. K. [*stamping angrily.*] – Bring him to me, I say. No more of your words!

BIDDY [*on leaving the room, aside*].—Oh, ye scolding baste! [*Re-enter with soldier.*]

MR. K.—Well, sir, am I a wild animal that you should fear me, or are you some prowling rascal, in soldier's clothes, trying to bamboozle the credulous hearts of women? Speak; don't stand there like a numskull.

BIDDY [*aside*].—Ah, the brute to spake the like o' that to the poor young man.

SOL.—I am neither a coward nor a rogue, sir; but having heard of your lady's goodness, and being in need of rather peculiar advice and immediate aid, I ventured to call on her for assistance.

MR. K.—And who are you that presumes to ask aid of a strange lady? Why not go to your kind? Any gentleman would help you, if your distress is not associated with dishonor. Prove that first, and I will then listen to your story.

SOL.—I can *prove* nothing at present, unless you are pleased to take my word on the honor of a gentleman.

MR. K. [*laughing.*]—Hear you that, wife? A "*gentleman!*" and begging!

SOL.—Sir, although the would-be recipient of favors, I am still free enough in manhood to ignore an uncalled-for insult. Even a *gentleman* may be placed in my position in these times of warfare and change, and especially a soldier should be free to ask a reasonable favor, and not be termed a *beggar!* *Time*, in this instance, is life or death, sir. Good-day. [*Turns to leave.*]

MR. R.—Stay, stranger. One of "Uncle Sam's boys" shall never say he turned from my door unaided. Indeed, I was jesting. My intention was not to wound your self-respect. Biddy, you gaping mortal, do you not see the gentleman standing?

BIDDY [*handing chair, aside*].—The auld sinner cotched it that time, sure!

MR. K.—Now be seated and tell me how we can be of service to you.

SOL.—Not to accept your apology would speak ill for my gentility. So, since I have your permission, I will speak direct to the point. There is in my company a little fellow of sixteen, who ran away from his home in the South, about a year ago; he has been my messmate and bedfellow during this time, besides fighting at my side in two battles. We became so much attached to each other, owing to the lack of other companionship. There are few among our fellow-privates that have enjoyed educational advantages, or can recall genial home associations as we can; thus, you see, we feel better to ourselves. I love him as a younger brother, and would sacrifice much to spare him trouble. Now, sir, being beyond communication with my own home, I would ask of you to take and protect this boy for a few days.

MRS. K.—Is he sick, poor child?

SOL.—I could almost wish he were. No, madam. We have, a short time since, received marching orders for the battle-field—to-morrow we engage with the enemy. But, through information gained this morning, he discovered that his father and two brothers are in the advance-guard of the opposing army. Unfortunately for him, our regiment is also ordered to the front. You see the predicament. The poor boy is nearly heart-broken. Our officers are too busy to pay attention to him, and say it is an excuse to skulk   You will, indeed, be doing a humane act to protect him until after the excitement of the battle is over; then, by properly representing the matter to the military authorities, he will be honorably discharged.

THEO. — Oh, papa, how terrible, if he must go!—perhaps be the death of one of them, or they may meet face to face in the fearful struggle.

MR. K.—Hasten, young man: he is welcome. I will keep him safe as if he were my own boy. But how will you get him here without being discovered?

SOL.—That advice I would ask of your wife—ladies always are quick in such matters. None are permitted to leave camp without an order—he will be suspected, were he to ask for one now.

MRS. K.   I have a plan. Have you a tent to yourself?

SOL.—Yes, madam—fortunately, we have not yet received orders to "strike tents."

MRS. K.—There is no time to be lost. Biddy shall go with you. A basket, containing fruit on the top, will conceal some female apparel—a sun-bonnet to cover his face. You must manage to dress him unseen—let him take the basket and walk away.

MR. K.—I have even a better plan. Biddy must take a friend with her, who will manage to disappear until the boy gets outside the camp. The guard will not know but the two coming out are the same that entered. The girl is safe enough. And thus there is no danger of discovery.

THEO.—I will go in Biddy's place. It will save time, and also be known only to ourselves. While the boy and I walk out, she can be entertaining the soldiers in the vicinity. May I go?

MR. K.—Yes—only hurry, before it is too late to effect the change.

SCENE II.—*Discovering the family, in seeming composure, interrogating a sergeant and soldier.*

MR. K.—Gentlemen, what means this intrusion?

SERG.—We have orders to search this house—we beg permission to proceed with our duty. A soldier lad has deserted from our regiment, and our superior officers have reason to believe him secreted here.

MR. K.—Tell your officers, my house is not a harbor for skulkers or cowards! Wife, call your servants that these men may continue their search unmolested. [*Mrs. K. leaves room—returns, followed by Biddy and colored girl.*] Now, men, do your duty. To my best knowledge, the persons in this room are the only living creatures in my house—unless, indeed, you capture the cat or a mouse.

[*Men bow, and leave room.*]

THEO.—Dinah, do you feel *queerish*?

COLORED GIRL.—Very chicken-hearted just now, Miss Kayser.

MRS. K.—Hush! listeners may be near.

MR. K.—Yes, this is a time of terror. This civil war— this breeder of strategy and deceit, poverty, and vice— nothing is sacred from its polluting influence. Why cannot nations leave this bickering? It seems as if one generation demanded revenge for the blood shed in that gone by; and ere the swords have lost their traces of human gore, a new generation rises up, with its inheritance of strife, to dabble its hands in deadly conquest. [*Enter sergeant.*] Well, did you find your man?

SERG.—We have found nothing, sir; but we have done our duty. [*Bows himself out. Colored girl is suddenly inspired—dances about the room—drops hoop-skirts and dress, discovers soldier-pants beneath—tears cloth from head, then steps in front of table, addressing Mr. and Mrs. Kayser solemnly.*]

BOY.—How can I thank you, sir, for thus befriending the boy, who would, otherwise, have been compelled to take up arms against his own blood—a loved father and dear brother. I know it is the duty of all to defend the nation's flag; but, sir, I could not raise my gun against the man who gave me birth. I will think over the question when wiser years are added to my understanding. As yet, my heart says—first, God; then the life that gave *me* life; and then my country's flag!

"ALL THE COMFORTS OF A HOME."

CHARACTERS.

Miss Caroline Palaver, æt. forty years.
Mrs. Palaver, somewhat decrepit—virago and mono-
maniac.
Mrs. Jinks, in search of board.
Hattie Jinks, } children of foregoing—nine and seven
Willie Jinks, }   years old respectively.
Mr. Lightfoot, collector.
Mrs. Pleasant, neighbor of the Palavers.

———

Scene I.—*A small room, plainly furnished—every thing old-
fashioned and musty—Mrs. P., broom in one hand and
duster in the other,* "*setting things to rights.*"

Mrs. P. [*adjusting ancient spectacles, and giving the
snuff-stick in her mouth another rub.*]—Here I keep a-
workin' and a-dustin'—a-workin' and a-dustin'—day in
and day out—day in and day out—and I'm scarce able
to do it—scarce able to do it [*reaches up to straighten an
old cloth stretched over a high-backed rocker to keep off
dust*]. Ugh! my shoulder! my shoulder! That ruma-
tiz in my shoulder! I can't last long—I can't last long
—and then she'll be alone—and who knows who'll have
her money, the little she's got—always givin' away and
givin' away to them Proud St. Church beggars! And
here I am a-workin' and a-workin', old as I am! I'll tell
'em—I'll tell 'em—how she uses me. I'll bring 'em here
to see the bed I lie in—not fit for the dogs—the hussy,
with all her pious, imperdent airs! [*dusting a covered
table, the legs tied up in papers.*] No such tables now-a-
days! Mr. Palaver paid seventy-five dollars for that
table—couldn't get it for that money these times. What
do I get now? The hypocrite! She hides every thing from
me. I'll know what she gets. Gives me nothing to eat
but crusts. She shan't have these things of mine in the
chest. I'll—I'll—[*shaking head ominously*]—I'll be the

death of her yet! Bah! here I scrub and scrub [*detecting a spot on the oil-cloth*] and who cares but to—[*listening—steps and a voice at the door—a rap—opens door and peers through—opens wider*]—Come in! Come in! Just come in! [*quite genial.*] Take a seat—take a seat now! [*to Mrs. J. and children entering.*]

MRS. J.—Is this Miss Palaver?

MRS. P.—You mean Cal'line—she's in—she's in! [*going to another door and calling*] Cal'line! Cal'line! Come down! Oh, take a seat, children. Such pûtty black eyes [*looking admiringly at Willie's eyes, with a smile and movement of the head*]. Black as coals! H—m—m! [*seats herself, and folding her arms, surveys the visitors.*]

MRS. J.—Your daughter, I suppose, takes pupils?

MRS. P.—Sometimes she does—since the death of him —twelve years ago, she does a great deal—does Cal'line —teaches in Proud St. Sunday-school [*going to the door and calling*]. Cal'line! Cal'line! do make a hurry!

MRS. J. [*going to wall to examine an ancient bead-worked sampler.*]—Beautiful! Beau—ti—ful!

MRS. P.—Cal'line did that when she wan't no bigger than that one [*pointing to Hattie*]. She's worked a great many—giv' away I don't know how many. She used to make the finest shirts I ever seed—giv' 'em to her friends —'most spiled her eyes! Them pûtty black eyes! [*looking at Willie, who turns away bashfully.*] What's his name?

MRS. J.—Willie.

MRS. P.—Willie? Such pûtty eyes! the dear child!

[*Door opens stealthily—Caroline enters, passes her hand over a scant, clinging dress, partially covered by a greasy old apron unaccountably patched—continues looking steadily at Mrs. J. as she advances, and bows.*]

CAROLINE.—I ought to apologize for keeping you waiting, but I was combing my hair [*combed very plainly down over her ears*], when I heard mother call, and I didn't stop to change my dress. [*Her lengthened face shortens in a semi-smile—gazes steadfastly—talks in slow monotone, without force, relieved by an occasional slow movement or gesture.*] I really ought to be ashamed of myself. I was quite busy in my room; and since it is vacation, I scarcely expected any visitor. We have very few visitors. Only our minister sometimes, or some pious person. I belong to the Proud Street Church. In fact, I have been a member almost from childhood. We live quite alone here—only mother and I—since father died.

Mrs. J. [*who has bowed, and said " Yes" many times during the foregoing.*]—I heard you recommended, Miss Palaver, as a person to take children to teach and, perhaps, board.

Caroline.—Yes, I have taught some since father died. I——

Mrs. P. [*interrupting.*]—The way she was raised—so delicate—never has touched a finger to work—since the death of him—since the death of him—such pretty little white hands—but now——[*lost in reverie*].

Caroline.—I have not found this place as good for a school as Broad street, where we used to live; but since we have lived here in Gouge street, I have been prevailed upon to take a few day-scholars. We have never taken children to board. We have sometimes taken a grown person or two, just for company. Miss Skowhegan—she boarded with us three years—couldn't bear to leave. I know very little about this neighborhood. I never meddle with the affairs of others, and let them say what they please. We generally think we can judge for ourselves. I believe the only thing I ever did hear that was said against me was that I was proud, because I didn't visit my neighbors. Did you wish to secure board for yourself?

Mrs. J.—Oh, no ! My husband is gone right smart He is on board of a vessel, and can get home only now and then. I board with my brother's family; but I find their children in the way. I want to go into company considerable myself, and my brother has company often; and when I heard of you I thought I would see if you would not board them. I am only twenty-eight, and find it too stupid sitting down to tend children. I never did care much for anybody's children; and I know I don't think much of my own. I want them well cared for, and I will pay you what you charge, if it is not unreasonable. I want you to teach them and keep them away from other children.

Caroline.—Well, I think, since we live in a plain, quiet

way, and would like a little care and company, that we
will take them. I am very fond of little children myself.
They seem so innocent! I will take them to Sunday-
school—shall I? [*Mrs. J nods assent.*] And then their
washing shall be done, and they shall be taught, and have
good, plain, nourishing food, and every comfort of a home.
I think, since every thing is so high, I must charge you
—— [*hesitating*] six dollars a week. That will cover the
cost of tuition and every thing. And I will see that they
want for nothing.

MRS. J.—Well, I can't have them with me, and I suppose I can't suit myself any better, nor provide for them
any better—so I will pay you what you ask. My name
is Jinks—I board at No. 37 Crooked street. You can ask
Mr. Stokes, the lumber-merchant at the corner, whether
I am responsible for the pay.

CAROLINE.—Oh, I'm sure you are, or we shouldn't take
them! When do you wish to have them begin?

MRS. J.—I would like to go away to-day, and if you
have no objection would leave them with you now.

CAROLINE.—Very well—any time you please.

MRS. J. [*to children.*]—Come here, dears! Let me
kiss you! Be good children and do as Miss Caroline
says, and perhaps next week I'll come and take you out
to Aunt Fanny's with me. [*Kisses them and rises to go.*]
There, dears! I'll send their clothes down this afternoon, Miss Palaver. Good-day, ma'am! [*To Mrs. P.*]
Good-day! Good-bye, children! [*Exit.*]

MRS. P.—Wa'nt that a quare woman? What did she
git married for! Sich an onhuman way of doin' business! If I had 'tended you in that way, where would
you have ben, I'd like to know, you mean, puling, whinin'
wretch! Curse the day you were ever born! You
needn't look at me so with them snaky eyes of your'n!
Stop—I say! Stop! [*Stamping violently.*]

CAROLINE.—Mother—mother! You are talking loud!

MRS. P. [*talking loudly.*]—Who are you, to correct
your own mother that way?

CAROLINE.—I didn't mean any thing. I thought in
my own house I might just speak. I only mean to sug-
gest—I think I am old enough to judge for myself.

MRS. P.—Hush! with all your imperdence! Stop looking at me so with your hypocritical airs! Don't I hate you! Just like that parson uncle of yours — that Methodist sneak who cheated me out of my inheritance! Me, his own sister—me, that's seen better days than this —me, that never touched my lily hands to work--and look at 'em now—ugh! Me, that had the handsomest foot and the trimmest figger for miles 'round —me, that used to dance and sing for father's guests – father, the handsomest man that ever was! Oh, that villain—that scoundrel! Little good did it do him—died sitting in his chair at his own table! [*While she gesticulates and talks loudly Caroline tries to divert the wondering children by calling them to her, asking their names, taking off their hats, etc.*]

MRS. P. [*dusting and soliloquizing.*]—And now she's brought this dirty baggage into the house—and who's to work for them? Not me—not me! Me, who am e'enamost gone! She a-fixin' herself up with the money she gets and goin' to Proud street meetins and leavin' me here to work! [*Exit.*]

CAROLINE [*to children*].—You mustn't notice what she says. She's an old lady. She's had a good bit of trouble. or thinks she has—and you mustn't provoke her. You must always clean your feet and step quietly and not talk loudly and ask me for what you want. I'll show you where I want you to sit and study and talk—and then after sundown, if it's pleasant, you may go and sit on the front door-steps and see the people go by.

HATTIE.—Can't we play any, or speak loud, Miss Car'- line?

CAROLINE.—Yes—when you're good. Willie, do you know your letters?

WILLIE [*lisping*].—No, ma'am—I geth I don't know nothin'.

CAROLINE.—Well, come with me, children!

MRS. P. [*shouting as they pass through the door.*]— Shut that door! Don't you come out here trackin' ove. the floor!

SCENE II.—*Caroline sewing patchwork in a room almo. empty—Children on a hard bench trying to keep quiet.*

HATTIE.—Miss Caroline, what makes you make me

wear a thick veil over my face when I go to Sunday-school? I haven't been out of doors hardly at all since I came here. I wish I didn't have to wear it.

CAROLINE.—Why, child, I wear one myself. I want you to keep your skin fair and to walk like a lady.

HATTIE.—It makes me so hot I can hardly breathe. I don't think it's a bit nice.

CAROLINE.—You shouldn't be giving your opinion about things till you are asked. You ought to be very thankful that any one takes such an interest in you. [*To Willie, wriggling in discomfort.*] Sit up there straight, Willie—like a gentleman!

WILLIE.—I don't like my papa muth! He bringth me thingth sometimeth—but Mithter Button at the sthore uthed to give me a pieth of candy every day. Can't I have thomething to eat, Mith Car'line?

CAROLINE—You are not hungry—are you?

WILLIE—Yith I am—I am jitht ath hungry ath a bear!

HATTIE.—Can't we have just a piece?

CAROLINE.—Go and tell Mrs. Palaver that Miss Caroline says you may have something to eat. Be very still! [*They go out, and soon return crying, each with a bit of bread. Mrs. P. follows.*]

CAROLINE [*rising*].—What is the matter? [*Children cry.*] Tell me!

HATTIE.—Oh, Miss Car'line [*boo-hoo*]! She got angry [*boo-hoo*], and beat me over the back! [*boo-hoo-hoo.*]

MRS. P.—Don't you come down agin a-botherin' me, and a-botherin' me, and beggin' for somethin' to eat—comin' down just after I cleaned the floor, and whinin' round, "somethin' to eat! somethin' to eat!"—jest as if you didn't have a slice of liver apiece this mornin' and hoe-cake enough—and every mornin' too! And didn't you roll up the mat a-scufflin' round? If you do it agin —— [*raises hand menacingly*].

CAROLINE.—Don't beat the child, mother!

MRS. P.—Hush your imperdence! Bringin' such rubbage into the house and a-makin' me do all the work and doin' not a thing yourself. [*Seizes a poker.*] Oh, you lyin', sneakin' thing! I'll pay you! [*tries to grasp Caroline's hair.*]

CAROLINE.—Don't, mother—don't, mother! [*half cry-ing*] don't pull my hair!
[*Knock heard at outside door. Mrs. P. desists, and goes away muttering. Caroline re-arranges things and opens door.*]

MR. LIGHTFOOT [*entering*].—Good-morning, Miss Pala-ver! It's the day for my call, I believe.

CAROLINE.—Yes, sir. I am ready with the twelve dol-lars; but, indeed, I think it's too much for poor women like us, with no one to provide for us.

LIGHTFOOT.—Mr. Lease is very lenient, I think, Miss. He has been offered fifteen a month several times.

CAROLINE [*handing money*].—I shouldn't think a rich man like him could think of asking more of me, because I'm an orphan with no father, or brother, or sister, and no protector.

LIGHTFOOT.—All right, Miss. Good-morning. [*Exit.*]

MRS. P. [*re-entering.*]—Cal'line, who was that?

CAROLINE.— Mr. Lightfoot—for the rent.

MRS. P.—Is he a-goin' to raise the rent this time?

CAROLINE.—He says Mr. Lease has been offered fifteen dollars.

MRS. P.—Mortal soul! What does the old skinflint think? Fifteen dollars for this old shell! There I stand, day after day, in that nasty, smoky box of a kitchen, nearly choked to death; and won't have the chimney fixed—no more mercy on the widder and the orphan! I wish I had him hung up in that chimney! There he'd hang till doomsday—see how *he'd* like smoke! What's the matter, Cal'line? [*who is holding her hand to her breast.*] Speak—can ye?

CAROLINE.—I have such a misery in my breast.

MRS. P.—Misery! Here I might be half dead with my shoulder, and crippled up as I am—who cares? Not you a-leavin' every thin' for me to do—and I don't complain a bit—*I* never complain.

CAROLINE.—I didn't mean to complain, mother; I only meant to answer your question.

MRS. P.—Go on—go on! You never know when to stop—old as you are and so aggravatin'!

CAROLINE.—I thought you asked me what was the

matter. I am sure I try to be unfeignedly thankful that I am so well as I am—I try to do——

Mrs. P.—Hear that! Hear that—will ye? Do stop that tongue of yours!

[*Caroline takes children and exit. Mrs P follows.*]

SCENE III.

CAROLINE [*sitting at table—brow knit — resting head upon hand*].—Oh, dear! Oh, dear! What shall I do? What shall I do? [*closing her eyes devoutly.*] This is a day of trouble--an orphan—no companion—nobody—nothing—only my little in the savings bank—all earned by my own labor and management since father died—and everybody bent on cheating me out of that! To be treated so in my own house, when I provide every thing, pay all the bills, and hold in from talking all I can so as not to cross her path. When father was here he could get away from it by leaving the house. And yet, peculiar as she is—strangely as she has always acted towards me—I should feel lonely without her in this cold, cruel world! Yes, heartless—as I have found it to-day. In the first place, I thought that market man ought to exchange that five cent note, which I find is counterfeit. I took it of him when I bought the liver. I never get any other meat when I can help it—it is so nourishing—and I always get of him. When I asked him if a piece of meat that laid there was lamb, he was very short and crusty; and when I asked him the difference between lamb and mutton, he laughed outright and said, "Why do they call the same girl at sixteen 'a tidy lass,' and at forty 'an old maid?'" I don't think that was any answer at all; and when I told him I thought he ought not to defraud me of five cents just because I had no father, nor brother, nor sister, nor companion, nor protector, and was an orphan, he only grinned the more, and said he guessed I was a nice old orphan, [*rising and walking a moment or two---re-seats herself*]. I shall not let those children go to the Proud St. excursion. Here they were sick last night because they ate too much, and I shall not trust them where I never have been myself—on cars or steamboat. I am always afraid of explosions

Mother is angry yet because I was up with them. I can make it pay, or I wouldn't have them, of course. What would she say if she knew that that minister whom she hated so, not only did not pay his board, but borrowed forty dollars and tried to get my watch? I am confident of it. Sing and pray as he did, too! Well, if he can get to heaven with it, I am sure I can without it. I wonder why our last boarders left so suddenly. I proposed to include washing and lights for only twice what I was getting. His partner didn't object—she only looked. They grumbled a bit, to be sure, when I couldn't make mother get breakfast till ten, or supper till late at night. I wish I could let that front room. Oh, dear! Let me see if the paper has any advertisements I can answer [*rising and looking for paper*].

Mrs. P. [*entering, muttering.*]—A pretty lie! A pretty lie! Who ever heard of such a thing? The meddling huckster's busy-body of a wife! [*discovering Caroline, softens tone.*] Is it Cal'line? I thought you were upstairs. [*Caroline passes quietly out, remaining just outside. Mrs. P., arranging mantelpiece, continues.*] She to dare to say I'm a neighborhood talk, and unless I stop scolding these children, there will be interference! I did give them water to wash their hands. Who brings it all? I should like to know what business it is of hern? [*loud rap at door—Caroline reappears—door suddenly opened.*]

Mrs. J. [*entering.*]—Where are my children?

Caroline [*coolly and calmly*].—How do you do, Mrs. Jinks? How providential your calling is! I was just thinking I would so much like to have you come and see the children—they were so sick last night and have had to be quiet to-day. They will be so glad to see you.

Mrs. J.—And well they may. I wonder they are alive. Where are my children? I ask you again [*goes to outside door and calls the neighbor next door*]. Mrs. Pleasant! Mrs. Pleasant! Come in here a minute, will you?

Caroline [*calls at inner door*].—Hattie! Willie! [*latter enter at same time with Mrs. Pleasant.*]

Both children [*rushing to mother and clinging to her*]. —Oh, ma—ma! Do take us away from here! Do—do —do!

Hattie.—You don't know what an awful woman she

[*pointing to Mrs. Palaver*] is! She beats me and Willie, and scolds us, and swears dreadfully!

WILLIE.—We don't get any thing to eat, ma!

CAROLINE.—Why Hattie! Why Willie! What makes you talk so? Don't you love your grandma? Don't you love Miss Caroline?

BOTH [*clinging to mother*].—No—no—we don't—we don't! Take us away, ma! Do—do—do!

MRS. J.—I don't care about having any words with either of you; but you must know that I have learned from those who have seen and heard what kind of treatment my children have received at the hands of both of you!

CAROLINE.—At *my* hands, Mrs. Jinks? Why I couldn't have done more for them if they had been my own children! Such care as I have taken of them—such a great responsibility! You have surely been misinformed. Will you give me the name of the person who has told you?

MRS. PLEASANT.—I will save Mrs. Jinks the trouble. I have been so worried by the treatment these poor children have had that I could endure it no longer, and I took means to inform their mother.

MRS. P.—So you're one of them gadding, dirty, mean, snivelling tell-tales, are you? Goin' round from house to house with your pack of lies—you talkin' about your betters who have rid in their own carriage—can't attend to your own brats, the nuisances, but must be meddlin' with other folkses! [*Looking around for something.*] You dirty, sassy critter—I'll teach you manners! Git out of my house, you trollop—git out! [*going towards her.*]

CAROLINE [*interposing*].—Mother, mother! Don't take on so! It is our duty to bear this persecution. It is for some good end, if we can't see it.

MRS. P.—Oh, you cantin' sniveller! You're in with 'em too—are you! I'll fix you! I'll fix you! Mind my words—I'll fix you! [*Exit in a rage, heard muttering in adjoining room.*]

MRS. J.—I said I wanted no words with you, and I will have none. Bring the children's hats—oh, here they are! [*putting them on.*] Here is your money [*throwing it to her*] —I'll send for their things within a half-hour. [*Rising with Mrs. P.*] Come, my dears! I may not be all that a mother should be, but I am mother enough to take you out of this hole, even if you do enjoy *all the comforts of* a *home!* [*Exeunt.*]

[*Caroline heard sobbing loud—curtain falls.*]

THE SUFFRAGE QUESTION.

CHARACTERS.

PROF. FAIRMAN.   DR. THOMAS.

Room in private house.

DR. T.—Were you serious, Professor, in that hurried chat we had the other day, when you stated that our American experiment of a republic must, as the case now stood, be regarded as a failure?

PROF. F.—Never more serious in my life, believe me, Doctor.

DR. T.—I have turned the matter over in my mind since, and examined it in every light in which I could place it, and I must confess that I cannot see sufficient reasons for agreeing with you. We are both at leisure for a while this evening. What say you to a talk on the subject? I am open to conviction.

PROF.—Your proposal is accepted; since, fortunately, we chance to belong to that rare class of disputants, who, if they cannot agree upon all points—and what thinkers can?—can at least agree to disagree as gentlemen. So much my modesty allows me to say—nor will yours prevent your endorsing it. Your last remark brings to my mind a character, who shall be nameless here, who declared that he was perfectly willing to be convinced—perfectly willing—but nobody could convince him! [*laughing.*] Nothing personal, Doctor, I assure you. But to the topic in hand. Are you prepared to maintain that the Government of the United States, as at present constituted, is a republic? Is it in reality, and more than in name?

DR.—Do you mean to ask whether I consider our government to all intents and purposes republican?

PROF.—I mean, is our government a government of the people by the people? That is my definition of a republic.

DR.—Perhaps not in every detail—but, certainly, for all practical purposes. That is to say, with a few amendments, it approaches probably as near such a form of government as is possible this side of Millenium—that good time coming.

PROF.—Ah! then you admit that some things are necessary? Of what nature, pray?

DR.—The most important involves the question of suffrage.

PROF.—Well——

DR.—I consider that we have made the elective franchise altogether too cheap an affair. To my view, we should, if it be possible, restrict the right of suffrage instead of extending it.

PROF.—And how?

DR.—I would have suffrage based upon property and brains—that is to say, I think no one should be allowed to vote who has neither an interest in the government based upon the property which he owns and which is, to a great extent, dependent for its value upon the nature of that government, nor intelligence sufficient to appreciate the various questions which will of necessity arise connected with the administration of that government.

PROF.—As to your first proposition—the property qualification—you would require a certain amount in fee, I suppose, of your voter?

DR.—Yes; not so large as to make an aristocracy of our voters, nor so trifling as to make the qualification merely nominal, like the payment of a poll-tax, for example, as is required in some States—which is so often paid by the party that wishes the particular individual's vote. The true mean between these extremes could be hit, I apprehend, if not at the outset, at least after repeated experiments.

PROF.—Granting that, how would you fix your standard of intelligence?

DR.—Why, in a country of free schools—where every one who will, can acquire, for almost nothing, a good English education—I should insist upon an ability to read and write—to read understandingly such works as would enable the citizen to comprehend the outlines, I will say, of our Constitution—and write a hand which should be as legible as that of ordinary men.

PROF —Any other changes?

Dr.—I think the period of probation required of foreigners before admission to the rights of citizenship should be extended.

Prof.—Take care, Doctor! You are treading on dangerous ground now! Well for you that these walls have no ears! You haven't forgotten the recent experiment in that line? "Up like a rocket—down like a stick!"

Dr.—I understand you; but I am none the less strenuous upon this point. Because bunglers initiate a good movement and fail—as they deserve—it is no ground for objection to renewing the same under better guidance.

Prof.—Would you lengthen the term of probation?

Dr —No—I should prefer the educational test—admit no man as a citizen who cannot meet the requirement I last indicated—to which should be added an ability to carry on ordinary conversation in our tongue. The latter, however, must, in a large majority of cases, be an incidental of the former.

Prof.—You would apply this test even if the would-be voter came up to your standard, so far as property is concerned?

Dr.—Certainly.

Prof. - Well—any others?

Dr.—None of importance, I believe. There are alterations involving minor considerations which might be advantageously made, but the two which I have named would, in my judgment, tend directly to introduce the others.

Prof.—Supposing these attained, your republic would be well afloat?

Dr.—Yes; we should have a government in which every man, if he chose, could participate. If he could not secure the right to vote, either upon the property basis or the educational, the fault would assuredly be his own. So far as the latter is concerned, I should favor compulsory legislation—somewhat on the Prussian system —requiring the attendance of all children, between certain ages, at school for a definite time.

Prof.—And this you would still call republican?

Dr.—Not in essence, probably, but in substantial results. If we take the property of the childless rich man to provide facilities for the education of the children of the quiverful poor man, it seems to me that the very least which the State can do is to see to it that those facilities are made use of by those for whom they are furnished—especially as we take this property upon the ground that intelligence is necessary to the existence of a republican form of government.

PROF.—Perhaps we should not disagree as to that under any form of government; but the question leads us somewhat outside of the record. When you said, a moment ago, that *every man* could, if he chose, participate in such a government, did you intend to make no discrimination regarding color?

DR.—None whatever.

PROF.—Then you have no horror touching the negroes voting?

DR.—Not if my tests are met.

PROF.—But, is that treating these "wards of the nation"—as the blacks have been so happily termed—is that treating them with the justice that they have a right to expect from us?

DR.—And why not?

PROF.—They fought for us when most we needed them. In consideration of such assistance, and as a means to an end we all desired to attain, we emancipated them. Now, the war over, they are left—the large majority of them—among former masters. There they must remain—there they undoubtedly prefer to remain. Under your plan very few of the adults can secure a vote. They will be compelled to wait until their children reach the age of manhood before they can even indirectly be assisted by the ballot. It seems to me, that by so dealing with them, the government would act with the grossest injustice. While claiming from them allegiance, taxes, and military service as citizens of the United States—a title which we have bestowed upon them in the most formal and solemn manner by express enactment—with their services for the cause of good government, as we termed it, fresh in our memory—we do yet, by adopting your plan, deny to the active, efficient, working men among them, the very ones, in hundreds of instances, whose good right arms helped us hew our way out of difficulty—that security for person and property which every government

N 2

in Christendom is bound to assure to its meanest citizen, or forever relinquish all pretensions to the designation of a government.

Dr.—I believe that every thing which the ballot would do for the blacks in the way of comfort and security, if they could have it at once, would be as effectually done by the certainty that they are to have it whenever they choose. I think this very course would act as an incentive to efforts which would never be made were the franchise to be given at once, unconditionally, into their immediate possession. From my familiarity with the negroes, I am confident that a greater proportion of the adults among them would make themselves able to stand the educational test—and in a shorter time—than of the adults of any other race among us—certainly than the Irish, the most dangerous element, taken as a mass, with which we have to deal.

Prof.—Possibly your views may be correct; but I still think that justice demands that we give all the blacks the ballot at once. They will, beyond question, at times misuse it. Who of us whites does not? And how many of us all the time? Yet, if they have the right to vote and vote against their own interests, they would soon see that themselves alone were blameable and the evil would, before long, correct itself.

Dr.—That might be. Did the question stand alone I should be disposed to make trial, perhaps, of the franchise among them at once; but I believe the time has come— and for the first time in our history as a nation—when we can make voting depend upon ability to vote intelligently So believing, I am anxious to introduce the test; and that, although I know that many excrescences and anomalies will thereby become apparent, and that injustice will in some instances be done. We cannot, of course, deprive the ignorant, uneducated, landless mass of voters, who are entitled to vote under existing laws of that right—and this will prove, for many years, a grievous trouble; yet a beginning must be made somewhere, and the lines of demarcation drawn distinctly. Time will rectify every thing. And I fear if we allow the present opportunity to slip through our fingers, so good a one may never again be offered us

Prof. —I reserve what might be said on that point for another stage of our discussion. Just now for something crucial. When you say *every man*, do you include woman under that general term?

Dr.—Only so far as she is represented by man.

Prof.—As I supposed. Then you would not give the right of franchise to her?

Dr —By no means. I am aware of the drift of your questioning. But I am ready to meet the issue now fairly.

Prof.—No doubt of that, Doctor; I am all attention. Why would you exclude woman from all share in the government of your revised republic?

Dr.—In the first place, I deny the premise universally, I believe, laid down by the advocates of female suffrage, who start with the proposition that the right of suffrage is a natural right, like that of life, of liberty, of property and the like.

Prof.—One moment, if you please. Do you class the right of government—that is, of forming political associations to govern and to be governed—as among natural rights?

Dr.—Certainly. But not the right of voting for a representative under any form of government; since this very representative government does not spring directly from the nature of man. The right of suffrage I assert to be, solely and exclusively, a political right, to which Providence has led man in the progressive course of history.

Prof.—I may be very obtuse, Doctor; but it is clear to my mind, that if the right of government is a natural right, it follows, as an inevitable corollary, that the right of each individual to have a voice in reference to that government—in other words, each individual's right to suffrage—is as fully and completely a natural, and not a political, right. Taking any other view, your natural right of government resolves itself—so far as the individual is concerned —into merely a right to be governed

Dr.—I fail to see that your corollary follows. To my mind, there is a very marked distinction between the two classes of rights. But I must object to being kept upon the offensive longer, as I have been thus far during our discussion. "Turn about is fair play." Open, if you please, Professor, with your arguments in favor of female suffrage.

PROF.—Shall we consider the natural rights question settled?

DR.—Yes—for the present.

PROF.—And as I put it?

DR.—No—no—by no means! But let me hear from you why woman should be allowed to vote.

PROF.—One reason, of weight with me, is, that the withholding of suffrage from her is a degradation of the sex which we are wont to laud most highly.

DR.—No more than women are degraded in those monarchies in which no princess can ascend the throne. In England, even; since she can there ascend the throne only when no brothers, even younger than herself, are left to wear the crown.

PROF.—Well—that does not meet my position. Because the degradation is no more marked in the case I put, than in the case put by yourself, I fail to see that my allegation is disproved.

DR.—But a political law regulates the succession, and no degradation follows.

PROF.—Why not under a political law, as well as under a natural law? Pardon me—but isn't a good friend of mine just now busying himself in an occupation which we used to call at school "begging the question?"

DR.—Go on with your arguments. A truce to badinage!

PROF.—If she cannot vote, she is not represented.

DR.—Indeed, she is—by her husband, her father, or her brother.

PROF.—But the votes of none of these may be deposited in consonance with her wishes.

DR.—Still she is represented. You overlook woman's true place in society, which is that of a member of a family. As such member, the head of that family represents her.

PROF.—Would you be content to have this species of representation carried as far as analogy would show? Should, for instance, the father of a family represent by his vote his wife and all of his children, even after the sons have reached adult years?

DR.—I can see no necessity for that.

PROF.—But this theory of representation, when pushed to logical results, inevitably leads to it. Waiving this—giving the right of voting to woman would highly improve and refine our elections, and not unwoman her.

DR.—There I disagree with you wholly. The division of labor—the very foundation of our whole economy—begins with the division of the sexes, and expands as a physiological distribution of employment, pursuits, and social relations.

PROF.—Well! If women are in fact represented at present, they are, as a class, represented by men as a class. Now, no class can ever really be represented by another; and the distinction between the sexes forms a distinction of class which no family ties can do away with.

DR.—According to this distribution, the political occupation ought not to be assumed by women, by parity of reasoning.

PROF.—Ah! Then the Indian is justified in reaching the conclusion that, inasmuch as men are physically fitted for adventurous occupation, hunting and war, all other work—all that is tiresome, degrading, uninteresting—falls naturally to women. Your argument is simply this: in the division of labor, beginning with the division of the sexes, is included a right on the part of men to draw the division where *they* please and to declare that their line is the line which Providence has drawn.

DR.—Woman, to my mind, exercises and ought to exercise much of this beneficial influence by her delicacy and modesty; and her legitimate influence in the proper sphere would be lost, were she to enter the arena of politics.

PROF.—I am of the opinion that the only way to give full play to the natural distinction between the sexes, is to place men and women on a footing of absolute social equality, which is impossible without political equality.

DR.—Would you have a woman vote by mere impulse and feeling, or is she to visit public meetings? What respectable man would wish his wife, his daughter, his mother, or his sister to do this?

PROF.—Prejudice has nothing to do with this question, which is one of justice and expediency alone. As the experiment has never yet been sufficiently tried, it is, taking the most cautious view, just possible that woman's influence in politics might be as great as the influence of politics on woman.

DR.—Probably at present her vote would be cast—that is, that of the majority—aright; but we must look to the future, when this public action, this understood departure from woman's true sphere, shall be carried out into all its inevitable results.

PROF.—I have no such outlook, not being a believer in progress backwards.

DR.—But women do have an influence at present—a great influence, in many cases, upon the votes of the other sex. Why not encourage her to develop that influence to the fullest extent?

PROF.—This influence, as now existing, is power without the sense of responsibility. Admitting, as you do, the influence of woman over the mind of man, I appeal to you, Doctor, whether it is not better that woman should be taught by the privilege of the ballot that they, no less than men, are responsible for the rational use of whatever power Providence has placed in their hands.

DR—Your manner of stating this question is, certainly, somewhat new to me, and, I grant you, deserving of serious consideration. And yet, granting the force of your arguments, I doubt much whether I can rid myself of the mountain of prejudice which, I will admit, rests upon me in connection with the subject. I do not deny that this ought not so to be—but that such is the fact, I frankly avow.

PROF.—I do not doubt that the same avowal would be made by the large majority of those who at present decry female suffrage, if they were as frank as yourself. One of the strongest indications of increasing civilization, as I regard it, is the growing disposition shown of late to examine this subject dispassionately. Few sensible men now attempt to sniff or sneer the question down.

DR.—But, Professor, how would you like to have a female President, and what would it lead to?

PROF.—Don't press me too closely there, else I may be forced into saying some things which might be construed into speaking evil of some of the dignitaries of our own sex whom we have had in that position—which may pure patriotism forefend !

DR. —Then you favor universal suffrage ?

PROF.—Yes, if we are to continue to call our government a republic.

DR.—It is solely because I see the disastrous results of our present approximation to universal suffrage that I favor the restriction of it, for which I have been contending with you.

PROF.—But the experiment of a republic can never be fairly made without it. For myself, I entertain grave doubts as to the success of the experiment ; but from the teachings of such a trial we shall, even if we fail, be better able to construct a system of government adapted to our needs and capacities. Theoretically speaking, universal suffrage should have a stimulating effect upon the popular mind. No part of the people should be left in an unhealthy state of indifference to political contests in which they can take no practical part. The activity of mind produced by an exciting election is an educating power of immense value. It is idle to suppose that any classes, if intrusted with the exclusive power of government, will care so well for the excluded classes as to compensate for the natural stagnation of mind among the latter. But my time is up [*looking at watch*].

DR.—I will think a while, Professor, and call this up again when we are disengaged. I must understand that you do not fall in with my views of a republic?

PROF.—You sketch me no republic—neither, on the one hand, the republic in which Hamilton and his adherents believed, nor, on the other, that which Jefferson and his school hold up to view. The truth is, all of us in theorizing systems of governments so color them with our preconceived notions, that, when they are finished and ready for operation, they might as well be labelled by one name as another. Your republic of to-day, now, Doctor, is, in effect, an oligarchy, an aristocracy, or a plutocracy—or, perhaps better, a compound of all. At all events, it bears no more resemblance to the ideal republic of theorizers than the horse which Baron Munchausen started with did to the horse which he drove back.

Dr.—How was that?

Prof.—The baron was attacked by a wolf. Fortunately he succeeded in creating a diversion from himself to his horse. The wolf began eating the unfortunate animal at the tail, and ate with such voracity that the Baron, taking advantage of the right moment, was able to drive home with the wolf harnessed inside the skin of his horse!

[*Curtain falls.*]

JACK AT ALL TRADES.

CHARACTERS.

SAMUEL STEADY.   THOMAS FLYAWAY

Room in a private house.

STEADY.—Let me see, Tom—how long is it since I've seen you? [*Meditating.*] Twenty years, as I'm living! Who would have thought it? I remember the last shake of the hand you gave me on the wharf. I was going to Montevideo, you know, for Leatherman & Co. Do you mind your parting advice to me? I told you I was going into the leather and tallow business. "Good-bye, Sam, old chum," said you, "life's a big game; but the game for you in life is the game of *hide and seek!*"

FLYAWAY.—Well, Sam, from all that I can see and hear you followed my advice very faithfully. Here you are comfortably located—name down among the big tax-payers of the city—President of one Life Insurance Company and director of I don't know how many Fire dittos, saying nothing of the like relation to a dozen or less heavy banking institutions—house in town, brown stone, swell front and trimmings—country seat with all the modern improvements, and luckily money enough to make it impossible for the fancy poultry and the blooded stock of the gardener and the manager to eat out your core! Egad, your nest is comfortably feathered, old chum! You played the game well, I grant you. I didn't dream for an instant, though, that you'd take my advice so literally. Now, candidly, Sam, what man in college would have bet on your head against mine for success in the world? Not one; and you know it. Don't imagine though, that I regret the hit you've made. I'm glad of it, my boy. You deserve it all, and more. You've always been a hard-working, persevering, stick-and-hang fellow; and I must say that Dame Fortune would have been a sorry jade not to look at you with a kindly eye. Over and beyond that, Sam, you have about you what most of those fellows of your crowd lack—a good heart, sound to the core. But, really, chum, isn't it strange how college calculations miscarry?

STEADY.—Partly so, and partly not. You mustn't forget, Tom, that we are, the most of us, somewhat callow at that era in our lives; and, at the time these calculations of which you speak are made, we live in a very small world—a world, too, which is by no means the real world in miniature—not capable of playing the part of microcosm to our macrocosm, as Waldo Bonner would have said in those days.

FLYAWAY.—Waldo Bonner! I declare I'd nearly forgotten him—the valedictorian of our class, too! What's become of him, besides the fact that he is D. D., and has written a score of treatises to establish the willingness of the human will or the divinity of deity?

STEADY.—Nothing of the kind, Tom. The last I heard of Wal, he was cashier in a hoop-skirt store.

FLYAWAY [laughing]—That poses me! But it's only one illustration out of a hundred which might be selected of the grand mistakes which smart college youths make when they attempt to locate each other according to their ideas of the eternal fitness of things. You remember Bumpus, of course—class ahead of ours—the clumsiest clown in the whole college—Terrapin we used to call him? Now what do you suppose he betook himself to?

STEADY.—Teaching dancing?

FLYAWAY.—He might as well as to figure as Principal of a Young Ladies' Boarding School. It seems, however, that that was his forte, for he has made money at it.

Think of Terrapin as Professor of Accomplishments and Graces! [*Both laugh.*]

STEADY.—Little Bartleby—Tom-tit, you know—after having had some half dozen duels—he was editor-in-chief and fighting editor of some tearing journal in the South-west—died a year before the war from a bullet received in a street encounter. The meekest, quietest, most inoffensive little chick in the whole college!

FLYAWAY.—Scrubb, too, who would appropriate every thing to which he could lay his hands—"convey the wise it call"—who was disgraced by his society for passing off some Scotch Dominie's production as his own—he is a leading and influential D. D. in one of the western metropolises, and is really doing a deal of good.

STEADY.—Here is Everman—class below—if ever man seemed predestinated for a foreign missionary it was he. What is he now? Here in town, one of the most ingenious and technical of criminal lawyers—very few Acts of the Legislature bearing upon crimes and their punishment that he can't drive his double team through. It's a queer world, Tom, this of ours! Circumstances seem to do so much and ourselves so little. The contradictions we meet in life cannot occur by chance—there must be some law governing them; but for me, I confess I know nothing of it, can shape nothing in imagination which will account for it, though I've bothered myself times without number with the attempt.

FLYAWAY.—A mercantile moralizer, Sam! Will that pass on 'change?

STEADY.—One can't help thinking, you know; and I see no reason why one shouldn't wander at times outside his own particular calling. "Once a huckster always a huckster," is one of those maxims which have more of sound than substance—truth sacrificed to a jingle. There is no more necessity for one who is engaged in mercantile life being so devoted to his business that he can think of nothing else than, as Sam Johnson puts it, for the driver of fat oxen to be himself fat. Now, to come home, chum—take your own case; I've heard of you from time to time, here and there, roaming up and down this land and other lands, a very Wandering Jew; and I have questioned for many an hour how it could be so. We used to talk the future over, you know, so often in No 21 Middle Hall. I've stuck to my text, while you——

FLYAWAY.— ——am nearly through with my sermon !

STEADY.—You've been tossed in such a sea of unrest that I wouldn't have believed it possible for you to sit and chat with me as long as we've been together now. It wouldn't have surprised me in the least, when I met you on the street yesterday, if you'd just shaken hand and said "Good-bye, Sam—excuse me this morning—I've an engagement in Sitka !"

FLYAWAY.—I'm settling down now, Sam.

STEADY.—We'll see—then I'll believe. But didn't I see your name in the newspapers, an administration or two ago, in connection with a good foreign appointment ?

FLYAWAY.—I reckon. I saw it myself—received congratulatory letters with requests to give friends a lift— read a very complimentary notice in a paper to which I had contributed.

STEADY.—And there was nothing in it after all ?

FLYAWAY.—Not for me – some better man got it. You see there was a little mistake made by the agent of the Associated Press. The lucky dog's name was Scud, of whom nobody had ever heard ; and as it so much resembled mine, of whom some little had reached the ears of political *quid nuncs*, I received the appointment——in the newspapers.

STEADY.—Now, Tom, you know all the salient points in my career, while I am pretty much in the dark as to your own. Enlighten me. Why haven't you succeeded ?

FLYAWAY.—But I have.

STEADY.—In what, pray ?

FLYAWAY.—In accomplishing nothing. But you want the points. You shall have them. I didn't take the valedictory at graduation, you know, although it was definitely settled in the class two weeks after I entered freshman that I was to have it in due course of time.

STEADY.— And so you might, if you had held to your work.

FLYAWAY.—There's your mistake, Sam. I did hold to my work, but couldn't hold to theirs. Preferred miscellaneous reading to the differential and integral calculus,

and so obtained a dissertation, or disquisition, or something of the kind—do you remember the name, Sam?
It is the only commencement that I ever assisted at. At
all events, it wasn't the valedictory. Well, I was to read
law. As my luck would have it, a slight obstacle inter-
vened—*pater familias* wouldn't furnish the funds.

STEADY.—Why so? I thought you were the apple of
his eye.

FLYAWAY.—And so I was—but, mark you, of *his* eye.
My visual organs were allowed but small play. Fact is,
he had selected an entirely different calling for me.
Other people can judge so much better than you can
yourself as to what you're adapted for. That is why I
was to learn manufacturing and become a cotton million-
naire.

STEADY.—I never should have attempted to manufac-
ture a business man out of you.

FLYAWAY.—That shows your ignorance, Sam. Hadn't
father succeeded as a manufacturer? Didn't I look just
like him? Then why shouldn't I succeed in the same
business? The reasoning, you will perceive, is unanswer-
able.

STEADY.—But, surely, you didn't start in that business,
Tom? A turtle would make as good a metaphysician.

FLYAWAY.—Rather faulty that simile, Sam. The turtle,
you'll observe, keeps his head to himself for the most
part—never thrusts it into the world, unless some advantage is to be gained by it. Why not a good metaphysician, then? No, I didn't go into manufacturing—except
sundry and divers reasons, why that business wouldn't
suit me. They amounted to nothing, of course; but the
result was that the family copartnership was dissolved,
and I took up Blackstone, trusting to chances. As soon
as possible I was admitted to the bar—hung out my
shingle - and attempted to practice for a year or two.

STEADY.—No longer? Didn't you succeed?

FLYAWAY.—To be sure I did. What a question! Wasn't
I declared by nearly all my seniors to be the most promising young man at the bar? So, in fact, I was—and it
was precisely that which troubled me.

STEADY.—How so?

FLYAWAY.—I promised altogether too much for my

comfort. It was the old story —debts and duns. Annoyed past longer endurance, I cast about me for some employment in which I might turn those talents, which everybody declared I possessed in such abundance, to some account. Naturally enough, I took to teaching.

STEADY.—You! A pedagogue!

FLYAWAY.—Precisely; and I may say, without undue vanity, that I acquired some little reputation in that delightful calling.

STEADY.—Delightful! If there be a dog's life led by any human being on earth, it is the life of a school-teacher.

FLYAWAY.—Your ignorance again, Sam. There is no occupation in which you can cover over so large a surface with so small an amount of brains—in the South, especially. Why I was a professor of ancient languages in a leading university in that section! No – you may abuse teaching as much as you like; but I assure you that few situations are more comfortable than that of the master of a popular school, with a good salary attached, provided you manage your cards right. There's Roper, now, of the class below——

STEADY.—That time-server! He never had an unselfish emotion in his life!

FLYAWAY.—All the better for his business, Sam! He has been for some time at the head of one of the most flourishing institutions in the country – receives, I think, the biggest salary paid to any public-school teacher. He had no trouble in making headway after he once got into the right track. At first, what were supposed to be his religious views prevented advancement; but, as soon as he comprehended the necessities of his position, he bravely rid himself of that incumbrance—and presto! the thing was done. Roper is now editor-in-chief of a leading educational journal – President of a State Teachers' Association—an acceptable lecturer at all education gatherings — has revised several German and Sanscrit works on educational topics——

STEADY.—What does he know about those tongues?

FLYAWAY.—Pooh, man! What difference does that make? More than all, he is editor of a very popular series of classical school-books, which brings him in a handsome sum. He has one of the best libraries in the States---all secured by writing puffs for publishers; married one of his pupils, an heiress; in short, is, every way considered, an ornament to society and a comfort to himself. With this before you, disparage teaching, will you?

STEADY.—How happened it, then, that you didn't tarry in such a pleasant tabernacle, Tom?

FLYAWAY.—That is a question which I have not even yet settled to my entire satisfaction. I either knew too little or too much - can't say which. The truth is, I never could assume a virtue which I didn't possess. I'll anticipate you, Sam; you needn't say that is because I never was familiar enough with virtue to make a successful counterfeiter. However that may be, such is the fact. This embarrassed me sadly at times. There are one or two branches which I feel myself somewhat competent to teach—no more. There are others in which I could act the smatterer's part; and still others in which I am a very ignoramus, and for which I haven't predilection sufficient to sustain myself while booking up in them. Now, as principal of a modern school, you are supposed able to instruct in all branches, no matter what your salary, "all the virtues"—as Cobbett said of the British soldier—"are expected for a shilling a day." I suppose I was too frank in such matters. Had I been a better man, I should have remained silent as to my abilities and inabilities, and not one in ten thousand would have been any wiser. Being, as you'll understand, somewhat knavishly inclined, I blurted out the truth. Besides, I think, I was rather independent--a failing which, fortunately, few teachers have. From some cause or other, enough to say that teaching and I disagreed, and that firm was broken up.

STEADY.—And then?

FLYAWAY.—And then I betook myself to politics. It was Dr. Johnson—wasn't it—who said that patriotism was the last refuge of the scoundrel? Edited a daily newspaper, and "stumped it" during a bitter campaign. We won, and I was offered an office commensurate with my services in behalf of the cause.

STEADY.—What! an attorney-generalship?

FLYAWAY.—Not so bad as that, Sam—an under-clerk·

ship in the Secretary of State's office! Eight hundred or eight hundred and fifty—I forget which.

STEADY.—You took it?

FLYAWAY.—Yes, in high dudgeon—threw up my position, and eked out a tolerable livelihood by writing for magazines and literary journals. Meanwhile I attended medical lectures.

STEADY.—For what purpose?

FLYAWAY.—To fit myself for a physician, to be sure. I had often thought of that well-known test of respectability—keeping a gig—and hoped sooner or later to achieve it.

STEADY.—But, seriously, did you turn medic.?

FLYAWAY.—Yes, in the far West—in Minnesota. And the joke was that during a two years stay in that State I never heard of but one sick person in the whole region round about; and he had been stranded there just dead with a pulmonary complaint.

STEADY.—How did you manage to live?

FLYAWAY.—By politics. I was sent to the Legislature, and believe I should have made a permanent investment in that stock, if, unfortunately, our party hadn't sunk into a minority so small that I feared I should die waiting for its resurrection. Then, having saved a few dollars—how I managed it, I can't, for the life of me, tell, but manage it I did—I went abroad, figuring as " Our Special Correspondent " for a brace of metropolitan journals.

STEADY.—Your signature?

FLYAWAY.—"Nameless here for evermore!" No—you can't catch me in that trap. I won't trust even you. The journals for which I wrote are at opposite poles in political sympathies, foreign and domestic; and you can understand my reasons for silence. Well, the war broke out— I returned—went into the army as a private—remained till the end—came out a colonel. Made a fair record for myself, I believe.

STEADY.—Yes, that you did, Tom—I heard of you, my boy, occasionally, and regretted, hundreds of times, the entangling domestic alliances which detained me here.

FLYAWAY.—I have never been embarrassed by such entanglements.

STEADY.—Why not? Too much of a vagabond—of a Bohemian? No chances?

FLYAWAY.—Oh, for that matter, I believe I've had offers enough—rather I should say have had opportunities enough to offer myself; but I have never yet decided that I am able to take care of myself.

STEADY.—Why not get one to take care of you?

FLYAWAY.—Excuse me, Sam—as Artemus Ward says, "not on purpose!" I prefer, while I live, attending to that department of business myself.

STEADY.—You said a bit ago that you are settled now. Do you mean here with us? What are you going into next? Railway engineering, or the drug business?

FLYAWAY.—Oh, I earn a comfortable livelihood by my pen. Have a book in press from which I hope something. And, if the worst comes to worst, shall fall back on politics. Our boys are at the top now in this latitude.

STEADY.—Well, old fellow, you know where to find me, and 1 needn't tell you that I shall always be glad to have you around.

FLYAWAY.—But madam——

STEADY.— —— is simply madam. I select my own friends, Tom, spite of your bachelor heresies on that matter.

FLYAWAY.—Sensible child! But, isn't selection one thing and obtaining allowance to enjoy quite another? Come, old fellow, own up!

STEADY.—Not in my establishment, Didymus. I paddle my own end of the canoe.

FLYAWAY.—Sensible to the last! I'll drop in on you often.

STEADY.—Do so—do so! Tom, do you ever think of that saying, "A Jack at all trades, and——"

FLYAWAY [motioning as if to box his ears].—You needn't finish it, Sam!

[Curtain falls.]

HELEN MACTREVER.

DRAMATIZED FROM J. LOFLAND'S

"SCENES AT THE BATTLE OF BRANDYWINE."

CHARACTERS.

COL. MACTREVER, an American colonel.
HELEN, his daughter.
DONALD, his son.
MAJOR SANFORD, a British captain.
MIKE, a watchman.
JUDGE ADVOCATE, OFFICERS AND SOLDIERS.

————

SCENE I.—*A room in Col. MacTrever's house—MacTrevet reading—Enter Helen.*

HELEN.—Dear father, I am almost afraid to venture my noble charger to-day.

COL. [*laying down his spectacles.*]—Why so, my child?

HELEN.—I had an ugly dream last night, and imagined I was lost in a woodland, whence I was carried off by a stranger.

COL. – Poh! poh! child, do you believe in foolish dreams? Do you not know that the Scripture declares that fools build upon dreams?

HELEN.—But, father, Milton also tells us that millions of spiritual creatures walk the earth, unseen, both when we wake and when we sleep, and may they not be commissioned to tell us of our danger? May they not whisper to us of good or evil during our dreams?

COL.—Why, really, you are becoming superstitious. I thought you had too much sense to entertain such nonsense.

HELEN.—Ah, father, it is not only the ignorant who are superstitious—if you are pleased to call it so. Many of the wisest men that ever dignified and adorned the pages

o

of history entertained such nonsense, and believed in
supernatural revelations.

COL. [*laughing.*]—Well, well, go take your ride, and if
none of the red coats carry you off I will be satisfied.
[*Curtain falls.*]

SCENE II.—*A room in Col. MacT's house—Enter Major
Sanford and Helen, in riding costume.*

MAJ.—Now, my good lady, you seem to have entirely
recovered from your fall, and are safe in your father's
house, and, although I would gladly tarry, I must not
forget that I am in the house of my professed enemy.
For your sake as well as my own I will haste away. But
I will soon meet you again [*bowing out, and Helen following*].
[*Enter Col. MacTrever. Looks around—paces the room
angrily.*]
[*Enter Helen*]
HELEN.—Oh, father, it was as I feared—my charger
frightened——
COL. [*angrily.*]—Can it be possible that Helen Mac-
Trever will stoop to the society of an enemy of her
country ? Can you countenance a foe to freedom who
this very day may imbrue his hands in the blood of his
brave brother who is now battling for liberty in the ranks
of the great and good George Washington ? For shame !
Let me never again see you bestow a smile upon an enemy
who would not hesitate to make midnight glittter with
your burning home.
HELEN.—But, father——
COL. [*agitated.*]—No buts, if you please; that red coat
shall never again darken my door if I can prevent it.
HELEN [*raising herself to her full height and assuming
an air of dignified importance*].—Let me inform you,
sir, without intending any disrespect, that the cause of
American freedom is as dear to my heart as to yours, or
to that of any other patriot; but, at the same time, I hope
I shall never forget that respect which is due to a flag of
truce and to the politeness of a well-bred gentleman, be
that gentleman a friend or foe to my country. Though

nationally at enmity, it is no reason that we should be individually so.

COL.—Very pretty logic, 'pon my word. Well, well, if you prefer the society of your country's bitter enemy, encourage him, and when his hands are reeking with the gore of your slaughtered brother and countryman, marry him, and go to England, and starve. You cannot remain with me, or expect a penny from one who bears the name MacTrever!

HELEN [*bursting into tears*].—Dearest father, he is nothing to me more than a friend, and, as he has always acted the part of a gentleman, I cannot but respect him as such.

COL.—I see how strong your friendship is, and it is with you as I have found it to be the case with every woman I ever knew : when she once fixes her mind upon a man, and she generally chooses the man that all the world beside would have rejected, not all the angels in heaven can persuade her to relinquish him. But be it so, you can repent at your leisure.

HELEN.—But, my dear father, what if we could win him over to the cause of American freedom? That would be a glorious achievement.

COL. [*his countenance relaxing.*]—Aye! if you could do that it would be glorious, and willingly would I give him your hand; but these red coats are true to old George, their master, and I'll have nothing to do with them.

HELEN.—But, father, you'll allow me to treat him civilly while endeavoring to win him over to our cause.

COL—Convert him! Folly, child, folly. I say I'll allow you to have nothing at all to do with him or any other cursed red coat. [*Exit Helen.*] [*Soliloquizing.*] I see! I see! "Frailty thy name is woman." [*Calls*] Mike! Mike!

MIKE [*outside*].—Ho, yer honor! [*Enter Mike, with spade in hand.*] Did yer honor call me?

COL.—Mike, put away your spade and take this gun [*hands him a rifle*]; and, mark you, if any man comes on the premises at dead of night fire on him.

MIKE.—Yis, an' be dad, sir, I'm the boy can do it, sir.

Col.—Now mind, Mike, watch well; keep your eyes open all night.

Mike.—Sure an' yer honor, it isn't Mike Maloney that would be spalpeen on guard.

Col.—Well, well, go ——

Mike.—Yis, Colonel.

[*Curtain falls.*]

Scene III.—*In a grove near Col. MacT's house—Mike seated by a bush with rifle, sleeping and nodding—Helen enters, disguised by throwing her brother's cloak on—Major Sanford approaches—Mike hears her step and wakens, levels his gun at Helen.*

Helen.—Ha! he comes. I see his graceful form amid the tall trees of the park. [*Major S. rushes towards her as if to embrace her. Helen raises her hand to bid him stop.*] Nay, nay, Major, we meet not here for a love-dalliance to-night, but on business dear to my heart and to my country.

[*Mike lowers his gun and listens.*]

Maj. S.—What are the terms you speak of?

Helen.—I can never consent to your proposition until you forsake the unjust cause you have espoused and join the glorious little band now struggling for freedom. In other words, I will never consent to give you my hand till you swear to betray General ——

Mike.—[*in undertone*].—Treason, by the dads!

Maj. S. [*starting.*]—Hark! did you not hear a voice?

Helen.—No; it was but the wind sighing in the trees.

Maj. S.—Could you love a traitor?

Helen.—Aye, when the traitor betrays a tyrant, and succors the oppressed. Indeed he is no traitor who betrays the vicious desires of a despot; and who, in espousing the cause of the injured, avenges their wrongs. No, Major Sandford, he can never merit the appellation traitor, who flies from vice to virtue—who forsakes a cause that is positively wrong.

Maj. S.—You are well skilled in moral philosophy, I see; but shall I turn against the land of my birth and the home of my fathers?

HELEN.—Are we not all of the same country? And were one part of your household to oppress the other, would you not espouse the cause of the oppressed?

MAJ. S.—I certainly would—but the oath of allegiance! Ay—the oath I should have taken to——

HELEN.—An unrighteous oath is not binding No, sir, an oath, extorted by a tyrant, to oppress the weak and enslave your fellow-man, is not binding—I say it is not binding in the sight of Heaven. God will never sanction an oath unholy in its object and in its end. [*Mike has fallen asleep.*] It is far nobler, and far less heinous in the sight of God, to break an unrighteous oath to a tyrant, than to fulfil that oath by crushing the oppressed, and carrying death and devastation to the homes of helpless wives and children. Your heart, Major, was never designed by Heaven to glut its vengeance on those who are struggling only for their rights, and have done no wrong.

MAJ. S.—Almost thou persuadest me to be a patriot— a rebel! But if I break my oath of allegiance, how could you place confidence in my oath to liberty?

HELEN.—I could place confidence in you, because you would act honestly to your conscience, and justly to the oppressed, by breaking an unholy oath to a tyrant. He who acts justly and honestly can never betray.

MAJ. S. [*Taking her hand and gazing at her.*]—In what then can I serve you?

HELEN.—You can serve me, or rather my country and the sacred cause of humanity, justice, and the rights of man, by assisting a handful of men to recover their birthright.

MAJ. S.—But in what manner?

HELEN.—By betraying General Howe, the jackall of the lion, George III., into the hands of the brave Washington, or those of any of his generals. This will be the first step. You have solicited my hand in marriage—but never until——

MAJ. S.—But should I fail—death, ignominious death, would be my portion.

HELEN [*solemnly*].—Should you triumph in the attempt, my hand and heart, and all that I possess of this world, shall joyously be given to you. But should you fail, and your life be the forfeit, then I swear to die with you.

MAJ. S.—Then, by heavens! for such a prize it shall be done, or I will perish in the attempt! But, Helen, this is a heavy undertaking—how shall it be accomplished.

HELEN.—Easily. I have laid the snare. The plan is this : Here are two letters [*handing them to him singly*]. This one is addressed to General Washington, asking him to appoint two or three officers, who shall meet the writer in the grove by the old Quaker meeting-house, on a certain night—at which time and place, the commander-in-chief of the British forces, General Howe, shall be betrayed into their hands. This other is addressed, as you may see, to General Howe, stating that if he will meet the writer in person, at the same time and place, General Washington shall be betrayed into his hands.

MAJ. S.—Capital! capital! I will send them.

HELEN [*seizing his hand*]. – Good-night, Major, good-night. May heaven bless you and our undertaking!

MAJ. S.—Amen, say I. Good-night. [*They turn and separate ; the Major attempts to put the letters in h's pocket, but accidentally drops the one to General Howe, leaving it unnoted behind ; Mike sees it and steals out and quietly picks it up.*]

MIKE [*looking at the address*].—I always thought that girl had a sneaking notion to the tory side.
[*Curtain falls.*]

SCENE IV.—*In Col. MacT's house—The Colonel has just arisen from bed, is yawning, and drawing on his boots— Enter Mike.*

COL —Well, Mike, what luck with the red coats?

MIKE.—Yer honor may well ask that, you may. While I was sittin', and sittin', and sittin' last night, watchin' for a red coat, who should come along with a coat and a hat on but a man, and he wasn't a man nither.

COL.—Well, what in the name of Banquo's ghost was it?

MIKE —Why, yer honor, jist as I was a goin' to shoot, I diskivered that it was Miss Helen that I tuck to be a man, so I didn't shoot, but I sot and sot and sot and

listened to her and some feller layin' a plot to betray
Gineral Washington into the inimy's hands and upsot
freedum and ivery thing. And here is a letter [*handing
it to the Colonel*] that the feller took from Miss Helen,
and he thought he put it in his pocket, but instid of that
he drapt it fernenst the summer-house, so I thought I'd
pick it up and bring it to ye.

Col.—Right, Mike, right [*takes the letter and reads it
excitedly*]. By heavens! that scoundrel has bewitched
my daughter, and he shall be arrested.

Mike.—Aha! yer honor, that's right; he's nothin'
nohow but a fortin hunter that wants to turn matrimony
into a matter o' money. They'll betray our Gineral this
very night.

Col.—Well, Mike, let not another word fall from your
lips on the subject, and the villian shall be caught in his
own trap and swing on the first tree

Mike.—Not another word, yer honor; no, no, no, not
another word; niver fear me, I'll be thrue to ye.

[*Curtain falls.*]

Scene V.—*In the grove—Enter two officers, sent by Gen.
Washington, and Maj. Sanford, from one side of the stage,
and Col. MacTrever, face muffled, with Mike and two
or three other stout men from the other—A pause.*

Maj. S. [*stepping firmly forward and layiny his hand
on Col. MacT's shoulder.*]—General, you are my prisoner!

Col. [*throwing off his disguise and laying his hand on
Sanford's shoulder.*]—No, by heavens! General Washington is not your prisoner, but, sir, I know you are
mine! [*whistles, and several stout men rush forth from
their ambush.*] Seize the villanous traitor! [*they seize
him.*]

Donald [*being one of the officers sent by Washington*].
—What means this?

Maj. S.—Let me explain this matter and you will not
call me a traitor or a villain.

Col.—Away with him, men! I have an explanation
of the whole matter in my pocket in a handwriting I

know as well as my own. Away with him ! I'll hear no more ! [*they pinion him and carry him to Col. Mac T's wine-cellar for safe keeping.*]
[*Curtain falls.*]

SCENE VI.—*In the wine-cellar—Major S. sitting on a wine cask.*

MAJ. S. [*soliloquizing.*]—Oh, woman, you are at the bottom of every thing. How many wars have you not incited? How many empires have flourished but to fall by your intrigues? The proud palaces of Priam and the lofty towers of Troy by your charms were laid level with the dust. Yea, by your fascinating influence in the garden of Eden, mankind fell But you have atoned— you have redeemed your character. By you was brought into the world that glorious character who hung the rainbow of redemption round the dying world. By you Christopher Columbus was enabled to discover a new continent. By you Rome was saved, and by you I shall yet be liberated from my perilous situation.

[*Curtain falls.*]

SCENE VII.—*In Colonel Mac T's bedroom. The Colonel sleeping, and the key that unlocks the wine-cellar hanging on the wall above him. Helen enters stealthily, and creeps along to her father's bed—tries to reach the key, and finds it too high : then turns and gets a chair from another part of the room, but does not observe that one leg of the chair is broken ; places it close by the bed, quietly steps on it, when it tilts, and she falls heavily on the floor. She lies perfectly still, fearing to move a muscle. Her father is partially waked, moves a little, and falls again into sound sleep. A second effort is successful, when she carries the key off in triumph.*
[*Curtain falls.*]

SCENE VIII.—*In the cellar.   Major S. in chains, sleeping, his head resting on a box or barrel.   The sound of a turning lock is heard at the door.*

[*Enter Helen.*]

HELEN [*laying her hand gently on his shoulder*].—Major, Major, awake! I am here to save you.

MAJ. S.—Why, Helen, have you ventured here? You will incur your father's vengeance. if discovered.

HELEN.—Fear not for me. Woman will dare any thing for the man she loves. Yea, when all the world forsakes, she will follow him to the dungeon, and, though covered with crime, will clasp the victim in his chains. But there is no time to be lost in the waste of words—you must fly this instant. I have come to save you, or perish in the attempt !

MAJ. S.—But by what means can I escape? There are watchful eyes about the building; and to elude their vigilance is impossible. I saw a guard, but a minute ago, pass the grated window, and he would recognize and stop me.

HELEN [*pauses in deep study*].—I have it! I have it ! Major, be of good cheer—I will save you !

[*Exit in haste.*]

[*Re-enter Helen, with one of her dresses, a long cloak and bonnet.*]

Haste! haste ! Put on this dress over your own, and you may pass out and be mistaken for me. Nay, not another word ! I will meet you to-morrow night at the old Quaker meeting-house. Away ! quick, quick !

MAJ. S. [*Imprinting a kiss on Helen's hand*]—Angel ! angel !

[*Curtain falls.*]

SCENE IX.—*In the street, outside the cellar.   Major passes in disguise.*

GUARD [*passing to and fro with gun*].—Hold ! [*approaching Major S., and looking into his face.   In guttural tones*]:—You may pass, madam.

[*Curtain falls.*]

Scene X.—*In a small, badly-furnished room. Major S. suffering from a wounded arm.*

[*Enter Helen Sanford.*]

Helen [*with joy on her face*].—Oh, my dear husband! here is a letter from my dear father—and hope whispers that it contains relief, or, at least, the promise of it. Something seemed to whisper that, in all our distress, a better fortune awaited us.

Maj. S.—Read it, Helen.

[*Helen opens it, and reads*]: "My once-beloved daughter—You have fled from my roof with a mean British spy, and have therefore forfeited my protection. You must bring stronger proof than you have yet brought to induce me to believe that a British spy was wounded in the cause of freedom. But, if you will leave your paramour [*pauses and weeps*], and return to me, I will, in mercy, guarantee to you a sufficiency to keep you from want; but otherwise, not a penny of mine shall ever bless a red-coat [*with excitement and grief she almost faints, and falls upon the floor*].

Helen [*recovering*].—Oh, God! Oh, God! What is to become of us? Universal distress pervades the country, and poverty stalks abroad. Cruel, cruel father, thus to reflect upon the character of a daughter, by calling her husband a paramour! I could have borne any thing else, but this is too severe.

Maj. S. [*sighing.*]—Well, it is useless to repine. We have one consolation—we are as low in the scale of poverty as we can sink; and if a change takes place, it must be for the better.

[*A loud knock at the door.*]

Helen [*opening the door, three stout men enter*].—Oh! on what errand have you come to this house of suffering? Our sorrows are great enough already, without the addition of any more.

First Officer.—We come, madam, to arrest a vile spy, who basely attempted at Chadd's Ford to betray the guardian spirit of America. Seize him instantly—he shall not escape again!

[*Second and* Third *Officers seize him and drag him to the door.*]

HELEN [*holding to her husband*].—Oh, for heaven's sake, have mercy on my poor husband!—he is innocent—he is not guilty of the charge!

FIRST OFFICER.—Away with the villain—and let not a woman's tears or a woman's prayers unman you!

[*They drag him out the door—Helen swoons and falls.*]
[*Curtain falls.*]

SCENE XI.—*Court-martial. Enter Judge Advocate, Major Sanford, Helen, jailor, and witnesses.*

JUDGE AD. [*seating himself and looking around.*]—We are now ready to proceed with the examination of witnesses who are here to testify concerning the conduct of the prisoner, who has been arrested under the charge of being a British spy. First witness, Michael Maloney.

MIKE [*stepping up hastily*].—Here am I, sir.

JUDGE AD.—Do you know the prisoner?

MIKE.—I do, sir, know him well.

JUDGE AD.—Where did you ever meet him?

MIKE. —Well, sir, to tell the truth, I never met him at all, at all.

JUDGE AD.—Did you ever see him?

MIKE.—Yis, faith, I did, sir, when he didn't see me.

JUDGE AD.—Well, Michael, how was that? Explain yourself.

MIKE.—Well, sir, that I wull. The Colonel, ye see, called me to him; and says he—Mike, says he—I want you to guard this house, says he, at night, says he, an' if any red-coat comes onto the premises, says he, shoot him, says he. Says I, I will Colonel, says I. So you see, I jist sot down behind a tree fernenst the summer-house. I hadn't sot there long, when sure enough here come the very feller, ye see, I was lookin' fur, and Miss Helen—that's the Colonel's daughter—met him there; and I didn't shoot, fur I was afeard of hitten her.

JUDGE AD.—Did you hear what he said to Miss Mac-Trever?

MIKE.—Hear him, is 't? That I did, yer honor—I

heard ivery word that come of his mouth as plain as I hear yer honor now.

JUDGE AD.—And what did you hear him say?

MIKE.—What did he say, sir? Why, yer honor, he said that if Miss Helen would help him, he would betray Gineral Washington into the hands of the inemy. That I heard, sir—and what more could ye ask agin him?

JUDGE AD.—Was that all you heard?

MIKE.—No, sir. They had a deal of talk; and when they parted, the chap dropped a letter unknown to himself, which I picked up and gave the Colonel; and if you could see that, ye wouldn't want any more.

JUDGE AD.—That will do, Michael. John Stone.

STONE.—Here.

JUDGE AD.—What have you to testify against the prisoner? Did you ever see him?

STONE. — I have, sir, often.

JUDGE AD.—Where?

STONE.—I saw him once in Colonel MacTrever's cellar.

JUDGE Ad.—Were you in the cellar?

STONE.—I was not, sir; but I was guarding the house, and saw him through the grated window.

JUDGE AD.—How did he come to escape?

STONE.—Well, sir, he was disguised as a lady, and I took him to be the Colonel's daughter.

JUDGE AD.—And you are sure that this is the man?

STONE.—I am, sir.

JUDGE.—That will do. [*A pause.*] Although two important witnesses, Colonel MacTrever and his son Donald, have not arrived, I think it unnecessary to delay the sentence, as the evidence heretofore brought to my notice, as well as that now given, is of such a character as leaves no room for doubt. And, sir [*turning to the prisoner*], I pronounce you *guilty* of the charges brought against you.

HELEN.—He is innocent! he is innocent! Heaven is witness he is innocent! [*Swoons and falls.*]

JUDGE AD.—Conduct the prisoner away.

[*Enter Donald and Colonel Mac Trever.*]

DONALD.—Nay, one moment! [*Looks steadily into the face of Sanford.*] It is he indeed! It is the man who, at the risk of his own, saved my life at the battle of Brandywine, when a powerful Hession had cloven me to the earth.

There must be some mysterious mistake about this matter, for I saw this man fighting like a tiger in the cause of freedom during the whole battle.

MAJ. S. [*handing Colonel Mac Trever a letter.*]—There, sir, if I may not yet dare to call you father, read that, and you will find in it an explanation of all this mystery, which has given us all so much trouble. [*A pause while the Colonel reads.*]

COL.—Judge, you must liberate the prisoner. He is entirely innocent, and deserves our highest commendation. We have all been cruelly deceived. A wicked haste in judgment has done this man great wrong, which all our apologies cannot right. [*Stepping forward and taking Sanford by the hand.*] My dear sir—*my son*—I am deeply grieved that I have thus wronged you and Helen. But I shall right this wrong by deed as well as word. Come to your home, my daughter, and bring your noble husband with you, and you shall share with us the comforts and honors we are able to enjoy.

JUDGE.—I release the prisoner to your custody, Colonel. Do with him as you will, and I fear not that the ends of justice will be answered.

[*Curtain falls.*]

TRUSTING TOO FAR;

OR,

LEARNING BY EXPERIENCE.

CHARACTERS.

MRS. ELTON, a woman easily deceived.
MR. ELTON, her husband.
MARY ELTON, their daughter.
MRS. BLACK, } Visitors.
MISS DUNN, }
PATRICK McGEE, a servant.
MR. GRAY.
CAPTAIN McCARTNEY.

SCENE I.—*City dining-room. Mr. Elton and daughter taking seats at the breakfast-table.*

Enter Mrs. Elton, in a flurry.

MRS. E.—It is too bad; never was there a woman so tormented.

MR. E.—What is the trouble now, my dear?

MRS. E.—Bridget has gone.

MR. E.—Bridget gone?

MRS E.—Yes, Bridget's gone!

MR. E. - When?

MRS. E.—Last night or early this morning.

MR. E.—Without her wages?

MRS. E.—No, indeed.

MR. E.—Then she gave notice of leaving?

MRS. E.—Not a word. She asked me yesterday for some money—said her mother was very sick, and if I would settle with her, she would go and take her some things. Her father was not well-doing, and she expected they were in need.

MR. E.—And you paid her?

MRS. E.—Yes, and gave her five dollars besides. Her wages seem such a trifle, if she wanted to get things for her mother, and I told her we could deduct it from our next settlement. She seemed so grateful——

Mr. E.—Where does her mother live?

Mrs. E.—She told me in Twenty-third street.

Mary.—Why, mamma, she told me last week that she had no mother.

Mr. E.—Ah! and she left last night, or this morning?

Mrs. E.—Yes; and took all, if not more, than belonged to her.

Mr. E.—Just as I expected. I warned you not to trust her.

Mrs. E.—Oh, yes—you warned me.

Mr. E.—Yes, I did; but where *experience* cannot teach, *advice* is of little benefit. Is this the fifth or sixth one who has played off the same game upon you? You will never learn.

Mrs. E.—No, I will never learn. You, Mr. Elton, had better take the kitchen cares on your own shoulders. I am sure I do the best I can.

Mr. E.—'Tis not what you do not do, Anna; 'tis what you do. Kind-hearted and unsuspicious yourself, the vile and dishonest are ever ready to take advantage of you.

Mrs. E.—Well, it does seem so. There was Ellen who went off taking two of my best dresses. I took her in through charity; the poor creature had no home she said, and then to go off as she did,—but if they act ungratefully it is no fault of mine.

Mr. E.—Yes, it is your fault; you place too much confidence in them from the first.

Mrs. E.—Well, I cannot bear the poor things to feel that I suspect them of dishonesty.

Mr. E.—And I think you do them more injury than good.

Mrs. E.—Why so?

Mr. E.—Well, it's seldom that a good girl seeks a situation, without a good recommendation. Those whom you have trusted came without, and you should have made them feel that they must prove themselves worthy before they won your trust

Mrs. E. [*laughing.*]—Oh, yes, Mr. Elton, it is very easy for you to talk, but you know I haven't the heart to practice your precepts. [*Rising.*] This will not do. I must assist Jane, or, to use her own words, she will be "kilt intirely wid the hard work."

Mr. E.—Introduce Mary into the kitchen; it is high time she was learning something besides lounging in the parlor. Come, daughter, let me see you remove those breakfast things

Mary.—Oh, papa, indeed I don't know how. It will soil my hands, and make them look so horrid when I practice my music lessons. [*Goes to work. Mrs. E. assists.*]

Mr. E.—Take care. They may spoil your fortune if you brown them by toil. I wish my daughter would try to cultivate good common-sense with her other accomplishments. [*To Mrs. E.*] I think, Mrs. Elton, I will employ a serving man. We can find sufficient for him to do, can we not?

Mrs. E.—If you do, I hope you will have better success than I have with serving maids.

Mr. E. [*laughing.*]—Well, don't you spoil them. Mary, be a good girl and learn to work, and when your mamma feels disposed to come with you, you may come down to the store and get that new dress we were talking about. [*Looking at his watch.*] It is time I was off. [*Exit.*]

Mary.—Now I just think it is too bad in papa, wanting me to go to work; just see, I know it will spoil my hands; may I not leave Jane finish this, mamma?

Mrs. E.—Your father told you to do it, and you will miss that new dress

Mary.—What time will you go with me, by ten or half-past ten?

Mrs. E.—That depends how well you work.

Mary.—Oh, I'll work ever so fast; now mind, I want a real nice dress.

[*Exit Mrs. E. and Mary with breakfast things.*]

Scene II.—*Mrs. E. and Mary on the street, in full walking-dress—Mary drops her pocket-handkerchief—A man with a hod near by picks it up.*

Irishman.—Hallo—hallo-o, madam, and this dainty belongs till yer, madam.

[*Ladies pausing. Man stepping forward, raises his hat, and presents the handkerchief.*]

MRS. E.—Honest man, you deserve better employment.

IRISHMAN.—Troth, ant it's no choice of me own, at all, at all; it's becase it's mesilf that's a stranger in the land. Sure if I was waitin'-mon for a leddy the likes of ye, it would be heaven intirely, it would.

MRS. E.—What is your name?

IRISHMAN.—Patrick McGee, yer honor; ant as honest a name as iver crossed the water.

MRS. E.—Well, Patrick, take this [*hands him her card*], and call at that place at two o'clock to-day; my husband will be at home then, and, I think, probably will give you better employment than carrying the hod. [*Turning to go.*]

PAT.—Heaven bless ye and yers foriver and iver.
[*Exit scene.*]

SCENE III.—*Dinner-table—Mr. and Mrs. E. and Mary.*

MR. E.—Bridget has not returned yet?

MRS. E.—Not she. Will you not advertise for another this afternoon?

MR. E.—Yes; and will advertise at the same time for a servant man. I would like a good-natured, trusty fellow, one who could turn his hand to any thing, and be generally useful.

MARY.—Ma, that man we met to-day was that kind, wasn't he?

MRS. E.—I cannot tell; he was intelligent-looking.

MR. E.—Who was he—some adventurer?

MRS. E.—He was an Irishman; honest, I think. We had evidence of that. Mary——

MARY.—Yes; I dropped my pocket-handkerchief, he found it, and instead of retaining it, he brought it and gave it to us.

MR. E.—Well, what became of him?
[*Enter maid. To Mr. E.*]

MAID.—A man wants to speak with you, sir.

MR. E.—Is he in the parlor?

MAID.- No, sir; he is in the basement.

MR. E.—Show him here.
[*Exit maid.*]

Mrs. E.—I think it is probable he has called, as I told him to do so.

[*Enter Pat.*]

Mr. E.—Well, what is your business?

Pat.—Yer good leddy, yer honor, may heaven bless her, tould me that if I would call, that mebbe yer honor would give me employment.

Mr. E.—How have you been getting your living?

Pat.—Carrying the hod, yer honor. Sure I don't like the business, honest though it be.

Mr. E.—How long have you been in this country?

Pat.—Six months, yer honor; and sorry was the day that I iver left me home in ould Ireland.

Mr. E.—What business did you follow there?

Pat.—What business bit me ain, yer honor; sure it is no honest callin' to be gaddin' 'round, 'tendin' to other people's.

Mr. E.—Well, but how did you live?

Pat.—Bless me soul, by eatin' and drinkin', yer honor.

Mr. E.—Yes! but didn't you work?

Pat.—Wark, be jabers and I did. Troth, but didn't I sarve wid as honest a mon as ever lived in Ireland, present company excepted?

Mr. E. [*laughing.*]—I don't think any of the present company ever lived in Ireland [*looking around*].

Pat.—Sure, and isn't it meself I'm maining; I never vouch for the honesty of strangers.

Mr E.—What kind of work can you do?

Pat.—What eny other mon can do, yer honor.

Mr. E.—Well, suppose you and I make a bargain What do you want per month?

Pat.—I want money, yer honor.

Mr. E.—Of course, but how much?

Pat.—What will yer honor be plazed to give me?

Mr. E.—Well, I suppose if I find you honest and trust-worthy, I will give eighteen dollars per month.

Pat.—Ant couldn't yer honor make it twenty? that would just be the even tens, and they are so much asier counted.

Mr. E.—If you do your duty I don't think we'll quar-rel about that; now go back to the basement and get your dinner.   [*Exit Pat*]

Mrs E.—Well, how do you like his appearance?

Mr. E.—He is dumb enough to be hones

Mrs. E.—Oh, I am sure he is honest!

Mr. E. [*laughing.*]—Remember your failing. [*Rising from the table.*]

[*Exit scene.*]

Scene IV.—*Mrs. E. in a parlor—Pat in a new suit of clothes, ushers in visitors—Enter Mrs. Black and Miss Dunn.*

Mrs. E.—Good-afternoon, ladies. Will you walk into the dressing-room and lay aside your bonnets?

Mrs. B.—No, thank you; we design only a short call.

Mrs. E.—It has been so long since you were here, that I shall only excuse your negligence by detaining you the remainder of the afternoon; so walk up and lay off your bonnets.

Mrs. B.—Oh, indeed, Mrs. Elton, it is impossible.

Mrs. E. [*to Miss D.*]—Do you not think she is jesting?

Miss D.—No; it is certainly impossible. Shall I tell you why?

Mrs. E.—Undoubtedly; but first be seated. [*Nodding to Miss D.*] Proceed.

Miss D.—She did not tell her good man, and his disappointment would be too great if she wasn't at the door to meet him when he came home.

Mrs. B.—I always make it a point never to absent myself from home during tea hour, without mentioning it to my husband before I go.

Miss D.—A very dutiful wife my little sister makes. Does she not, Mrs. Elton?

Mrs. E.—I think so.

Mrs. B.—Not more than I should be. Mr. Black's business calls him away so much that I should fear he would feel that I set but very little value on my home and his society, if I should carelessly absent myself in the few hours that business permits him to spend at home.

[*Pat shows a ragged-looking woman and child in.*]

Pat.—Sure, madam, it's a gintleman you made of me,

and won't ye do somethin' for this poor crature? Heaven bless ye.

MRS. E. [*annoyed.*]—Patrick, why didn't you take them to the basement? [*To the woman.*] I am engaged now. I have no time to attend to you. [*Taking her purse she hands her money.*] Patrick, show her out.

MRS. E.—New servants are often so annoying. We have lately employed Patrick, and I don't know whether we will be able to teach him any thing or not. He seems honest.

[*Bell rings. Pat ushers in Mr. Gray and Captain McCartney. Mr. G. shakes hands with the ladies and introduces the Captain. Mrs. E. invites them to be seated. Pat remains on the stage, taking a seat rather back of Mrs. E.*]

MRS. E.—Why, Mr. Gray, I understood you were absent from the city. When did you return?

MR. G.—Last week only. Oh, yes, I made quite a tour during the summer. I think every one should see something of their own land before they visit other countries. I expect to start on a tour through Europe next year.

MISS D.—Will you go to Rome? How I envy you!

CAP.—Then you are fond of travelling, Miss Dunn?

MISS D.—Indeed I am, but I have had little opportunity of gratifying it.

MRS. B.—Your tour did not extend very far through the Southern States, I suppose, Mr. Gray?

MR. G.—No, not very far. Had my health permitted I should have enjoyed following in the trail of Sherman, on his way to Atlanta.

MRS. E.—From appearance, Captain, you have seen something of the South or Southern people. I see you carry your arm in a sling.

CAP.—Yes, I was wounded in the shoulder about a year ago. I have not been able for duty since. I hope to return at an early day, probably next week.

MRS. B.—Have you been with the army since the first breaking out of the rebellion?

CAP.—No, ma'am; I was in Dublin then.

PAT [*speaking aloud*].—Thin it's the ould country yer from? Give us a sheek iv your hand for the sake of the swate ould place.

Mrs. E. [*rising to her feet.*]—Patrick, you here?

Pat.—It's meself shure, and didn't I tell Mr. Elton that I could do what any other mon could, and isn't it meself what can entertain the ladies and gintlemen, when he is absent?

Mrs. E. [*going to the door.*]—Patrick, I wish to speak to you.

[*Exit Pat and Mrs. Elton.*]

Mr. G.—That man is tipsy.

Mrs. B.—He certainly acts strangely.

[*Enter Mrs. Elton.*]

Mr. G.—How long has that man been in your employ?

Mrs. E.—Only to-day; came at noon.

Mr. G.—He has been drinking.

Mrs E.—I fear he has; he appeared to be perfectly sober when my husband employed him, but he took him up and had him fitted out with a new suit of clothes, and I suppose he had to stop on his return and drink in honor of them.

Cap.—No doubt; that is a failing so many of my poor countrymen have.

[*Pat's voice heard at a distance, singing "Lanighan's Ball"—" Me father he died and he made me a man agin." Enter bearing a waiter with glasses and pitcher.*]

Pat.—And it's whiskey punch it is to warm ye when ye'r cauld, or make ye young whin ye'r auld. [*Staggering, catches his foot in the carpet and falls near Miss Dunn— gathering himself up.*] Och, me dear leddy, did it get over ye? The nasty baste, ant it was too heavy for me, and pulled me down, the dirty critter.

Cap. [*taking hold of him.*]—Come, my man, I think you would make a better soldier than a waiting-man.

Pat.—Soldier do you main? Niver while my name is Pat McGee. I'll never disgrace its beauty by fighting for the nagers.

Cap.—I have fought against oppression, and hope to do so again.

Pat.—That's where two Irishmen differ just as much as chalk and cheese. It is a family brawl, and an Irish- man ought to have nothing to do with it. They don't belong to the family.

Mr. G.—Then, I suppose, Irishmen do not vote.

PAT. [*excited.*]—Yis, they do vote!

MR. G.—Oh, then, they belong to the family.

[*Enter Mr. Elton.*]

MR. E.— Good-afternoon [*bowing*]. What is the matter here? What does all this noise mean?

PAT.—Main, jest! Why, yer honor, it mains that just when I was showing these leddies and gentlemen how beautifully I could entertain them, and was jest bringing some of the crater to cheer their spirits whin the nasty baste got too heavy for me.

MR. E.—Take yourself off now. I want nobody in my employ who acts in this manner.

PET.—Faith, ant didn't I tell you I could do what any other mon could?

MR. E.—And I told you to do as I bid you. I didn't bid you get drunk. Be off!

PET.—Plase, sir, and you niver tould me not to.

MR. E —Be off with you! I don't want you here!

PAT. [*crying.*]—Must I put on thim ould clothes again? I thought it was a gintleman you made of me intirely.

MR. E.—Be off with you! clothes and all!

PAT.—Ant do ye main they are mine? [*brightening.*] God bless yer honor! Ant may the divil blow me the night and the day, if iver I forgit to bless yer honor! And it's niver a cint will I charge ye for this day's work, at all, at all. [*Staggering, he bows himself out, singing :*]

" Now I'm goin' back agin, as poor as I began,
To make a happy girl of Moll, for sure I think I can.
My pockets they are empty, but my heart is full of joy.
Auld Ireland is my country, and my name is Pat Maloy."

[*Mr. Gray introduces Mr. E. and Captain McCartney.*]

MR. E —I pity the poor fellow, but there is no dependence to be put in such a character.

CAP.—Not a bit, not a bit!

[*Ladies rising to go.*]

MRS. E.—Well, I am sorry you have been so annoyed. Pray call again soon. Don't be so formal.

MRS. B.—Thank you, I shall look for you to return mine. Do not let it be long.

MRS. D.—You, Miss Dunn, might often drop in. You have no household duties to look after.

Mr. E.—Ladies, do not hurry off because I have come in.

Mrs. B.—Certainly not; but it is fully time we were going.

Mr. G.—Captain, if the ladies do not object, we wiii walk up the street with them, as our way leads in the same direction.

[Exit all.]

Scene V.— *Supper-table — Mr. and Mrs. Elton ana daughters.*

Mrs. E.—Ha! ha! Sir Wisdom, and how do you like the experiment?

Mr. E.—So well, I shall try it again.

Mrs. E.—How much did the suit of clothes cost?

Mr. E.—Not over ten dollars. Poor fellow! I pitied him.

Mrs. E.—Oh! you did!

Mr. E.—Now, Mrs. Elton, don't be sarcastic. You know it was all your fault.

Mrs. E.—My fault?

Mr. E.—Yes. You recommended him.

Mrs. E.—True; but you knew my failing.

Mary.—Has Patrick gone?

Mr. E.—Yes. Were you not at home this afternoon?

Mary.—No. I was out with Anna Stephens at her cousin's. I was telling them about Bridget. She used to live there, mamma, and went off in the same manner.

Mrs. E.—Then I am not the only one she has humbugged.

Mr. E.—And won't be the last. I think it will be well for us both to resolve now to employ no one without a good recommendation.

Mrs. E.—I hardly think that is right. Every one must have a start somewhere. And although I have been cheated a number of times, I have not lost all faith yet; but will try to be more guarded in future.

[Curtain falls.]

READING WORKS OF FICTION.

A DEBATE.

PRESIDENT [*rapping upon desk*].—The Lyceum will please come to order. The first business this evening is reading the minutes of the last meeting.

A MEMBER.—I move, Mr. President, that the reading of the minutes be dispensed with.

[*Motion seconded, put, and declared carried.*]

PRESIDENT.—The next business in order is the report of the Committee on Debate, Mr. Fisher, chairman.

FISHER.—The Committee have agreed upon the following question for discussion this evening: RESOLVED, *That the reading of works of fiction should be discountenanced.* Disputants upon the affirmative, Messrs. Ames, Brown, Chase, Day, Eames, Fay, Good, Hope, Ivins and Jones; negative, Messrs. Airy, Booth, Cass, Dilks, Easy, Fisher, Green, Hale, Ingalls and James.

PRESIDENT.—The debate being next in order, it will be necessary to select a chairman of debate.

A MEMBER.—I move that Mr. Judgment acts as chairman.

[*Motion seconded, put, and carried.*]

CHAIRMAN [*taking chair*].—The Lyceum has heard the question selected by the Committee. Mr. Ames will open in behalf of the affirmative.

AMES.—Mr. Chairman—ladies and gentlemen: The question assigned for this evening's discussion resolves itself into the simple proposition, that the reading of works of fiction is productive of more injury than benefit. I am, to the best of my ability, to maintain the affirmative; and I do so, sir, upon this ground, among others, that the reading of such works unfits one for the actual, practical duties of life. Using the word "novels" as tantamount, for the purposes of this debate, to the phrase "works of fiction," I assert that the writers of novels deal with unreal characters, living, moving, and having their being in an unreal world. The characters sketched,

oftentimes with consummate ability, are at best but dis·
tortions or caricatures of the men and women of every-
day life. They are placed in such positions as will best
enlist the interests of the reader, regardless of the requirements of truth. As a general thing, they are pushed
to extremes, such as in this work-day world of ours we
never encounter. Either the good are perfect, or the bad
have so many redeeming traits about them that one is at
loss whether to style them bad or good. Every thing is
wrested from its actual surroundings as we find them
about us. Even in those novels which profess to have a
moral bearing, virtue and vice are so confounded in the
characters that the dividing line is very often undistin-
guishable, or virtue is portrayed with such drawbacks
as to make vice appear lovely and desirable by contrast

These works constitute the exclusive reading of
numbers — of the rich and the idle, who, from their
position of ease and leisure, have it in their power to
influence others to an extent entirely disproportioned
to their worth ; they form the reading of most men
in their hours of leisure — a principal part of the
reading of women—and, most unfortunate of all, a
large proportion of the reading of the young, of those
whose judgment is immature, who are mere creatures of
impulse and passion and swayed this way and that as the
novelist may choose.

Now, Mr. Chairman, this life of ours is a serious affair.
About it cluster the sternest realities ; on its conduct depend the most momentous issues. Rightly to live demands the most careful painstaking. No effort can be
spared to enable us to fulfil all the requirements which
our position in this world of being lays upon us The
farther we move from the actual practical facts of life,
the nearer we approach to wrong-doing, the more readily
we yield ourselves an easy prey to the temptations to evil
which beset us upon every side.

This hazard the novel-reader runs — fascinated with the
charms of the work which he peruses—transported out
of himself, for the time being, away from his own world,
from the men and women whose destiny is his, into an
idealized world, furnished with such inhabitants and furniture as suits the whim or caprice of genius. Taken

captive by what he reads, real life seems wanting in savor. The zest of healthy existence is gone; the duties devolving upon him become irksome; responsibility is shirked whenever it is possible; and he degenerates into a listless dreamer, caring nothing for the goal towards which he should ever press, utterly unfitted for the scene of action in which he has been placed.

Such, sir, I believe to be the effects of novel-reading; and for this reason, saying nothing now of others, which will doubtless be presented hereafter, I most earnestly advocate the affirmative.

CHAIRMAN.—Mr. Airy upon the negative.

AIRY.—Mr. Chairman: While I have no objection, speaking for myself only, to adopt the interpretation of the question given by the gentleman whom I follow, it must be distinctly understood that my colleagues are not to be bound by it, unless they choose. We understand the term "works of fiction" to include imaginative poems as well as novels, much of history so-called, no little of what passes current as biography—all writings, in short, which do not, throughout their entire extent, in general and in detail, adhere to the actual truth—which are not based, and always and everywhere based, upon facts.

So much for our construction of the question. As the gentleman, however, has chosen—and with excellent judgment, as I apprehend, considering the side which he is to maintain—to restrict it to novels, I meet him upon that limitation, and contend that so far from discountenancing novel-reading, we should encourage it and further it—encourage it, precisely as any judicious person should encourage any other kind of reading, with proper checks and cautions.

For, sir, let it be understood at the opening of this discussion that we are not to be forced to undertake the defence of novel-reading in those cases, if such there be, where it constitutes the sole reading of the individual. The confinement of oneself to the perusal of any class of human productions, I care not what, will perforce result in a one-sided, ill-balanced, unfinished person. Some variety is indispensable to culture, to that growth which should be the object of all reading.

When, therefore, the ground is taken that novel-read-

ing is to be discountenanced, the gentleman must mean,
if any thing is meant, that no novel is ever to be read by
any person.   But, sir, I will not narrow the question to
this extent.   The position I assume is, that novels are to
be read, regard being had to their class, as history is to
be read, as biography is to be read, as poetry is to be
read, as books of travel are to be read.   In other words,
as man's physical development is not to be secured by
bread alone, so his mental development is to be sought
by the perusal of a variety of intellectual productions of
other minds, in which variety works of fiction, or novels,
find their fitting place.

When the gentleman essayed to delineate the novel, he
seemed to forget that it is as broad and as deep as life
itself—that all shades of character, both of the individual
and of the nation, are delineated by the novelist—that it
has been made the vehicle of social improvement, of moral
reformation, of religious instruction; that its pages have
branded vice with marks as ineffaceable as any which the
preacher or the professed moralist has used; that virtue,
as recognized by the great and good of Christendom, has
been held up to reverence and regard as embodied in
heroes and heroines, who would be models in any age or
land.   His characterization I pronounce unjust and limited
—as unjust as would be the selection of Sir John Mande-
ville as a fair representative of writers of travels, or of
Hume or Gibbon as the type of a Christian historian.

Why is it, Mr. Chairman, that the novel exercises the
influence that it does upon the age—an influence greater
than that of any other work?   Is it possible that the
false, vapid thing which the gentleman outlined exerts
that influence?   No, sir; no shadowy, vague, illusive un-
reality could sway the mind thus; substance and strength
are requisite.   These the novel of worth possesses in an
eminent degree.   By means of it we are brought near to
our fellow-men, through the medium of that faculty of
our nature—the imagination—which the Creator intended
should be appealed to for the conveyance of instruction.
So far from mingling with unreal men and women, we are
brought in the closest possible contact with our brothers
and sisters, fellow-toilers with us, strugglers for the same
great end, sharers of a common fate, whose joys are our

joys, whose sorrows ours. They breathe as we breathe, work as we fain would work, or, if haply succumbing to the wrong, we see, in what leads to their misdoing, pitfalls which we are to avoid.

Believing the true novel, sir, to rank among the most valuable instrumentalities for mental culture and moral development, I advocate the negative of this question.

CHAIRMAN.—The question having been opened upon both sides, gentlemen will follow in debate as assigned.

BROWN.—Mr. Chairman : The gentleman will pardon me, but he misapprehends the point we make : which is, in effect, that this reading of works of fiction cannot, from its very nature, be hedged in and confined as he would prescribe. Its fascination is such that the reader is held a willing captive ; his chains he would not break if he could. Such I understand to be the view taken by my colleague, who opened the debate. Novel-reading grows by what it feeds upon. The more you give, so much the more is desired. The habit is readily confirmed ; and when once you yield to the witchery of the spell your self-control is, as a general thing, forever gone. .

Nor need it surprise any that such should be the fact. Consider the ease with which your average work of fiction is perused—how one's mind floats along with the current of its thoughts—that no concentration of faculties is required—that, in short, it is read without effort and remembered without trouble.

Such works—and of this staple are the most of our works of fiction made up—do certainly, Mr. Chairman, unfit us for the active conflict of life, and should, on that account alone, be carefully avoided by one who would make of himself all that the Creator has given him opportunity for becoming.

BOOTH.—Mr Chairman : " Still harping on my daughter !" I do not see that the gentleman just seated makes the discrimination upon which we insist. All works of fiction are not alike, any more than all men, all histories, all biographies, all works upon natural science are alike. Of each there are all conceivable shades, from the very good to the utterly and deplorably worthless. As was insisted by my friend who preceded me upon the nega-

tive, we are not tied to the extreme; attention should in
fairness, be directed to the best specimens of the class
under discussion. Show us that such works are objectionable, and the affirmative is maintained—otherwise not.
Take the Waverley Novels, for instance. I contend that
the student can obtain a more correct idea of the life of
the times introduced therein by Scott than can be secured
by the investigation of any and all historical documents
bearing upon the same era. The reader is placed so completely in communication with the characters represented,
and those characters are so faithful to the prototypes in
actual life upon which they are built, that we cannot but
identify ourselves with the course of action which they
adopt and become ourselves part and parcel of that past
which the genius of the author so vividly, so truthfully
portrays. The foundation of historic truth upon which
these works rest is incorporated into our stock of information—incorporated, it must be remembered, in a shape
which we can readily manage—and we thereby, I assert,
gain more solid results than would be possible for the
average reader from any other source. Besides, the al-
lusions and incidental remarks made in such works lead
us, all unconsciously, into other fields of investigation,
in which we become eager gleaners for facts which would
have remained forever unsought, had it not been for the
charms of the novelist's pages.

The very fact, sir, that—as the gentleman has stated—
but little concentration of faculties is requisite for novel-
reading, establishes the truth of our side of the question,
when we take account of what material the great mass
of readers must ever be composed—how ill-adapted for
more labored, more solid (as some would call it) reading;
for, surely, if works of fiction exist which are not objectionable upon any tenable grounds, better that they
should be read than that nothing should be perused.

CHASE.—Mr. Chairman: I do not believe it true that
the average man or woman is so hampered as to be
obliged either to read works of fiction or to dispense
with reading altogether. In these days when the press
teems with works dealing in all conceivable subjects,
treated in every possible manner, it is impossible that it
should be so. He who runs even may now-a-days read—

and read understandingly too —works in almost any branch of intellectual effort. Think, sir, how science is popularized—its great truths stated and illustrated so that the weakest capacity can not only comprehend them, but will feel an interest excited which will not rest until questionings are pushed farther and farther, adding at each advance new and valuable information.

Now, sir, not the least objection to the reading of works of fiction is, that it deprives the mind of this needed ali- ment—that it substitutes the palatable for the nutritious. It is imperious, exacting, as has been well asserted— "bearing, like the Turk, no brother near the throne." In this world it is easier to do wrong than to do right; and I count it among the most deplorable facts that there should be a class of works into the reading of which the young so readily glide, where they so gladly linger, when by doing so they shut themselves out of a range of inter- esting reading which is at the same time profitable—like Dr. Johnson's tea, cheering but not inebriating.

Take the study of natural history, by way of illustra- tion of my position. Who that has seen the intense eagerness with which a boy listens to the crude harangue of the showman at a menagerie—hanging upon his every word, reluctant to pass on although the same monotonous recitation he knows is all that will compensate him for remaining—who can doubt that, if in the hands of this boy a work on natural history adapted to his ca- pacity were placed, he would readily follow its lead and acquire therefrom tastes and aptitudes which would shape his whole future course for the better? And the same may be said of any branch of natural science, the study of which can be made so interesting and profitable that I confess to having little, if any, patience with those who would allow the young to feed upon the dry husks of novel-reading.

Cass.—Mr. Chairman, I grant you, sir, that the greatest caution is requisite relative to the kind of reading which is placed in the hands of the young—caution bearing not only upon works of fiction, but as well upon works of every kind. Why, sir, there are professedly truthful works—works based upon undoubted facts—which no judicious parent would give to his children. But, sir, children do not constitute the whole of this world's inhabitants, and because certain restrictions may be necessary in their case, it by no means follows that we children of a larger growth are to be hemmed in in like manner. The milk for babes is exchanged, when manhood's estate is attained, for strong meat.

To my mind, Mr. Chairman, the gentleman last upon the floor dwelt upon a small, and, comparatively speaking, insignificant department of the subject.

DAY.—Mr. Chairman: I cannot agree with the gentleman in his estimate of the importance of the views which my colleague advanced. I think no question so momentous as that involved in the start which shall be given to the young in the matter of reading. It is the old maxim of the twig and the tree, and we cannot well be too solicitous as to the bias which tender minds will receive from the books which they read.

To works of fiction they will take as naturally as the duckling to the water, and very often, sir, with the same untoward issue. Such works need no digestion, but are at once assimilated into the mind, unlike history, philosophy and political treatises, which are comparatively tough and solid food. I would have the young furnished with reading which should require thought, that the discipline which is the condition of growth may commence at an early period.

DILKS.—Mr. Chairman: The gentleman would not surely rob childhood of its chiefest joys—those inimitable fairy tales which all of us remember with such delight, which peopled our young world with visions of beauty by day and by night—with glories which never set, but remain with us through life. Going back to my early days, I can recall nothing which so powerfully influenced me—and for good, as I verily believe—as those nursery stories which I drank in from my mother's lips, which are associated with her at this moment in my mind, through the quiet splendor of which, toned down with years which have sped, her angel face even now looks lovingly upon me.

Believing, sir, as I do, that many a work of fiction is as valuable an instructor in morals, as ardent a persuasive to right as the world can furnish—and that more characters have been shaped by novels than by sermons—I could not remain silent while such works are—as they have been here this evening—calumniated and traduced.

EAMES.—Mr. Chairman: Are we not wandering somewhat from the subject? Life is too short to enable any of us to read every thing that has been written in by-gone days, that may yet be written while we are on the stage of action. A selection, then, must be made, and it is upon the nature of this selection that our question now hinges.

I concur fully with the gentlemen who contend for a variety in reading. I would have neither the young nor the mature bound down to one kind simply; and were there no other facilities for obtaining refreshment and recreation from the exhausting reading which in the main ought to claim our attention (since the elements of development are found in it to the highest degree) than what the work of fiction affords, I, sir, should most earnestly advocate an infusion of such reading.

This is not, sir, in my judgment, the case. Perhaps nothing more distinctly stamps the present age on its intellectual side than the versatility displayed in every department, by means of which all capacities are ministered to. Contrast, for example, the historical writings of a Niebuhr or an Arnold with those of a Rollin—of a Macaulay with those of a Robertson; and it will at once be seen what new life has been imparted to themes which, not many years ago, were wont to be deemed the dryest and most repelling. And the same holds good, to a greater or less extent, in every nook and corner of the domain of intellectual effort. The very novels of the day have been compelled to take their cue from this great change. The namby-pambyisms of scarcely more than a quarter of a century since have been forced to give place to a more vigorous and energetic species of writing, which professes—whatever the result may show—to have a definite purpose, and that a commendable one.

While, sir, I see such a wide range from which to select—a range which will recreate and refresh as well as interest—outside of the acknowledged works of fiction, I must claim, aware as I am of the deteriorating tendencies of such reading, that it ought to be discountenanced in every way. Sure am I, sir, that were the novel entirely excluded, its place would be found to be better and more fully supplied.

EASY.—Mr. Chairman: I must do my friend whom I follow the justice to say that he alone, of all the disputants who have hitherto spoken upon the affirmative, meets the question at issue in a manly, straightforward manner. I shall endeavor so to present my views, in the few moments which I shall occupy, as to reciprocate the frankness which he has shown.

There are certain minds among adults, as well as among the young, which require to have their reading weighed out to them. From such I should certainly keep the novel, were it in my power, as also I should the profound treatise on political economy, or the highly-wrought imaginative poem. Such minds are abnormal, however; and our discussion does not concern them.

If the reading of works of fiction is to be tabooed, then do we say that the average reader will be harmed rather than profited thereby. And why, Mr. Chairman? Because appeal is made to the imagination alone, or for the most part. But has not instruction been imparted in all ages through such instrumentality? Have not the wise and good availed themselves of it? Did not the Great Teacher himself, when on earth, constantly speak to man as a being having imaginative faculty? Shall we blot out the parables? Take from the New Testament every appeal to this faculty of our nature, and what have you left? What novelist but has dealt in the imaginative that he might the more deeply set home the great truths he would enforce?

Can it be, sir, that a class of writings, which has been sanctioned by the best of all times, is to be thrown aside?

FAY.—Mr. Chairman: Our position appears, as the debate progresses, to be somewhat misunderstood. We do not maintain that no appeals to the imagination are to be made. We are well aware of the extreme difficulty in carrying on even the commonest conversation upon the tritest of topics without a resort to it. What we do assert is, that works which are confined exclusively to such appeals are objectionable, in that they make this faculty an

P 2

absorbent of all the others—that they disturb the equilibrium of the mind, and render us, to a certain extent—graduated by the intensity of our devotion to them—incapable of exercising that deliberate, healthy judgment, which, as responsible moral beings, we should exercise.

Not that some works of this class may not be mainly free from such injurious tendencies—for that would be to claim what we cannot make good ; but that the prevailing drift, the general tendency is bad, for the reason given. To this we add the undeniable fact, that this species of literature, more than any other, makes abject slaves of those who should be independent free agents. I trust I have made myself understood ; and that our position, so stated, will be that against which the attacks of the negative are directed.

FISHER.—Mr. Chairman : I am glad to have the position of the affirmative so fully set before us ; because, during this debate, their ground has shifted so much that I was unable to determine with precision what must be said.

I differ with the gentleman in my estimate of the proportion of the healthful and the pernicious works of fiction. He admits that there are some whose tendency is beneficial. I claim that such is the tendency of the large majority, especially of the productions of modern writers. The Christianity of the age has not been without its influence upon these productions ; and I regard the writings of Dickens, of Thackeray, of Mrs. Craik, and many others, as entitled to be ranked among those which make their readers wiser and better men.

GOOD.—Mr. Chairman : The gentleman, when speaking in such high terms of modern writers of fiction, must surely have overlooked the fact that the majority of them are to be found among the immature and inexperienced. The greater part of new-fledged writers essay the novel. A few, indeed, dabble in poetry, mostly imitative ; but the novel is the port whence, as a general rule, they spread their sails to the breeze.

Very many novel-writers are women—young women. Now, I indulge in no tirade upon the sex when I assert that their experience of life is not such as to make them safe guides. They see but little of the actual movements of the world, and that little is very circumscribed. Even when they deal, as they mostly do, with the great passion, love, they can only speak from their own limited experience, if any they have, or from the confidences of female friends, who can never impart those shades of feeling, those delicate traceries of thought, which are essential to a correct portrayal of this or any other passion of our nature. What is the result? Half-views of life, sentimentality in place of sentiment, false morality, and a train of other ills. Shall such writers be our Mentors, Mr. Chairman?

GREEN.—Mr. Chairman: I leave the gentleman to his fate at the hands of those whom he so mercilessly stigmatizes; nor need he expect from me the slightest sympathy, whatever may befall him.

Were there no other reason, Mr. Chairman, to be urged in behalf of works of fiction, the simple fact that they refresh us toilers along the world's hot and dusty thoroughfare, would of itself alone make me their advocate. When fatigued with the cares of business, wearied with the work of the day, what a delightful retreat they afford us! What a solace amid misfortune! How exhilarating to mingle in the world they disclose to our view—to chat with their men and their women – or, in the higher order of imaginative writings, to catch at times glimpses of what has never yet been seen save by the eye of faith – that bright side of the imagination—to bask in beauties that are bathed by

" The light which never yet was seen on sea or land— The consecration and the poet's dream !"

Who, Mr. Chairman, would forego that immortal poem to which the sightless bard, fallen on evil days, dedicated the full maturity of his genius—the Paradise Lost—for all the "over true tales" that were ever written or the "Stories founded on Fact" with which our Sunday-school libraries abound?

HOPE.—Mr. Chairman: Have gentlemen never heard that " Truth is stranger than any fiction "? We move in the midst of events which, could their impelling causes be thoroughly comprehended, would hold us rapt in wonder Were we masters of the hidden springs of even the most trivial actions, we should not need the aid of another's imagination to furnish us with food for thought and reflection. Indeed, did we address ourselves to the business of life as we ought, the investigation of what passes for facts—naked, Gradgrind facts—would afford full play for every faculty of our nature, the imagination included.

When I see the slight attention which is paid by the most to any kind of investigation—the reluctance with which concentration of mind is secured—the aversion to tracing an effect back to its cause—the shallowness which passes for wisdom—the superficiality which, by its un-blushing effrontery, looks out of sight thoroughness and method—all of which I do not hesitate to attribute to the morbid craving for such *pabulum* as works of fiction furnish—when I see all this, and contrast it with what should be our characteristics as rational creatures, I say most emphatically that I should greatly rejoice—and so would every well-wisher of his race—could every work of the kind under discussion be forever removed from sight and memory.

HALE.—Mr. Chairman: Is it indeed true that life is to be devoted to hard thinking? Must we work on, work ever—no relief, no holiday? Did even the Fall include all this, what of us were left which were worth the in terest of any order of beings?

We need, sir, at times to avoid thought. The iron crown should not always pierce our temples. If we would preserve our sanity, there must be moments when we can yield ourselves to whatever surrounds us—when listless-ness may brood over us with healing in its breath – when freedom from the pressure of the world of mind and of matter may be ours to enjoy as we will.

He who has no such moments is a visionary or a mad-man. Workers of fiction open the portals of such de-lights; and for myself, speaking of the great relief they have imparted to me, I say wide open, and yet wider, may they ever stand!

IVINS.—Mr. Chairman: Conceding the justice of the gentleman's claim, we need not resort to the pages of fiction for relief. Our thoughts, whether we will or not, are not to be avoided. It is our duty to see that they are supplied with the right materials for digestion.

I need not, at this stage of the discussion, elaborate what has been already so ably and so exhaustively advanced—namely, that works of fiction do not supply this; but I will only ask your attention to the statement that our minds will never acquire strength, save as work is furnished them for their employment. What the writer of fiction presents is already digested and codified; no effort is required of the reader; his mind is, therefore, kept undisciplined, and remains dwarfed, stunted, infantile ever.

INGALLS. —Mr. Chairman: A distinction must be drawn between protracted, sustained thought upon topics demanding it, and that kind of thinking which imposes no such tax upon the mind, which, like the boy's whistle, thinks itself.

With the former kind, every growing man and woman must, if true to the demands of his nature, be for the most time busied; but there come moments, as has been so well said, when, in order to continue such a course of thought, we must be placed, by some means or other, in the latter category.

This, we contend, the perusal of works of fiction secures for us as no other resort can.

CHAIRMAN.—Mr. Jones will close the debate in behalf of the affirmative—Mr. James in behalf of the negative.

JONES.—Mr. Chairman—Ladies and gentlemen: After the patient attention with which you have honored us it would be trespassing too much upon your kindness, were I to weary you with any extended remarks at the close of this debate. Upon this I shall not venture.

Bear with me but for a moment while I bring before you the grounds upon which we rest our advocacy of the affirmative.

We contend that the perusal of works of fiction incapacitates the mind for vigorous action—tends, rather, to dwarf and stunt it, and renders the reader alike unwilling and unable to fight the good fight; that the fascination of such works keeps the reader constantly on the *qui vive* for further supplies of the same nature; that ample ministrants for the development of our imaginative faculty, to which alone such works cater, are to be found in the truths of life, in those grand facts, whose laws and history it should be our earnest endeavor, as it is our highest employ, to investigate and comprehend; that, in

fine, when we take into consideration our high destiny—
when we reflect that

"Not enjoyment and not sorrow
  Is our destined end or way;
  But to act that each to-morrow
  Find us farther than to-day"—

we are forced to the conclusion, from which there can be
no escape, that the serious things about us are ample
enough to exercise our every faculty, and that any neglect
of such exercise—which the reading of works of fiction
almost always occasions—defeats the primal end of our
being.

Entertaining these views, Mr. Chairman and ladies and
gentlemen, we shall entreat your suffrages in behalf of
the affirmative.

JAMES.—Mr. Chairman—Ladies and gentlemen: A
word from me, and we will relieve you from what, I fear,
has proved the tedium of this debate.

A varied reading, coupled with a careful observation,
makes the fully-equipped man. To exclude works of
fiction from such variety would, we maintain, be as ab
surd and unjust as to forbid the sense of smell to a man,
because, forsooth, he could be said to enjoy existence
without it. To deprive us of the advantages resulting
from the reading of works of fiction would be to cut us
off from avenues of pleasure and instruction which the
great and good have opened before us. Giving all due
weight to the realities of life, there are different ways of
presenting them, one of which is to be found in works of
the class whose perusal we advocate.

We cannot forget that the most gifted minds have
thought it no unworthy employment to prepare such
works for our perusal; that in the experience of each of
us, intervals occur which can be filled so satisfactorily
by no other means—when we are led willing captives,
kissing the silken chains which sweetly constrain—when

"Though inland far we be,
Our souls have sight of that immortal sea
Which brought us hither—
Can in a moment travel thither,
And see the children sport upon the shore,
And hear the mighty waters rolling evermore."

Appealing to the consciousness of each of you for the truth of our assertion, we ask you to record yourselves upon the negative.

[*Chairman puts the question to the audience—decided majority in favor of the negative—adjournment moved and carried.*]

THE ARCADIAN CLUB;

OR,

THEORY vs. PRACTICE.

Dramatized from Bayard Taylor's "Experiences of the A. C."

DRAMATIS PERSONÆ.

MR. SHELLDRAKE.	MRS. SHELLDRAKE.
ABEL MALLORY.	FAITH LEVIS.
HOLLINS.	PAULINE RINGTOP.
ENOS BILLINGS.	EUNICE HAZLETON.

PERKINS BROWN, boy of all work.

SCENE I.—*Mr. Shelldrake's parlor.*

[*All present engaged in animated conversation.*]

ABEL.—Yes ! I also am an Arcadian. This false dual existence which I have been leading will soon be merged into the unity of Nature. Our lives must conform to her sacred law. Why can't we strip off these hollow *shams*, and be our true selves,—pure, perfect, and divine !

MISS RINGTOP [*heaving a sigh, and speaking in a sickly sentimental tone*].

"Ah ! when wrecked are my desires
    On the everlasting Never,
And my heart, with all its fires,
    Out forever,
In the cradle of creation
Finds the soul resuscitation."

MR. S. [*turning to his wife.*]—Elviry ! How many upstairs rooms is there in that house down on the sound?

MRS. S.—Four, besides three small ones under the roof. Why, what made you think of that, Jesse?

MR. S.—I've got an idee while Abel's been talking. We've taken a house for the summer, down the other side of Bridgeport, right on the water, where there's good fishing, and a fine view of the sound. Now there's room enough for all of us,—at least all that can make it suit to go. Abel, you and Enos and Pauline and Eunice might fix matters so that we can all take the place in partnership and pass the summer together, living a true and beautiful life in the bosom of Nature. There we shall be perfectly free and untrammelled by the chains which still hang around us in Norridgeport. You know how often we have wanted to be set on some island in the Pacific Ocean, where we could build up a true society right from the start. Now, here's a chance to try the experiment for a few months anyhow.

EUNICE [clapping her hands].—Splendid! Arcadian! I'll give up my school for the summer.

FAITH L. [knitting.]—It will hardly suit me to go. My home duties require my presence there.

MISS R.—" The rainbow hues of the ideal,
Condense to gems, and form the real."

ABEL [pushing both hands through his hair, and throwing his head back].—Oh, Nature, you have found your lost children! We shall obey your neglected laws! We shall hearken to your divine whispers! We shall bring you back from your ignominious exile, and place you on your ancestral throne.

ALL.—Let us do it! By all means, let us do it!

HOLLINS.—I have an engagement to deliver lectures during the summer in Ohio, but this delightful prospect induces me to postpone them till Fall. I could not miss such a sojourn in Arcadia.

EUNICE.—What shall we call the place?

ABEL [rolling his eyes].—Arcadia!

HOLLINS.—Then let us constitute ourselves the Arcadian Club! I think this title exceedingly appropriate.

ENOS.—In order that we may avoid gossip in case our plan should become generally known, suppose we only use the initials—the A. C.

[General assent.]

ABEL.—Our preparations need not be extensive. But little change of clothing will be required. Gentlemen, two shirts will be enough. You can wash one of them any day and dry it in the sun.

MR. S.—There is a vegetable garden down there in
23

good condition. I should think that might be our principal dependence with a supply of flour, potatoes and sugar.

ENOS.—Besides the clams.

EUNICE.—Oh, yes! we can have chowder parties. That will be delightful!

ABEL [*groaning*].—Clams! Chowder! Oh, worse than flesh! Will you reverence nature by outraging her first laws?

ENOS.—Excuse me, I forgot.

EUNICE [*mischievously*].—Ditto.

[*Exit Scene.*]

SCENE II.—*A pleasant cottage on the island—Perkins greets them at the door with a wild whoop, tossing his straw hat into the air—Enter Mr. and Mrs. Shelldrake, Abel, Hollins, Enos, Miss Ringtop and Eunice.*

MR. S.—Here we are! At Arcadia at last!
[*Joyful exclamations.*]

MISS R. [*looking out the window*]—

" Where the turf is softest, greenest,
    Doth an angel thrust me on—
Where the landscape lies serenest,
    In the journey of the sun."

EUNICE.—Don't, Pauline! I never like to hear poetry flourished in the face of nature. This landscape surpasses any poem in the world. Let us enjoy the best thing we have rather than the next best.

MISS R. [*sighing.*]—Ah, yes! 'tis true:

" They sing to the ear, this sings to the eye."

[*General unpacking*]

MRS. S.—Now, for our first meal in Arcadia!

[*Mrs S. and Perkins retire to the kitchen. Eunice and Miss R. unpack dishes and set the table. Miss R. smiles as she says: " You see I also can perform the coarser tasks of life." Mrs. S. sends in onions, lettuce and radishes, which, with bread, constitute supper. No salt is allowed: but Perkins fills a blacking-box lid with some for his own*

*use.   They seat themselves at table—Enos by the side of
Perkins.*

EUNICE [*eating lettuce*].—Oh, we must send for some
oil and vinegar. This lettuce is very nice.

ABEL [*in astonishment*].—Oil and vinegar !

EUNICE [*innocently*].—Why, yes, they are both vegetable substances.

ABEL.—All vegetable substances are not proper for
food. You would not taste the poison oak, or sit under
the upas tree of Java.

EUNICE.—Well, Abel, how are we to distinguish what
is best for us ? How are we to know *what* vegetables to
choose, or what animal and mineral substances to avoid ?

ABEL [*with a lofty air, touching his temple where the last
pimple was about healed*]—I will tell you. See here :
My blood is at last pure. The struggle between the
natural and unnatural is over, and I am beyond the
depraved influences of my former taste. My instincts
are now therefore entirely pure also. What is good for
man to eat, that I shall have a natural desire to eat;
what is bad, will be naturally repelled. How does the
cow distinguish between the wholesome and the poi-
sonous herbs of the meadow? And is man less than a
cow, that he cannot cultivate his instincts to an equal
point ? Let me walk through the woods, and I can tell
you every berry and root which God designed for food,
though I know not its name and have never seen it before.
I shall make use of my time, during our sojourn here, to
test by my purified instincts every substance, animal,
mineral and vegetable, upon which the human race sub-
sists, and to create a catalogue of the *true food* of man.

[*Perkins dips his onion into the salt on his knee, and
nudges Enos, who partakes slyly also. Accidentally the
lid falls to the floor.*]

ABEL [*stretching his long neck across the table*].—What's
that ?

ENOS [*embarrassed*].—Oh, it's—it's only—only chloride
of sodium——

ABEL.—Chloride of sodium ! What do you do with it ?

ENOS [*boldly*].—Eat it with onions. It's a chemical
substance; but I believe it is found in some plants.

[*Eunice suppresses a laugh.*]

ABEL.—Let me taste of it. [*Stretching out an onion Enos hands the box-lid; Abel dips the onion, bites off a piece and chews it gravely.*] Why [*turning to Enos*], it tastes very much like salt.

[*Perkins bursts into a spluttering yell, discharging the onion top between his teeth across the table. Enos and Eunice join in the laugh.*]

ABEL [*gravely*].—There's no objection to that. Let it appear upon our table.

[*They push back from the table, which Mrs. S. and Perkins clear off.*]

HOLLINS [*leaning back lazily*].—My friends, I think we are sufficiently advanced in progressive ideas to establish our little Arcadian community upon what I consider the true basis; not law, nor custom, but the uncorrupted impulses of our nature. What Abel said in regard to dietetic reform is true; but that alone will not regenerate the race. We must rise superior to those conventional ideas whereby life is warped and crippled. Life must not be a prison, where each one must come and go, work, eat, and sleep, as the jailor commands. Labor must not be a necessity, but a spontaneous joy. 'Tis true, but little labor is required of us here : let us, therefore, have no set tasks, no fixed rules; but each one work, rest, eat, sleep, talk or be silent, as his own nature prompts. [*Perkins chuckles.*]

MR. S.—That's just the notion I had when I first talked of our coming here. Here we're alone and unhindered, and if the plan shouldn't happen to work well (I don't see why it shouldn't though), no harm will be done. I've had a deal of hard work in my life, and I've been badgered and bullied so much by your straight-laced professors, that I'm glad to get away from the world for a spell and talk and do rationally without being laughed at.

HOLLINS.—Yes, and if we succeed, as I feel we shall, for I think I know the hearts of all of us here, this may be the commencement of a new epoch for the world. We may become the turning-point between two dispensations; behind us every thing false and unnatural— before us every thing true, beautiful and good.

MISS R. [*sighing.*]—Ah, it reminds me of Gamaliel J. Gauthrop's beautiful lines :

"Unrobed man is lying hoary
  In the distance gray and dead,
There no wreaths of godless glory,
  To his mist-like tresses wed;
And the foot-fall of the ages
  Reigns supreme with noiseless tread."

ENOS.—I am willing to try the experiment; but don't
you think we had better observe some kind of order, even
in yielding every thing to impulse? Shouldn't there be,
at least, a platform, as the politicians call it—an agreement by which we shall all be bound, and which we can
afterwards exhibit as the basis of our success?

HOLLINS.—I think not. It resembles too much the
thing we are trying to overthrow. Can you bind a man's
belief by making him sign certain articles of faith? No,
his thought will be free in spite of it. Let each one only
be true to himself, be himself, act himself, or herself, with
the uttermost candor. We can all agree upon that.
                    [*Exit scene.*]

SCENE III.—*An obscure grocery with the sign Water
Crackers—A woman at the counter —Enos and Abel,
walking in front of it, enter—Abel goes sniffing round,
pausing over some smoked herring.*

ABEL.—Enos, I think herring must feed on sea-weed.
There is such a vegetable attraction about them. [*Next
smells a Rhode Island cheese.*] Enos, this impresses me
like flowers—like marigolds. It must be [*sniffs again
and again*], really—yes, the vegetable element is pre-
dominant. My instinct towards it is so strong that I cannot be mistaken. May I taste it, ma'am? [*The woman
slices off a thin corner and presents it to him on the knife.
He tastes it.*] Delicious! I am right. This is the *True
Food.* Give me two pounds of cheese and a pound of
water crackers, ma'am.
                    [*Outside.*]
ABEL.—Let us sit down a little while, Enos. Will you
have some of this cheese?

ENOS.—No, thank you [*sits down and takes a book from
his pocket and reads*].

ABEL.—My natural instincts towards it are so strong that I cannot resist longer [*eats ravenously, cutting off slice after slice*]. Oh, Enos, it is glorious to possess such purified instincts; to know to a certainty exactly what is good for us to eat—[*suddenly leans back and groans—having eaten the two pounds, or appeared to—writhes in severe pain*].

ENOS [*looking up from his book*].—What is the matter, man? Are you sick?

ABEL.—Terribly sick! Oh! ooh! ooh! [*attempts to get up, but is not able.*]

ENOS [*chuckling to himself*].—Shall I go for a doctor?

ABEL.—Wait! I shall be better. Oh, dear! oh! oh! [*shows signs of nausea—Enos holds him up.*]

ENOS [*aside*].—His instincts *are* strong—stronger than his poor stomach!

[*Curtain falls.*]

SCENE IV.—*A sitting-room—The members of the A. C. assembled for reading—Hollins reading aloud from Bulwer.*

HOLLINS.—"Ah, behind the veil! We see the summer smile of the earth! Enamelled meadow and limpid stream; but what hides she in her sunless heart? Caverns of serpents or grottoes of priceless gems? Youth, whose soul sits on thy countenance, thyself wearing no mask, strive not to lift the mask of others! Be content with what thou seest, and wait till time and experience shall teach thee to find jealousy behind the sweet smile, and hatred under the honeyed word."

MISS R. [*in a sing-song voice.*]

"I look beyond thy brow's concealment,
I see thy spirit's dark revealment,
Thy inner-self betrayed I see,
Thy coward, craven, shivering Me!"

HOLLINS.—We think we know one another, but do we? We see the faults of others, their weaknesses, their disagreeable qualities, and we keep silent. How much we should gain, were candor as universal as concealment. Then each one, seeing himself as others see him, would truly know himself. How much misunderstanding might be avoided, how much hidden shame be removed, hopeless, because unspoken, love made glad—in short, how much brighter and happier the world would become, if each one expressed everywhere and at all times his true and entire feeling. Why, even evil would lose half its power. Come [*turning to Enos*], why should not this candor be adopted in our Arcadia? Will any one—will you, Enos—commence at once by telling me, now, to my face, my principal faults?

Enos [*thinking for a moment*].—You have a great deal of intellectual arrogance, and you are physically very indolent.

Hollins [*with surprise*].—Well put! though I do not say that you are entirely correct. Now what are my merits?

Enos.—You are clear-sighted, an earnest seeker after truth, and courageous in the avowal of your thoughts.

Abel [*looking shyly at Hollins*].—Do you know that I begin to think beer must be a natural beverage? There was an auction in the village to-day, as I passed through, and I stopped at a cake-stand to get a glass of water, as it was very hot There was no water—only beer; so I thought I would try a glass, simply as an experiment. Really, the flavor was very agreable. And it occurred to me, on the way home, that all the elements contained in beer are vegetable. Besides, fermentation is a natural process. I think the question has never been properly tested before.

Hollins.—But the alcohol!

Abel.—I could not distinguish any, either by taste or smell. I know that chemical analysis is said to show it; but may not the alcohol be created, somehow, during the analysis?

Hollins.—Abel, you will never be a reformer until you possess some of the commonest elements of knowledge.

Abel [*sarcastically*].—*Commonest elements of knowledge!* Hollins, your mind is material and grovelling. But I disdain to say more. Perkins, bring up three bottles of that beer I put in the cellar. [*Perkins obeys, bringing the bottles and glasses. Abel drinks one bottle at a draught, and offers the beer around. All refuse, but Hollins and*

Shelldrake, who divide a bottle.] The effect of beer depends, I think, on the commixture of the nourishing principle of the grain with the cooling properties of the water. Perhaps, hereafter, a liquid food of the same character may be invented which shall save us from mastication and all the diseases of the teeth.

ABEL [*getting tipsy*].—Oh, sing, somebody! The night was made for song!

MISS R. [*in a screeching voice*]—

" When stars are in the quiet skies,
  Then most I pine for thee ;
  Bend on me, then, thy loving eyes,
  As stars bend on the sea."

ABEL.—Candor's the order of the day, isn't it?

HOLLINS.—Yes! yes!

MISS R.—Certainly.

ABEL.—Well, then, candidly, Pauline, you've got the darn'dest squeaky voice——

[*Miss Ringtop gives a faint scream of horror.*]

ABEL.—Oh, never mind! We act according to impulse, don't we? And I've the impulse to swear! and it's right! Let Nature have her way! Listen! Darn it! darn it! darn it! darn it! I never knew it was so easy. Why, there's a pleasure in it! Try it, Pauline! try it on me!

MISS R.—Oh! ooh! ooh!

HOLLINS.—Abel! Abel! the beer's got into your head.

ABEL.—No, it isn't beer—it's candor! It's your own proposal, Hollins. Suppose it's evil to swear : isn't it better I should express it, and be done with it, than keep it bottled up to ferment in my mind? Oh, you're a precious consistent old humbug, *you* are! [*He jumps up, and goes off dancing, singing :*]

" 'Tis home where'er the heart is."

EUNICE [*in alarm*].—Oh, he may fall into the water!

SHELLDRAKE.—He's not fool enough to do that. His head is a little light—that's all. The air will cool him down presently.

[*Exit Scene.*]

Scene V.—*A garden—Abel and Eunice present—Enos looking on unobserved.*

Eunice.—Come, Abel, please do not go so near the water.

Abel [*catching Eunice's arm and holding her*].—This is fate—destiny. Ah, Eunice, ask the night and the moon, ask the impulse which told you to follow me! Let us be candid, like the old Arcadians we imitate. [*Eunice starts and endeavors to leave.*] Eunice, we know that we love each other, why should we conceal it any longer? Let us confess to each other. The female heart should not be timid in this pure and beautiful atmosphere of love which we breathe. Come, Eunice, we are alone; let your heart speak to me.

Eunice.—I will not hear such language. Let me go back to the house.

Abel [*groaning*].—Oh, Eunice, don't you love me, indeed? [*unloosens his hold.*] I love *you*— from my heart I do. Yes, I love you. Tell me how you feel towards me.

Eunice [*earnestly*].—I feel towards you only as a friend; and if you wish me to retain a friendly interest in you, you must never again talk in this manner. I do not love you, and I never shall. Let me go back to the house.

Abel [*groaning*].—Oh, Eunice, you have broken my heart! [*sits down, covers his face with his hands and begins to cry.*]

Eunice.—I am very sorry, Abel, but I cannot help it.

[*Exit Eunice and Abel.*]

[*Enos comes forward—sitting down and meditating— Miss Ringlop enters and takes a seat at his side, shakes back her long curls and sighs, looking at the moon.*]

Miss R. [*in a sentimental voice.*]—Oh, how delicious! How it seems to set the spirit free, and we wander off on the wings of fancy to other spheres.

Enos.—Yes, it is very beautiful, but sad when one's alone.

Miss R.—How inadequate is language to express the emotions which such a scene calls up in the bosom.

Poetry alone is the voice of the spiritual world, and we, who are not poets, must borrow the language of the gifted sons of song. Oh, Enos, I *wish* you were a poet! But you *feel* poetry, I know you do. I have seen it in your eyes when I quoted the burning lines of Adeliza Kelly, or the soul breathings of Gamaliel J. Gauthrop. In *him* particularly I find the voice of my own nature. Do you know his "Night Whispers?" How it embodies the feeling of such a scene as this!

"Star drooping bowers, bending down the spaces,
And moonlit glories sweep star-footed on."

Ah, this is an hour for the soul to unveil its most secret chambers! Do you not think, Enos, that love rises superior to all conventionalities? that those whose souls are in unison should be allowed to reveal themselves to each other regardless of the world's opinions?

ENOS.—Yes.

MISS R. [*in a tender voice.*]—Enos, do you understand me?

ENOS.—Yes.

MISS R.—Then our hearts are wholly in unison. I know you are true, Enos. I know your noble nature and I will never doubt you. This is indeed happiness.

"Life remits his tortures cruel,
Love illumes his fairest fuel,
When the hearts that once were dual,
Meet as one in sweet renewal."

[*Lays her head on his shoulder.*]

ENOS [*starting away from her in alarm*].—Miss Ringtop, you don't mean—that——

MISS R.—Yes, Enos, *dear* Enos, henceforth we belong to each other.

ENOS [*greatly agitated*].—You mistake—I did not mean that—I didn't understand you. Don't talk to me in that way! Don't look at me that way, Miss Ringtop! We were never meant for each other! I wasn't——you are so much older—I mean different. It can't be—no, it can never be! I never thought of such a thing! Let us go back to the house—the night is cold.

[*Exit Enos.*]

Miss R. [*singing disconsolately :*]
"The dream is past, the hope has fled,
Love's fairest flowers lie crushed and dead."
[*Exit scene.*]

SCENE VI.—*A room at Shelldrake's—Mr. and Mrs. Shell-drake, Abel ana Hollins engaged in loud conversation—Perkins Brown sitting on a low step.*

HOLLINS.—Now, are you sure you can bear the test?

SHELLDRAKE.—Bear it? Why, to be sure! If I couldn't bear it, or if you couldn't, your theory's done for. Try! I can stand it as long as you can.

[*Enos and Eunice enter, hand-in-hand, unobserved.*]

HOLLINS.—Well, then, I think you a very ordinary man. I derive no intellectual benefit from my intercourse with you; but your house is convenient to me. I'm under no obligations for your hospitality, however, because my company is an advantage to you. Indeed, if I were treated according to my deserts, you couldn't do enough for me.

MRS. S. [*wrathfully.*]—Indeed! I think you get as good as you deserve, and more too.

HOLLINS [*with a condescending look*].—Elvira, I have no doubt you think so, for your mind belongs to the lowest and most material sphere. You have your place in nature, and you fill it; but it is not for you to judge of intelligences that move only on the upper planes.

SHELLDRAKE.—Hollins, Elviry's a good wife and a sensible woman, and I won't allow you to turn up your nose at her.

HOLLINS.—I am not surprised that you should fail to bear the test. I didn't expect it.

SHELLDRAKE.—Let me try it on you. You, now, have some intellect; I don't deny that; but not so much, by a long shot, as you think you have. Besides that, you're awfully selfish in your opinions. You won't admit that anybody can be right who differs from you. You've sponged on me for a long time; but I suppose I've learned something from you, so we'll call it even. I think, however, that what you call acting according to impulse is simply an excuse to cover your own laziness.

PERKINS [*jumping up*].—Gosh! that's it! Ho! ho! ho!

HOLLINS [*exasperated*].—Shelldrake, I pity you. I always knew your ignorance, but I thought you honest in your human character. I never suspected you of envy and malice. However, the true reformer must expect to be misunderstood and misrepresented by meaner minds. That love which I bear to all creatures teaches me to forgive you. Without such love, all plans of progress must fail. Is it not so, Abel?

SHELLDRAKE [*contemptuously*].—Pity! Forgive!

MRS. S. [*rocking violently in her chair.*]—Ts, ts, ts, ts, ts!

ABEL.—Love! There is no love in the world. Where will you find it? Tell me, and I'll go there. Love! I'd like to see it! If all human hearts were like mine, we might have an Arcadia; but most men have no hearts. The world is a miserable, hollow, deceitful shell of vanity and hypocrisy! No, let us give up. We were born before our time. This age is not worthy of us.

[*Hollins stares.*]

SHELLDRAKE.—Well, what next?

ENOS.—My friends, let the disgraceful scene we have just witnessed terminate our foolish experiment. Our Arcadia has proved a failure. Let us go back to the world from which we have so foolishly sought to divorce ourselves, satisfied that it is only in human intercourse with the *many*, and not the exclusive *few*, that we are to attain the greatest degree of happiness. For my part, I shall leave to-morrow, and Eunice has promised to go with me. Be assured that if the true Arcadia ever breaks upon our vision, we shall enter it through the gates of home comfort and domestic happiness.

[*Curtain falls.*]

THE TOWN MEETING.

CHARACTERS.

'SQUIRE FUNGUS, Moderator.
JOTHAM SCRIBBLE, Clerk.

DR. BORAX,
DEACON WHIMPER,
'SQUIRE GUMP,
MR. TIMMS,
MR. FUSSY, } Citizens. {
MR. LAWYER,
MR. OLDTIME,
MR. WILLING,

MR. DIGGER,
MR GROVEL,
MR. SCRIPTURE,
MR. CARPENTER,
MR. FOREMAN,
MR. TWADDLE,
MR. TWITTER,
MR. WATTS,

A hall, with men and boys in great confusion. Groups in earnest conversation.

CITIZEN [*taking off hat and mounting a bench speaks loudly to insure a hearing*].—Fellow-citizens! As it is the hour named for the meeting [*Cries of* "No!"—"No!" —"Wants five minutes!"—"All right!"—"Go ahead!"] —the hour named for the meeting, I move that 'Squire Fungus act as Moderator. [*Cries of* "No!"—"No!"— "Dr. Borax!"—"Deacon Whimper!"]

ANOTHER.—I second the nomination.

FIRST CIT.—Those in favor of 'Squire Fungus acting as Moderator of this meeting will give their assent by saying "Aye." [*Shouts of* "Aye!"—"Aye!"] Contrary-minded will say "No!" [*Shouts, but fainter, of* "No!" —No!"] The ayes have it, and 'Squire Fungus—— [*Cries of* "Doubted!"—"Doubted!"—"Count the vote!"] The vote is doubted! All will please be seated! [*After some disorder the citizens take seats.*] Those in favor of 'Squire Fungus acting as Moderator will please rise and remain standing until they can be counted. [*Cries of* "All up!"—"Sit down, Smith!"—"You've no vote!"— "Up! Up!"—"Down—down!" *Citizen points with finger and counts aloud.*] Twenty-four ayes. Those opposed will p.ease to rise and remain standing till counted. [*Ayes sit. Noes rise in confusion. Citizen counts as before.*] Eleven noes. [*Noes sit.*] The ayes have it, and 'Squire Fungus is elected Moderator of this meeting. 'Squire, will you please take the chair?

MODERATOR.—1 thank you, friends and fellow-citizens, for the honor which you have conferred upon me, and will try to discharge the duties of my position so as to meet your approbation. To complete the organization a Clerk will be necessary. Will some gentleman make a nomination?

THIRD CIT.—1 nominate Jotham Scribble.

[*Seconded, put and carried. Clerk takes seat.*]

MODERATOR.—The Clerk will read the call for this meeting.

CLERK [*reads*].—The legal voters of the town of Epsom are hereby warned to meet in special town-meeting (a petition to that effect having been preferred to us in writing signed by Nathan Nute and thirteen others, legal voters of said town), at the Town Hall, on Wednesday, the sixteenth day of October, A. D. 18—, at three o'clock P. M., to take into consideration the following question : *Shall the Board of Supervisors be directed to appropriate a sum of money for the purpose of building a new school-house in said town ; if so, what sum shall be appropriated?*

(Signed)   WILLIAM WATTS,
                            ROBERT GOING,
        Majority of the Board of Supervisors

Given under our hands this Sept. 20, 18—.

MODERATOR.—Gentlemen, you have heard the call for this meeting read. What action will you now take upon it? [*Several citizens spring to the floor, shouting "Mr. Moderator !"—" Mr. Moderator !" and endeavor to catch the Moderator's eye.*] Gentlemen [*rapping earnestly*], you must preserve order, or we cannot proceed with our deliberations ! Let me urge upon you now the importance of conducting our proceedings with dignity and decorum. 1 recognized Mr Timms first—Mr. Timms has the floor. [*Rest seat themselves.*]

TIMMS.—I move, Mr. Moderator, that this meeting do now adjourn. [*Cries of* "Second the motion !"]

FUSSY.—Mr. Moderator, I move that we proceed to business to once't. ["Second that !"]

MODERATOR.—A motion to adjourn is before the meeting, which takes precedence of every other.

FUSSY.—I want to be heerd a bit on that are motion.

MODERATOR [*rapping*].—A motion to adjourn is not debatable. I will put the motion.

[*Motion put and lost by a decisive vote.*]

FUSSY.—Mr. Moderator.

MODERATOR.—Mr. Fussy has the floor.

FUSSY.—I now put forward my motion agin that we go to work about the business that we're here for. I for one don't want to be foolin' away my time here the whole arternoon doin' nothin'. I say let's git to work and do what we're a-goin' to, and then git hum.

MODERATOR.—Will the gentleman be good enough to reduce his motion to writing, or at least put it in such a shape that the Chair can submit it to the meeting?

LAWYER.—Mr. Moderator!

MODERATOR.—Mr. Lawyer has the floor.

LAWYER.—I believe, Mr. Moderator, that the gentleman's motion did not obtain a second. Am I right, sir?

MODERATOR.—You are right—perfectly right — Mr. Lawyer.

LAWYER.—Then, sir, according to parliamentary law, there is no motion before the meeting.

MODERATOR.—None, sir, whatever.

LAWYER.—Then, sir, I beg leave to offer the following : [*reading*] RESOLVED, *That the Board of Supervisors be instructed to appropriate the sum of —— dollars for the erection of a new school-house ; said school-house to be erected as soon as possible, and that its location be left to the judgment of said Board.* I move you, sir, that this resolution be adopted. [*Lawyer hands motion to the Moderator.*]

CITIZEN.—I second the motion.

LAWYER [*recognized by Moderator*].—I offer this resolution, sir, for the purpose of testing the sense of this. meeting. It will be observed that four distinct propositions are embraced in my resolution. 1st, Shall a new school-house be built? 2d, If yea, at what cost? 3d, Shall it be built at once? and 4th, Shall the Supervisors settle the location of the building?

I am indifferent as to the shape which the discussion may assume; for I suppose I do not err when I speak of a discussion as likely to ensue—["Certainly not!" "We'll discuss it!" *Moderator raps and calls* "Order, gentlemen, order!"]—I thought my experience in this town was not so far at fault. Well, then, sir, as the matter will, I cannot doubt, be thoroughly ventilated by the able gentlemen whom I see all around me, I would propose, as a matter of convenience and for the sake of expediting business, that my resolution be divided, and I call for the reading of the first section.

MODERATOR.—The clerk will read the first section of the resolution before the meeting.

CLERK [*reads*].—RESOLVED, *That the Board of Supervisors be instructed to appropriate the sum of —— dollars for the erection of a new school-house.*

LAWYER [*recognized*].—This presents the first point for our consideration: Shall we build a new school-house? If this meeting shall agree to this, we can then decide as to the sum which shall be inserted in the blank.

Upon this question, Mr. Moderator, I have simply to say here in open town-meeting what I have said upon so many occasions in private, that I am strongly in favor of the new building. The affair which now stands us instead of a school-house is a nuisance, an eye-sore, and a disgrace to any community.

OLDTIME [*recognized*].—Well, sir, Mr. Moderator, I go agin the new buildin'. Ain't our taxes hefty enough now, I should like to know? My boys and gals were edecated in the school-house which we have, and ef it was good enough for them, I don't know why it ain't good enough for other folkses' children. I should like to know where on airth the money's to come from. People come into our town with scarcely a shirt to their backs and their heads crammed full of new-fangled notions, and think they 've nothin' to do but to vote away the money of us old residenters. I declare to you, Mr. Moderator, ef this kind o' carryins-on don't stop pooty soon, I'm goin' to move outer town. I can't stand it much longer. Why

don't you fix up the school-house you have now? What
are you a-goin' to do with it ef you build another? Use
it for kindlin', I s'pose, for some of those new-comers
who can't airn enough to keep their fingers warm, and so
have to cenamost, if not quite, steal their fires. Where's
your money comin' from? How many among them as 'll
vote for the new buildin' will have to pay any taxes on
it? I'd like to have them as favors it show their hands.
Here's mine [*taking a tax-bill from his wallet, exhibiting
it*]—and it's receipted—nineteen dollars and sixty-four
cents. Let's hear how much you new-buildin' voters can
say for yourselves as to payin' taxes. That's what **we**
property-owners want.

WILLING [*recognized*].—If the money-question is to be
so persistently thrust into our faces, I am ready to meet
it here and everywhere. I say, sir, it is a burning shame
that a town which has assessed taxable property amount-
ing to nearly a million of dollars—nine hundred and
ninety-seven thousand three hundred and fifty dollars'
worth, to be exact—for a town of such wealth to stand
higgling about putting up a decent, comely building in
place of the shell we now have—which I wouldn't so
insult my Suffolk pig as to offer to put him in—to hear the
palaver and the howlings that have been made is enough
to make some other people anxious to get out of town.

For three successive town-meetings, now, we've had
this matter staved off, and on the most parsimonious
grounds. I am disgusted with it, for my part; and I say
now that we'll fight this matter through till we carry our
point, if it has to come before every town-meeting that
is held while one of us lives. I've no children to educate,
as you all know; but when my children did go to school,
I would never have suffered them to stay a day in such a
rattle-trap as that concern some of you call a school-
house, if I'd had to build one out of my own pocket.

All this talk about taxes is neither here nor there. The
children of this town, whether of rich parents or of poor
parents, must be educated; and we are in honor bound,
as civilized Christian men, to furnish them with a comfortable building. I despise this whining in one breath
and bragging in the next about the amount of taxes paid.
If no one in favor of a new school-house paid a dollar of

taxes, I should still vote for it. Whether I pay any tax or not, you can any of you very easily ascertain.

DIGGER [recognized].—I don't see, Mr. Moderator, as there's any need of anybody's gittin' putcheky about this business. I b'lieve this is a free country, and a man can say what he thinks about this business, whether it agrees with the big bugs' notions or not. That's my kink, anyhow. Some folks [looking at Willing] can let on's much as they please 'bout havin' no children to edecate and the like o' that; but, then agin, some other folks have hearn of sich things in this world as some folks gittin' married agin—and then what about our new school-house?

I think, too, it's 'bout right not makin' a heap of difference as to whether you pay much tax or not. I don't pay any more than I can help—and that's little enough, you all oughter know—but I ain't a-goin' to encourage my children to put on stuck-up airs as they will, sartin sure, if they're a-goin' into a bran-new gimcrack of a school-house, when the one they go to now's better than I ever seed when I's a boy, though I didn't go to school much. I tell you, Mr. Moderator, I'm down on this stuck-up business, and naterally I'm down on the new school-house.

GROVEL [recognized].—Mr. Moderator: All I've got to say is, ef folks are so pesky anxious to git a better school-house and the heft of the town don't want it nohow, why don't they stop their braggin' 'bout what they'd do and what they wouldn't do and set about buildin' a buildin' to suit themselves and pay for it, like men, outer their own pockets? I've got a lot o' ground I'd sell 'em at a reasonable figger; and I guess some of my neighbors has, too, who don't want no buildin' neither.

SCRIPTURE.—Mr. Moderator: As clergyman of this parish and Chairman of your School Board, to which latter position you have elected me for so many years, I regret exceedingly the personal turn which this discussion is taking. Let us, Mr. Moderator, approach this matter in a calm, dispassionate manner. Crimination and recrimination can do no good. Do let us act as brethren in talking about a matter which so deeply concerns us all as children of a common Father. I need not give this meeting my views upon this question. You all know them,

since I have submitted them at length to you in my
annual report for the past five years.

FOREMAN [*recognized*].—I've been turnin' this matter
over in my mind consid'ble, Mr. Moderator, since we had
the last town-meetin' on it, and I've about concluded that
I've been wrong in opposin' the new building ["Shame!
Shame!" *from the opposition*], and I shall vote for it
to-day.

CARPENTER [*recognized*].—Me, too, Mr. Moderator, if
they do cry "shame!" I own up I am ashamed of havin'
been led by the nose so long by sich critters, and I'm in
for the new school-house arter this, from Genesis to Rever-
lation.

TWADDLE [*recognized*].—Mr. Moderator, bein' that I've
no job to git by the new buildin' [*looking at Foreman and
Carpenter*], I shall stick to my principles and vote "no"
every pop.

[*Lull in the debate.*]

MODERATOR.—Has any gentleman any further remarks
upon the question as divided? If not, the chair will put
the question.

TWITTER [*recognized*].—Mr. Moderator, I jest want to
give fair notice now, that ef we're voted down—which I
don't cal'late on - we shall take out a conjunction to stop
your proceedin's.

[*Cries of* "Question! Question!"]

MODERATOR.—The question is called for. ["Read it!
read it!" "Let's know what we're votin' on!"] If gentlemen will preserve order [*rapping*], the Clerk will read
the section of the question before the meeting.

CLERK [*reads*].—"RESOLVED, *That the Board of Supervisors be instructed to appropriate the sum of   dollars
for the erection of a new school-house.*

MODERATOR.—As many as are in favor of the question
as read ["Standing vote—standing vote!"] will rise and
remain until they are counted. [*Ayes rise, and Clerk
counts.*] Be seated, gentlemen. Those opposed will rise.
[*Noes rise, and Clerk counts.*] The question's carried—
twenty ayes to fifteen noes.

LAWYER.—Mr. Moderator, I move that the blank in the
section adopted be filled by the insertion of the words
"five thousand."

["Oh—oh !" *from opposition.*]
WILLING.—I second the motion.
MODERATOR.—The question is before you, gentlemen.
Any remarks upon it?
FUSSY [*recognized*].—Reelly, Mr. Moderator, I voted for
the new buildin', but this looks like pooty tall figgering.
I think we ought to git a good 'un for a power less money.
I move we say a thousand dollars,
DIGGER.—I second that thousand.
OLDTIME.—Goodness gracious, Mr. Moderator, where
are we drivin' to? Five thousan' dollars for a school-
house! Why, my whole farm ain't worth mor'n four
to-day. If we must have a buildin', let's not be onrea-
sonin'-like 'bout it. I move we make it five hundred.
FUSSY.—I second that motion.
TWADDLE.—I move we make it three.
[" *Question—question!*"]
MODERATOR.—Let us understand the question. Mr.
Lawyer moves to fill the blank with the words "five
thousand", so that the Board, if that carries, will be
instructed to appropriate five thousand dollars for the
erection of the building; Mr. Fussy moves to amend by
inserting one thousand dollars; Mr. Oldtime moves to
amend by inserting five hundred dollars; Mr. Twaddle
moves for three, but his motion did not obtain a second:
—Mr. Lawyer, do you accept either amendment—that of
Mr. Fussy, or that of Mr. Oldtime?
LAWYER.—No, Mr. Moderator, I cannot. If we are to
have a building, let us by all means have one which shall
be an ornament to the town. We should build not merely
for to-day, but, so far as we can anticipate, for the wants
of the future inhabitants of our town. I have consulted
with experienced builders about the matter, and I am
satisfied that the sum I have named is the least for which,
at present prices of materials and labor, we can procure
such a building as we need. And allow me to express
my surprise, Mr. Moderator, before resuming my seat,
that any who earnestly favor the new building should
name such paltry sums as have been mentioned in our
hearing. That an opponent of the measure should advocate a mere pittance, I can understand; but why any
friend should do it is to me inexplicable. It wears very

much an Ensign-Stebbins' garb. He, you may remember, Mr. Moderator, was in favor of the Maine Liquor Law, but opposed to its being put in force.

FUSSY.—If Mr. Lawyer means me, I don't know why I hain't as much right to my 'pinion as he has to his'n, ef he did make the motion.

MODERATOR.—The question will first be put upon the smallest sum—five hundred. [*Motion put and lost.*] Next upon one thousand dollars. [*Same result.*] Lastly upon the original sum, five thousand dollars. [*Same result, to the evident surprise of the Moderator and others.*]

'SQUIRE GUMP.—Mr. Mod-e-ra-tor !

MODERATOR —'Squire Gump has the floor.

'SQUIRE—Mist-er Mod-e-ra-tor! When I was in the Le-gis-lá-ter, sir—hem [*clearing throat*]—such things frequently happened, sir. Now, sir—hem—we've voted down each and every sum named. As a comprómise, Mr. Moderator, I propose that the blank be filled with the words "three thousand," sir—hem! That hits about 'twixt wind and water—hem—and in the Le-gis-lá-ter, sir, I never knew it to fail—hem!

LAWYER.—I second the motion.

MODERATOR.—Are you ready for the question? [*Put and carried.*]

LAWYER [*recognized*].—I now call for the reading of the second section of the resolution.

MODERATOR.—The Clerk will read the second section as divided.

CLERK [*reads*].—*Said school-house to be erected as soon as possible.*

LAWYER [*recognized*].—As, after the previous votes, there can be hardly any doubt as to this section carrying, I move its adoption without discussion.

WILLING.—I second the motion. " If when 'twere done 'twere well done, then 'twere well 'twere done quickly." Don't Shakspeare say something like that?

OLDTIME [*from his seat*].—What's he got to do with the new school-house, I'd like to know?

MODERATOR.—Are you ready for the question? ["Question!"—"Question!" *Put and carried.*]

LAWYER [*recognized*].—And now, Mr. Moderator, I call for the reading of the third and last section.

CLERK [*at the direction of Moderator reads*].—*And that its location be left to the judgment of said Board.*

LAWYER.—I move its adoption, Mr. Moderator.

CARPENTER.—I second the motion.

MODERATOR.—The section as read is before you, gentlemen. Has any one any thing to say upon it before the question is put to the meeting?

DR. BORAX.—Mr. Moderator!

MODERATOR.—Dr. Borax has the floor.

BORAX.—I have remained silent, Mr. Moderator, during our deliberations up to this point; but I am compelled to declare my dissent from this section. There is no reason why we should not fix the location ourselves here in town-meeting assembled. Why leave it to the Board of Supervisors, each member of which has property which he would like to dispose of for this purpose?

WILLING [*interrupting*].—If the Doctor will allow me, are we not all in the same predicament? How can we hope to arrange it here, then?

BORAX.—Well, then, Mr. Moderator, why not vote to have the building located in the centre of the town? This will accommodate a greater number, certainly, than any other location can.

LAWYER.—Begging the Doctor's pardon, Mr. Moderator—but would he locate at the geographical centre or at the centre of population?

BORAX.—At the centre of population, certainly.

LAWYER.—Then—asking the Doctor's pardon again for my interruption—should we be providing for the necessities of the future, as wise men ought?

BORAX.—Why not, Mr. Moderator, leave the whole matter in the hands of a Committee? It does rest in my mind that the plan proposed is not the best one, though I do not wish to seem captious.

WHIMPER.—Mr. Moderator!

MODERATOR.—Deacon Whimper has the floor.

WHIMPER.—I think, Mr. Moderator, the location had best be put in hands of the School Board.

SCRIPTURE.—Mr. Moderator!

MODERATOR.—Rev. Mr. Scripture has the floor.

SCRIPTURE.—As Chairman of the School Board, Mr. Moderator, I must, in behalf of my colleague, decline in advance any such responsibility as the worthy Deacon suggests. We are too well aware of the thankless nature of such a task to care to take such a burden upon ourselves. Fix upon the location here, leave it to the supervisors, or submit it to a special committee; but I entreat you, gentlemen, not to throw the responsibility upon the School Board. We have full enough of trouble already for our comfort, if I may be allowed the expression.

LAWYER [*recognized*].—I am well aware of the delicate nature of the task contemplated in the section of the resolution before the meeting. The location of any public building—especially of a school-house—is, as a general thing, the signal for the manifestation of no little dissatisfaction. It will be too near to some, and too distant from others. Yet the question of location must be met in some way; and I could think of no better plan than the one proposed—leaving the matter in the hands of those who, as fathers of the town (elected too, I believe, by almost a unanimous vote), may well be judged most competent to consult and provide, to the best of their ability, for the wants of all their children.

WATTS.—Mr. Moderator !

MODERATOR.—Mr. Watts has the floor.

WATTS.—Mr. Moderator : Although it chances to be correct—fortunately so, shall I say ?—that the members of the present Board of Supervisors are each of them, more or less, interested in real estate in this town, yet I take it upon myself, as President of the Board, to say that no such consideration will influence in the slightest degree their action relative to the location of the proposed new school-house, should this meeting choose to submit it to us. Indeed, I may say here that all temptation is happily removed, inasmuch as no less than five eligible central lots have been offered to us, free of expense, should the building be voted by the town.

BORAX.—This, Mr. Moderator, removes every objection; and I am glad that I am citizen of a town which can claim so many citizens of such unwonted liberality.

LAWYER.—I call for the question.

MODERATOR.—The question is called for. Those in favor of its adoption will say "Aye." [*Nearly all shout* "Aye.*] Those opposed, "No." [*Messrs. Oldtime, Grovel,* *and Twitter, only,* "Noes."] The ayes have it, and the third and last section is adopted. Any further business, gentlemen?

WILLING.—I move we adjourn.

GUMP.—Mis-ter Mod-e-rat-or: Before that motion is put I would like to say a word.

WILLING.—I withdraw my motion.

MODERATOR. — 'Squire Gump has the floor.

GUMP.—Mis-ter Mod-e-rat-or: We haven't finished our business yet—hem—in a par-lia-ment-a-ry manner—hem! Leastways, not as it used to be done here when I was a member of the Le-gis-la ter. We've only adopted the re-so-lu-tion by sections—hem. I now move you, Mis-ter Mod-e-rat-or, sir, that the whole resolution be adopted — hem!

LAWYER.—The 'Squire is right [*bowing deferentially to 'Squire*]. I second the motion.

[*Moderator puts the motion, and declares it carried — only three "noes" as before.*]

WILLING.—I now renew my motion, Mr. Moderator, that this meeting do now adjourn.

OLDTIME.—Before that are motion's put afore us, Mr. Moderator, *I'd* like to propound a question : Where on airth's your three thousan' dollars for a new school-house comin' from?

[*Outbursts of laughter—amidst which the motion to adjourn is put and carried.*]

Good=Humor

FOR

Reading and Recitation

BY HENRY FIRTH WOOD
Humorist and Reciter

Paper Binding, 30 Cents
Cloth, 50 Cents

The title of this volume accurately and faithfully describes the character of its contents. It is believed to be "good humor," and the rendition of the selections is calculated to put the audience in an equally "good-humor."

Mr. Wood, one of the most popular humorists of the day, presents in this volume one of the very best collections of humorous recitations ever offered to the public. Many of the pieces make their first appearance in this book, several among the number being original creations of the compiler. Considerable space has been devoted to the popular dialect fancies of the day, which are so much in demand at the present time. While all of the selections are exceedingly laughable, special pains have been taken to prevent overstepping the bounds of propriety, and there is, therefore, nothing that cannot be appropriately given before the most cultured and refined audiences.

No reader, who wishes to keep abreast of the times, can afford to be without this volume, as its selections are indispensable to his repertoire.

Sold by all booksellers, or sent, prepaid, upon receipt of price.

The Penn Publishing Company
923 Arch Street, Philadelphia

Choice Dialect

FOR READING AND RECITA-TION

By Charles C. Shoemaker

Paper Binding, 30 Cents

Cloth, 50 Cents

This popular and attractive volume contains a rare collection of Choice Dialect of every variety, covering a broad range of sentiment, and suited to any public or private occasion where readings or recitations are the order of entertainment. The transitions from grave to gay, from humorous to pathetic, and from the simply descriptive to the highly dramatic, will be found unusually wide.

Many of the selections have never before appeared in print, and a number of others have been specially arranged for this volume. It is believed that the book will meet the wants of those who are partial to selections in dialect, but whose good taste and good sense are often shocked by the coarseness that too frequently prevails in books of this character.

Among its contents will be found selections in all dialects, such as Irish, Scotch, German, Negro, etc., and representing all phases of sentiment, the humorous, pathetic, dramatic, etc., thus affording full scope to the varied attainments of the reader or reciter, and adapting it eminently to the needs of the amateur and professional elocutionist.

Sold by all booksellers, or sent, prepaid, upon receipt of price.

The Penn Publishing Company

923 Arch Street, Philadelphia

Choice Dialogues

Humorous Dialogues and Dramas

By Charles C. Shoemaker

Paper Binding, 30 Cents

Cloth, 50 Cents

After the severe labors of the day every one enjoys that which will afford relaxation and relieve the mind of its nervous tension. For this reason the humorous reading is so heartily received and the humorous dialogue so vigor· ously applauded. Humor has its legitimate field, but it .s always attended with one great danger, that of descending to the coarse and vulgar. And just at this point lies the merit of this book. The dialogues are humorous without being coarse, and funny without being vulgar. Many of them are selected from standard authors, but a number of others have been specially prepared for the book by experienced writers.

All the dialogues are bright and taking and sure to prove most successful in their presentation. They can be given on any ordinary stage or platform, and require nothing out of the ordinary in the way of costuming. They are adapted to old and young of both sexes, and are suitable to all occasions where good, wholesome humor is appropriate and will be appreciated.

Sold by all booksellers, or sent, prepaid, upon receipt of price.

The Penn Publishing Company

923 Arch Street, Philadelphia

Classic Dialogues and Dramas

By Mrs. J. W. Shoemaker

Paper Binding, 30 Cents

Cloth, 50 Cents

This book embraces scenes and dialogues selected with the greatest care from the writings of the best dramatists. It is, therefore, valuable not alone for public and private entertainments, but to individuals for the opportunity it affords for literary study. It is rarely, if at all, that such a collection of articles from the truly great writers is found in one volume.

As would be expected a number of the strongest and most familiar scenes from the plays of Shakespeare have been inserted, but selections from Sheridan, Bulwer, Schiller, and others equally prominent have also been made. Many of the dialogues are such as would prove acceptable in the form of readings or recitals, and for this reason the value of the book to many persons is greatly increased.

It is a volume that appeals most forcibly to the teacher and advanced student, and its contents will find acceptance most readily with audiences of the highest culture and refinement. With such environment the dialogues will prove very acceptable and enjoyable.

Sold by all booksellers, or sent, prepaid, upon receipt of price.

The Penn Publishing Company

923 Arch Street, Philadelphia

Eureka Entertainments

Paper binding, 30 cts.   Cloth, 50 cts

The title of this volume expresses in a nutshell the character of its con-tents. The weary searcher after ma-terial for any and all kinds of enter-tainments will upon examination of this book at once exclaim, " I have found it." Found just what is wanted for use in day school, Sunday-school, at church socials, teas, and other festivals, for parlor or fireside amusement—in fact, all kinds of school or home, public or private entertainment.

Perhaps a better idea of the value of the book can be had by direct reference to some of the features it con-tains. From the long list the following are selected as representative:

S Supper and Sociable
Girls' Buck Saw Exercise
The Peak Sisters
A Vernal Tree
A Lemon Party
A Brown Sociable
A Night Cap Sociable
A Poverty Party
Among the Trees
Harvest Home Sociable
The Old-Fashioned Dis-trict School
A Pansy Party
The Temple of Fame

An Evening with Art
An Emblem Service
The Old Curiosity Shop
Hints for Thanksgiving
For Christmas Time
Parlor Base-Ball
The Kalendar Kermesse
Quaker Meeting and Soci-able
The Cob Web Party
Acting Proverbs
Shadow Pantomimes
The Children of the Bible

Full directions accompany all the entertainments, so there will be no doubt about their success even at the hands of the most inexperienced.

Sold by all booksellers, or sent, prepaid, upon receipt of price.

The Penn Publishing Company
923 Arch Street, Philadelphia

Holiday Selections

FOR READINGS AND RECITA-TIONS

By Sara Sigourney Rice

Paper Binding, 30 Cents

Cloth, 50 Cents

The selections in this volume are adapted to all the different holidays of the year, and are classified and arranged in the book according to those days and occasions. Fully half of the pieces are for Christmas, but ample provision is also made for New Year's, St. Valentine's Day, Washington's Birthday, Easter, Arbor Day, Decoration Day, Fourth of July, and Thanksgiving. The selections in all cases are strictly appropriate to the occasions for which they are designed.

The volume has been prepared by one of the most prominent elocutionists of the country, who has tested the value and effect of its contents, and thus proved that the pieces are in touch with popular sympathy. Much of the material is from the pens of our most recent and taking American writers, while the remainder is from the classic and ripened experience of English authors. It is a volume that cannot fail to meet most acceptably a widespread demand, and the varied character of its contents makes it as serviceable in midsummer as in midwinter.

Sold by all booksellers, or sent, prepaid, upon receipt of price.

The Penn Publishing Company
923 Arch Street, Philadelphia

www.ingramcontent.com/pod-product-compliance
Lightning Source LLC
Chambersburg PA
CBHW020619030726
47497CB00007B/2314